THE ICONIC

TME BOX

THE ICONIC

TIME BOX

R. Bruce McGill

Another Quality Book Published By:
LEGACY BOOK PUBLISHING
1883 Lee Road, Winter Park, FL 32789
www.LEGACYBOOKPUBLISHING.com

The Iconic Time Box

Published by:
LEGACY Book Publishing
1883 Lee Road
Winter Park, Florida 32789
www.LegacyBookPublishing.com

2018© R. Bruce McGill
Printed in the United States
ISBN: 978-1-947718-14-2

Cover Design by Gabriel H. Vaughn

Acknowledgements

I would like to thank Gabriel Vaughn, an accomplished writer in his own right, for his help in adding color to this novel as my ghost writer.

I would like the thank my mother Joan McGill and my sister Linda McGill for their tireless efforts in helping me flesh this book out and for supporting me to write this book. I would also like to thank my brother and sister in-law for their contributions.

Furthermore, I would like to thank my friend Chris Bawiec for his input and being there for me to bounce ideas around.

Lastly, I would like to thank Josh Gerson for his ideas which helped to bring the machine to life.

Chapter One

What Just Happened?

It was a cool, clear night near the middle of winter. The small town was illuminated by the full moon and the stars glistened like a million tiny lights in the night sky. In the yard of a stately home in an upscale community, the trees possessed a ghostly glow.

A brilliant light and a loud sound pierced the night suddenly; a tall gray and seemingly insignificant box seemed to materialize out of thin air. The box was enveloped in a green, phosphorescent glow that slowly brightened into a golden amber tint. The crude, upright, rectangular contraption stood as if it were a fixture near an old shed. Without warning, smoke began pouring from the roof of the booth. Within a few seconds, its doors flung open and a tall and slightly muscular young man named Duncan Sims jumped from the smoking hulk, clutching a laptop computer against his chest. He landed hard with his face down on the ground. Rising to his hands and knees, he coughed uncontrollably for he had been overtaken by smothering noxious fumes.

Finally catching his breath, he rolled on his back. Lying in the thick, cold grass he then turned over and looked back at his handy work as it became fully engulfed in swirling, white smoke.

"Oh, my God," he gasped as the tall box began

to grow dim. Smoke continued to billow out as Duncan ran his hand through his hair, his fingers getting stuck in its tangled mess. He continued to lie there, breathing the cool night air. His lungs were burning like a forest fire in his chest.

His eyes were watering, as his lashes were dusted with ash and his face smeared with soot. His previously white shirt was stained with grass and dirt. After a moment, he gathered his strength and sat up, continuing to cough.

He watched as his invention began to grow even dimmer, and then went slowly dark; the once vibrant noise subsided and ceased.

Duncan frantically reached around for his laptop. When he had grasped it, he quickly opened it to make sure it was still working. He was relieved when the screen lit up, illuminating his face in a familiar soft glow against the chilly, moonlit night. If someone were to look at him in that moment, they would see wild, dark hair splattered with white ash and deep green eyes. Duncan, though somewhat frantic, wasn't out of his mind, but he was on the mission of a lifetime.

The yard around him became still and silent; the only sounds he could hear were those of the night—crickets and the boisterous noise of vehicles in the distance passing on a nearby highway.

Duncan pushed himself up on his feet and brushed himself off—his jeans streaked green from the grass—and shook his head in disbelief.

"I can't believe this. It's ruined! How the heck am I supposed to find all those parts again?" Duncan said aloud, his mind spinning with worry. He paced in front of the invention he was once proud of, his fingers interlocking at the back of his neck and the promise of a headache beginning to throb at his temples.

His attention was soon drawn away from the smoking kiosk as he heard the crunching of leaves and the sound of an older man's voice. It was a neighbor, Professor Wofford Batton. "Duncan...Duncan Sims?" the professor called to him.

"Yeah?" Duncan replied, regaining his breath.

"Are you okay? What happened?" the professor asked as he looked over toward the box. Smoke was still pouring upwards as if it were a raging furnace.

"Professor Batton?" Duncan inquired, as he only vaguely recognized the man in the dark. He could smell the tobacco from the professor's pipe, its potent smoke curling in the air. It was a sweeter scent in comparison to the acrid stench that had flooded his nose earlier.

"That's right, Professor Batton. How are you Duncan? You look like you have had a rough night, son," the professor remarked with a pleasant smile, seemingly undaunted by the sight. Duncan appraised him; he appeared to be out of place or time even, dressed in a dark blue long sleeved shirt buttoned to the top and a brown sweater vest. He didn't know what to make of him.

"That's an understatement," Duncan gruffly retorted.

"Well, what happened son?" the professor asked again. Maybe it was just his round wire rimmed glasses, but Duncan noticed an odd glimmer in his eyes and wondered if he had seen him appear out of thin air.

"You would never believe me if I told you," Duncan quipped.

"Oh, I don't know, Duncan. I've seen a lot of weird things in my lifetime. Weirder than you look now, anyway, so try me."

Duncan looked at the professor, his eyes still watering and smeared. The man was right; he probably did look a mess. He had known Professor Batton for years, but he had always been a somewhat distant figure and Duncan did not wish to divulge anything about what had transpired. How would he ever understand? No one would.

"I would really rather not talk about it, professor," he half-muttered to himself. "No offense."

"Okay, Duncan, but it looks like you need to talk to someone."

Duncan rubbed his neck, feeling the grit of sand under his fingers. He had started to feel itchy all over after his tussle in the grass.

"It suffices to say this has not been my night," he finally admitted sharply.

"Well, I am sorry, Duncan. I kind of eavesdropped on you earlier while I was walking my dog, but did I hear you say something about time travel?" the professor asked inquisitively.

Duncan, somewhat shocked, looked directly at the professor while watching him fiddle with a pocket kerchief.

"Uh...yeah," Duncan replied as he coughed once more. *Does he really know anything about time travel? Could he really know what I've been doing?* Duncan thought to himself.

"If you tell me what is going on, then maybe I can help you," Professor Batton offered.

"Help me? Help me how?" Duncan asked, raising an eyebrow.

"Well, you might be surprised, Duncan, but time

travel has long been a passion of mine."

Duncan stood up and looked directly at the professor, pondering if he should say anything. He felt he needed to tell someone—someone that actually understood what he was trying to do—but should it be the professor?

The professor met his gaze and stood perfectly still, as if giving him an open invitation. "Come on, Duncan. Let me help you."

Duncan stood there for a moment, hesitantly weighing his options. "If I tell you what happened, it goes no further. Do we have a deal?" he insisted, looking sternly at Professor Batton. At least he would be able to discuss this with somebody that understands what he is talking about.

"Of course, Duncan; you can trust me," the professor reassured. He straightened his glasses and waited for Duncan to speak.

"Well, it all started two days ago, while I was working on an experiment..."

Chapter 2

Recollection

TWO DAYS EARLIER.......

Duncan stood for a moment in the early light of day, gazing at his home-made, would-be, time machine.

Soon baby, soon we will show everyone! he confidently thought, patting the side of the box in earnest. He smiled, day-dreaming about attainting his goal. Everything was coming together now.

He reached into his jeans pocket, grabbed the antique looking key, and unlocked the tall, wooden box. He opened its door and stepped inside. It was dark and filled with low-dollar technology that Duncan had scavenged from junkyards.

He felt his heart rate increase as he was about to test all his theories. There was an energy he felt here that he could not explain. He began tinkering with a mass of wires and odd switches. He hooked up his personal laptop, solid black and scratched from numerous mishaps, and turned it on. Duncan then opened a dialog window and ran a file he had created so he could check the coding for errors. His long, deft fingers raced quickly over the keyboard.

For weeks, Duncan had been working on the circuitry between his laptop and the onboard electronics of his box. Soon, he would be ready to test this theory and try his experiment.

Time flew by as he was absorbed in his work, and soon Duncan's girlfriend, Jamie Connors, walked up from behind him. So consumed by his work, Duncan had let the hours tick by unknowingly, so much so that Jamie was able to enter virtually unnoticed. He smelled a sweet perfume just before he felt her wrap her arms around him in affection. She caught him off guard in the cramped space. Duncan quickly turned around in surprise to see Jamie's sweet face.

"Did I startle you?" she asked with a chuckle, her teeth glistening in her perfect smile.

"Uh...no. I was just so engrossed in wiring circuits that I did not hear you come up, but I am always glad to see you," Duncan said fondly as he took Jamie's perfectly manicured hands in his. He stepped out of his box and wrapped his arms around Jamie and they exchanged a quick, but passionate, kiss.

Jamie and Duncan had only been a couple for a little over a year and their love had blossomed into a deep relationship; however, while Jamie was ready to take the next step, Duncan was hesitant.

"Are you wiring the lights up, or the sound?" she asked inquisitively while pushing a strand of long, brown hair behind her ear.

"Well, neither really. I am just adding a few more components in for an experiment."

"An experiment? What kind of experiment?" she asked, peering towards the box.

Duncan cleared his throat. "Oh, let's just say I have a few ideas about what I can make this thing do," he said confidently.

"You're not gonna tell me are you?" she asked, crossing her arms and cocking her head to the side.

"Uh, not just yet, but I will show you soon enough," he said as he quickly ran his finger down her nose with a smile.

Jamie lips curled into a smile. "I can hardly wait. So when is the big convention?"

"It's still a ways off, but I will be ready long before then."

"Got something big planned, do you?"

"Oh yeah, and it will amaze even you," he grinned.

"Well I think you're pretty amazing as it is," she said, her shiny white teeth gleaming up at him in a joyful smile.

Duncan took her hand again and looked into her eyes. They were a soft hazel, different from his deep green ones.

"No babe, we're amazing. You are my life, Jamie, we were made to be together," he charmed in a soft, tender voice.

"You make me feel so good when you say things like that," she blushed through a sweet smile.

"It is how I feel," he said affectionately.

"Me too," she whispered, as she ran her other hand down his cheek, still looking into his eyes.

"Good, now hand me that pair of pliers on the ladder, will ya?" he asked, giving her a quick kiss on the forehead and spinning around.

Jamie was taken aback, rolling her eyes as the moment went from being romantic to requesting a tool. *Duncan's typical tunnel vision and persistence for his mission changed the declaration of love and appreciation to back to work.*

"Sure, nothing says romance like you are my life babe, now hand me the pliers," she mocked playfully as she handed them to Duncan.

"Hey, just be glad I didn't ask for the hammer," he mused.

"Ha, ha," she offered, rolling her eyes again. "So where are we having lunch today?"

"I am not sure; I figured we would just play it by ear. Anyway, it's only 11:00 a.m.," he pointed out.

"I know, but until you get another car, we have to walk into town and that will take at least twenty minutes."

Duncan noticed Jamie getting a little impatient, tapping her foot lightly on the ground.

"Oh, yeah. Well just let me attach a couple of breakers to this circuit and then we'll go."

Jamie stood outside the box, turning away with her arms crossed, as Duncan stepped back inside. He was unaware, however, that he had inadvertently struck the main power switch and turned it on as he attached the breaker.

Suddenly, there was a burst of energy and light. There was the sound of a powerful surge. The sudden increase of power jolted his laptop and inadvertently started the code Duncan had typed in running. It was an obscure equation that was based on the work of Nikola Tesla that Duncan had found online on one of his marathon searches for all things related to time travel.

The equation was, in fact, a partial equation for opening a rift in time. As the code ran, a strange occurrence took place.

Somehow the machine Duncan had assembled punched a small hole through the fabric of the universe and created a breach window into time. All of a sudden, to Duncan's amazement, he heard what sounded like himself and Jamie arguing, but he could only make out a few garbled words. He was baffled by this, but he was even more startled when he began seeing a blurry vision from an event vortex which looked like himself and Jamie standing in darkness. He was curious, nevertheless. He quickly reached up, turning the power off. Jamie, while she was standing at the door, heard the commotion, and looked inside the box, bewildered.

"What was that?" she asked. "It sounded like some kind of surge and I thought I heard people yelling," she said in astonishment.

"I didn't realize the main power switch was on. I must have bumped it; it's pretty cramped in here. I am not sure what those other sounds were," Duncan replied, running a hand through his hair nervously.

While he was unsure what had happened, he played it off as if it were nothing. *She did not see the vortex,* he thought to himself. He was completely at a loss for an explanation.

"Well just be careful, please," Jamie said, concern flooding her voice.

"It's okay now, I turned it off."

Jamie was still wondering what this experiment might be, but she trusted Duncan and quickly dropped it. She turned her attention back to their lunch plans.

"So, how about pizza for lunch?" she asked, twisting her long hair into a loose braid, her perfectly manicured nails catching the light.

Duncan was still puzzled by the voices he had heard but could not make sense of what it had been, so he remained distracted.

"Fine...anything you want," he replied as he looked around and checked his laptop for any clue as to what had just happened.

"Oh really, anything I want, huh? Well then,

how about an engagement ring?" she quipped, eyes focused on the door of the box.

"Yeah sure, anything you want. Wait, what?" Duncan snapped back to reality at her words and he stepped back out of the box, looking at Jamie intently.

"Sorry, I shouldn't have said that," Jamie said apologetically, her eyes flicking from the box to the ground. She may have apologized, but she was not really sorry; she wanted Duncan to ask her to marry him.

"No, it's okay. I just feel like, well, I mean I..." Duncan tried to speak his mind, but stumbled over his words clumsily.

"You mean what?" she pressed.

"It's just, well, I've been thinking of our future," Duncan said, looking down as he moved some leaves with his shoes nervously.

"You have?" she asked. Her hopeful tone was not a least bit subtle.

Duncan grasped for what to say next; he loved Jamie very much, but he did not feel he was ready for marriage—at least not yet. *How do I say this without sounding like I am putting her off,* he thought to himself.

"Yeah, babe. I mean I really think, I...I mean I really want for us to—" Duncan tried to articulate his thoughts as he was still stumbling over his words.

Duncan's cell phone began to ring, buzzing loudly in his pocket. At first he hesitated for a few seconds to answer it, as he and Jamie stared at each other in the awkward moment of silence. Finally, he held up his finger as if to say one moment to Jamie, then he answered the call.

"Hello? Oh hey, Logey! What's up man?" Duncan

said into his phone, gripping it tightly. He was slightly relieved for the interruption.

"Perfect timing Logan, as usual," Jamie said under her breath in a sarcastic whisper.

Logan was Duncan's best friend. He was also Jamie's friend and had introduced them, but he had a rather bad habit of unintentionally coming between them, particularly when Jamie wanted Duncan's attention.

"Yeah bro, me and Jamie are gonna walk into town and get some pizza in a few. You want to meet us there?" Duncan asked. His free hand was placed on the back of his neck as he paced in front of the box, hoping the awkwardness of the conversation had passed.

Jamie gestured with her hands as she shook her head for Duncan to not invite Logan. While Jamie had nothing against Logan, she wanted some time alone with Duncan. As of late, though, Duncan seemed to have less and less time for her.

"No, man, it's cool; she won't care," Duncan assured, as Jamie glared at him.

She finally resigned herself in defeat and yelled into the phone. "Hi Logan. No, I don't mind. Are you at least gonna buy for a change?"

Duncan was slightly embarrassed and tried to excuse Jamie's comment. "No she is just kidding, man. Oh, you will buy? What? Did you win the lottery or something?" Duncan said in light sarcasm, seemingly stunned by the offer.

Logan had the reputation of being cheap and, at times even leeching, and it was a surprise to Duncan and Jamie that he would offer to buy lunch.

"What? He is actually offering to pay? I may pass out!" Jamie remarked snidely as Duncan continued to talk to Logan, shielding the phone with his hand.

"Yeah, okay. Then we will meet you there in say twenty five minutes, okay? Okay see you then, bro."

Jamie was still shocked that Logan would offer to buy them lunch. "What? Did he inherit some money or something?" Jamie asked, at a loss for words.

"Nah, he is just doing some side work for Retz's dad. I guess he is feeling generous for a change," Duncan shrugged.

The moment passed and Jamie tried to prompt Duncan to return to the conversation they were having before Logan had interrupted. She moved closer to him, putting her chest against his and embracing him lightly.

"Great. Now where were we?" she asked.

Duncan attempted to dodge the issue as best he could, disentangling himself gently and bending down to retie his shoe. It was an uncomfortable conversation for him.

"We were closing up the time machine—I mean the box—and heading into town."

Jamie was undeterred by Duncan's effort to change the subject. "That is not what I meant and you know it," Jamie scolded. "Wait, did you say time machine?" she continued, as if she had misheard.

"Uh, well yeah. It's supposed to be a replica of a time machine, right? Now come on and we can talk about it while we walk," Duncan said aloofly, looking up at her while he fiddled with his laces.

He stood up and pulled the door shut to his replica, would-be time box, and locked it. He put his arm around Jamie as they began walking from his yard and down the street towards town. After a short distance, Jamie looked over at Duncan who was keeping his eyes forward.

"Duncan?" Jamie prompted with a concerned look.

"Yeah, babe?" he answered as he looked towards her.

"Aren't you going to say anything?" she asked with an urgent tone.

"Sure, what would like me to say?"

"I would like you to finish what you were saying before Logan called," she said in a clearly aggravated tone.

Duncan cleared his throat nervously; avoiding her eyes, he took a deep breath. "All right, all right. Well, I was saying that I've been thinking about our future."

"And?"

"Well... Jamie you know I'm not in good shape right now financially and..." He began before Jamie cut him off.

"That does not matter to me, Duncan. I love you!" Jamie said, sounding exasperated in frustration from hearing his excuse.

"I know. And I know money doesn't matter to you now, but what about later?"

Duncan loved Jamie very much, but he never felt he was good enough for her. He wanted to give her everything, or at least a good life, but it seemed unlikely, given his current situation.

"Duncan you won't always be this way," Jamie reassured, placing her hand on his chest, but Duncan took her comment the wrong way.

"What do you mean 'this way?'" Duncan asked in a slightly annoyed tone, his eyes darkening.

"Don't get upset. I just mean one day you will

find your place and be successful," Jamie shrugged.

Duncan looked down at the sidewalk, feeling even worse about the situation.

"Well for now, I don't feel like I fit in anywhere. Sometimes I wish I could escape all of this..." Duncan said, waving his arms in the air.

Jamie abruptly stopped her stride. Duncan turned back to look at her. She seemed to have taken the comment personally.

"All of this? Does that include escaping me?" she asked pointedly, placing both hands on her hips.

"No, of course not, babe. Without you my life would be empty," Duncan assured trying to diffuse the last comment.

"Then what *do* you mean?" she asked, wanting clarification.

"I mean...I mean, Jamie, you know I love you. I just want the best for us. And I know you want to get married. So do I—one day. But right now is not the time."

Jamie was slightly hurt by his comment. To her, love was not based on a person's worth or how much they earned, nor where they were in life. "Not the time? What do you mean?"

"Just—well, where I am in life right now is not where I need to be. Do you know what I mean?" he sighed, slightly frustrated. *How else could I explain it?*

"I guess so. But happiness does not wait for anyone, Duncan. We have to grab hold of it while we can," Jamie persisted, grabbing his hand and squeezing his fingers.

"Yeah, but you deserve better than what I am right now," Duncan said, shifting his weight uncomfortably.

Jamie answered him in a reassuring tone. "What you are right now is what I love! I'm really scared that if we wait that...our love could grow cold and fade."

"That's not going to happen. I promise," Duncan reassured with a smile.

"I've never felt like this about anyone. I don't want to lose this, Duncan," Jamie reiterated. Her eyes pleaded with him to agree with what she was saying.

"Don't talk nonsense. We were destined to be together. Now, it's a beautiful day, so let's just enjoy it. Okay?" Duncan said while thinking this stroll to the restaurant has become like taking a walk with your greatest fears.

"I want all of our days to be beautiful days..." Jamie replied quietly.

"They will be, babe....they will be."

Jamie leaned her head on Duncan's shoulder as they walked slowly, arm-in-arm, under shady oaks. They walked across the brick streets in the cool of the day with the sun peering through the old oak trees making a canopy over the sidewalks. Jamie tilted her head to see two neighborhood boys chasing one another on their front lawn. She looked up admiringly at Duncan, daydreaming of a better tomorrow with him. Duncan met her eyes and looked up to see the faded white fences and a rusty tire swing. Duncan escaped through *his* dream of a better tomorrow.

They made a pretty picture—a couple in love walking down the street. But it would only take a glimpse below the surface to see that not all was perfect between them.

CHAPTER 3

Pizza and The Professor

Parked in front of the pizza restaurant, Logan sat impatiently swinging his legs over the tailgate of his faded black pickup truck.

He was slightly annoyed that his friends were late. Finally, he saw Duncan and Jamie approaching. They walked up to where he was seated on his truck.

"What? Did you guys take the scenic route?" Logan asked in a slightly annoyed tone.

"We were just enjoying the walk," Duncan answered casually, his shoes crunching on the loose gravel as they approached.

"Yeah, I'll bet you were," Logan replied snidely as he gave Duncan a slanted look.

"You're one to talk. How come when it comes to eating you're always early, but any other time you're late?" Jamie replied in a chiding tone.

"It's called being a guy, Jamie. One day you'll get it," Logan replied in his typical cavalier way.

"I doubt it," she quipped.

Logan hopped off of the tailgate and pushed it shut. The trio walked up the street, with Logan somehow managing to make his way into the middle of them. He sprinted ahead to open the door for Jamie in a dramatic gesture, and she rolled her eyes as she passed him. When they entered the restaurant they chose a table near the center of the sparsely filled eatery.

They were greeted by the aroma of parmesan cheese and tomato sauce, the slight sounds of chatter were heard from conversations of the few customers there and functional rings of the cash register. They paused for a moment to find their regular booth.

Jamie and Duncan sat together while Logan made his way toward the counter to order their pizza. As Logan passed by, he saw a friend of his and Duncan's seated at a table alone writing on a sheet of paper and sipping coffee. He walked up and knocked on the table, quickly getting the attention his friend who was listening to music on a set of headphones.

"Chris, what's up man?" Logan grinned, knuckling a greeting with his fist.

Chris pulled his earphones out and laid them on the table.

"Hi, Logan. I'm just working on some lyrics for my new album," Chris explained.

"Are you still gonna play at Ryan's Party?"

"Yeah, I've got some new songs I want to try out, so that should be a good opportunity to test them."

"Right on. I'll let you get back to it. See you later," Logan said as he departed for the counter.

"See ya, man," Chris replied politely as he turned back to his writing.

As Duncan and Jamie waited at the table, Jamie peered over to see an older man seated at another table near the front window of the restaurant.

She leaned over to Duncan and whispered, "Hey, isn't that that crazy old professor?" Duncan turned and looked toward the older man. He sat distinguished and upright, seemingly unaffected by the world around him.

He was seated with a book in one hand and a fork in the other, gold, round rimmed glasses peeking out just over the top of the book.

"What? You mean Wofford Batton?"

"Yeah, he is a real weirdo. He always keeps to himself and he is always alone," Jamie noted, her tiny nose scrunching with distaste.

"Maybe because he never got married? Is that what you mean?" Duncan mocked with a grin.

"No, he just never speaks to anyone and you rarely see him out of his home," Jamie said. Her long, straight hair did little to hide her glaring as she kept tossing it over her shoulder and continuing to comment.

Duncan, feeling that Professor Batton was kind of a kindred spirit, spoke in his defense.

"Jamie, some of the most brilliant people are the most eccentric and tortured of souls. Maybe he just prefers his solitude."

"Hmm, or maybe it's because he never got married!" she said with a smirk.

"Funny. He seems to have made it through life without needing a wife. From what I've heard, he used to be quite famous and a great inventor," Duncan taunted.

"Maybe so, but he gives me the creeps," Jamie said as she nervously moved a salt shaker back and forth on the table.

Their attention was soon drawn from the old professor when Logan returned to the table.

"All right, one large double pepperoni coming up. You guys ordering anything?" Logan joked.

"Ha-ha. Well, if you're willing to share that sounds

good. I'm starving," Duncan eagerly remarked.

"I'll think about it," Logan said with a laugh, sliding into the booth next to Jamie.

Logan also noticed the old professor sitting at the front end of the restaurant.

"Hey Dunc, look over there. Isn't that crazy old Wofford Batton?"

"Oh, not you, too? Yes, that's Wofford and no, he is not crazy. He is just a recluse," Duncan again defended.

"I just wonder what he's doing out of his coffin before sundown," Logan said with a cracked grin.

"Aw come on. He is not that bad, Logey," Duncan fidgeted with his straw casing, folding it into a tiny accordion.

"Yeah? And just how do you know?" Logan asked, as if to imply something comical with a slight smirk.

"When I was younger I used to mow his yard. He was always good to me," Duncan pointed out.

"Uh huh. He was probably just planning for the day when he could turn you into one of his own kind," Logan taunted as he smirked and made a face at Duncan.

"Funny, Logey. I wouldn't be so quick to judge. He happens to be quite rich from what I understand," Duncan replied in a light scold.

"Well as long he is over there and I am over here we will be just fine."

As the three sat talking, the waiter delivered three drinks to the table and Logan grabbed a straw and tossed it at Duncan, hitting him in the nose. Jamie chuckled at Logan's gesture.

Chapter 4

Einstein and The Eldridge

Later that evening, Duncan was back at home in his room, seated at his computer. He dug through a pile of disorganized notes on his desk to find his mouse and he began researching theories on time travel, his right index finger clicking open a bunch of articles at random.

He had begun this process weeks before. Pretty soon, he found an obscure website which stated, "Time Travel is indeed a real possibility, say scientists."

As Duncan clicked on the site, he saw a number of diagrams, equations, and elaborate theories on how some believed time travel could be achieved. He found one in particular which interested him greatly because the theory involved the use of light and sine waves of sound.

At the bottom of the page he clicked on a thumbnail icon which opened an old black and white picture of Professor Albert Einstein standing next to a chalkboard. On the board was written an equation very similar to the one Duncan had used from Tesla. The subtitle beneath the photo read, "Einstein's relative time thesis." Duncan was entranced at what he was seeing. He quickly grabbed a composition book and a pen out of the drawer of his desk and wrote the equation down.

In anticipation, he then opened the "run dialogue" window on his computer, typed in the equation, and ran the code. To his surprise, a weird image began to manifest on his screen; it was a stream flowing in a figure eight with overlapping paths that seemed to appear at random. Duncan was puzzled by this, he knew it meant something but he wasn't sure what.

He went back to the website and started reading more on theories about time travel, looking for anything he could find to add to his own research.

His eyes were glued to the screen—barely blinking as the black text became a blur in front of him—he was reading so fast.

One theory in particular stated that sine waves, such as those used in audio recordings, radio, or television broadcasts, should be able to be traced.

The theory stated that wherever a certain set of chords or frequencies have been sounded abroad, modern technology could trace its waves of origin. This is because such waves resonate outwardly from their original source, whether it was the first time they were ever sounded or anytime they were sounded since. Therefore, they should be fixed points in time, and thus, always traceable if mankind could ever find a way to locate such sounds, theoretically.

Other theories claimed that a precisely modulated pulse made with laser emitters, when coupled with sound, should be able to open a door into time. This would allow explorers to pass through with ease.

Duncan was now more intrigued than ever. He sat back in his chair and rubbed his eyes, thinking about his own theory which involved using his own laser pulse emitters to create rifts in the space-time continuum. He also thought about his own experiences, like earlier in the day when he heard what seemed to be himself and Jamie arguing. All of this had given him some food for thought.

This has to be why I heard myself and Jamie arguing this morning. What I heard had to have come from the future at some point, he thought.

He stood up, walked over to his closet, and began to pilfer through a bunch of boxes. As he was rummaging, he found an old picture of his grandfather standing next to a United States naval vessel. Near his grandfather in the picture was a sign that showed two number designations. One sign said CVE-60; the other below it said DE-173. Duncan knew that his granddad had been in the navy, but he did not know in what capacity. Duncan took the photo and clinched it between his teeth before grabbing two large speakers from his closet and walking back to his computer. He opened a search engine on his desktop and typed in the two number designations. He first typed in CVE-60, which returned the result: Carrier Vessel Escort number 60 U.S.S. Guadalcanal was the carrier that captured the German submarine U-505 which is now housed at the Museum of Science and Industry, also known as M.O.S.I., in Chicago.

Duncan did not know what exactly his grandpa had done in the navy, but he knew he had not served on a carrier. Then, Duncan typed in the second number designation and, to his shock, he became wide eyed as he read Destroyer Escort number 173 U.S.S. Eldridge, the destroyer famed to have disappeared in a naval endeavor gone awry known as the "Philadelphia Experiment." Duncan knew this story all too well. He had read the book and seen several movies about this legendary ship.

No wonder grandpa never said anything about this. It was highly classified and I read that Albert Einstein was rumored to have been involved with this experiment, but could this equation be the answer? He pondered.

Along with the picture of his granddad was a birthday card which read, "From Grandpa to Duncan, my gosh, four years old already. How time flies. I know you will do great things one day, little man. Love you always, Rex Sims (Grandpa)."

Duncan quickly hooked up a set of speakers to his computer. He intended to run Einstein's code in hopes of breaking through the dimensional barrier to see if he could recapture the same effect and hear what he had heard earlier that morning.

While the equations ran as a sub routine, Duncan began to hear some odd sounds vibrating from the speakers. It was as if many people were talking all at once and he wondered who or what they could be. He increased the volume, his ear drums buzzing, and saw what appeared to be flashes of light in his room; yet, they seemed to be coming from no specific direction.

What the…? No, it must be my imagination, it could not be that easy, Duncan thought in dismay. All at once, the code stopped and he looked around, wondering if he now had the key to puncturing the walls of time.

Duncan reset the code and tried it again; this time he heard voices and other noises and he saw the same flashes again. His heart began to thud in his chest as he kept on reading. He couldn't figure out what was happening, so he looked for information about atmospheric disturbances associated with Einstein or Tesla's work on the internet. He found several pages concerning Nikola Tesla and The Philadelphia

Experiment and read about events which happened to the U.S.S. Eldridge, some of which were quite lengthy.

Duncan shut his eyes and felt them sting from staring at his screen for so long. His brain had been in overdrive for hours and he didn't realize how drained he felt, yet exhilarated at the same time. He looked at the clock by his bed and saw that is was three a.m. He was exhausted, but he felt he was really onto something.

"Could this be the answer? Can I use my own theory along with Einstein's code and do what no one else has yet achieved?" he muttered to himself.

Duncan stood up from his desk and collapsed onto his bed. As he laid back with one arm behind his head, he reached over and picked up a Bible from his bedside table and turned to the Book of Revelation, Chapter One. He began to read about John the apostle being taken to the future.

John saw the future. There has to be a way to travel through time, Duncan assured himself.

Duncan laid his head back with the Bible open on his chest and began to ponder these things, but the pull of the soft pillow was a battle he wasn't going to win. Duncan soon fell asleep.

Chapter 5

Parents Just Don't Understand

Duncan's mother, Shellie, was always very supportive of him and tolerant of his research. Most days she was, at least. Unfortunately, today would not be one of those days. Today, she had enough of Duncan and his 'experiment.'

She woke Duncan abruptly by popping him on his leg with one of his own shoes which she had grabbed as she entered his room.

"Duncan?! Duncan? Wake up! You cannot sleep all day," she screeched in an angry tone. Her dark hair was up in a chiffon bun, and her makeup was applied impeccably even though she was just at home.

Duncan jolted awake, pulled the covers over himself, and turned on his side. "All right, all right, I am awake already," he yawned.

"What are you doing in bed? Do you know what time it is?" she inquired angrily.

"I had a late night doing some research."

"Research? You need to research getting a job. If your father knew you were still asleep he would blow the roof off this house."

"Okay, I said I was awake. Sheesh," Duncan replied angrily as he stretched, his strong back muscles flexing as he moved.

"Duncan, I know you have your own priorities but you are twenty four years old and you haven't had a job in seven months. Don't you think it's time you started thinking of your future?" Shellie interrogated. Her hands were on her hips as she looked down at his sleepy form.

"Yes, mom. I have been rushing to complete this experiment. It might be the catalyst that gives me the success I need."

"Experiment? What experiment? Building that prop?" Shellie questioned with sarcasm.

"It's not a prop. I'm onto something big. In a few days, I will know if it works or if it's a dead end," Duncan said defiantly, slapping his palms against the mattress.

"If your father catches you sleeping in, you'll be a dead man. The world is not going to stop turning for you." She looked around the room, almost as an afterthought. "Also, your room is a mess, mister. What is wrong with you?"

"Nothing is wrong with me. Listen, I will go look for a job this morning, okay?" Duncan answered in an annoyed tone.

She continued to berate him as he sat up on the edge of the bed. It was the same old story, but from the tone in her voice he knew he had to do something today.

"Good, then at least your dad will know you are trying. He works hard Duncan, and he expects you to do the same," his mother said as she hovered over him.

"I know what he expects. I hear it every day," Duncan protested.

Duncan and his dad had a history of butting heads over Duncan's seemingly blatant disregard for being in the working class.

"Yeah? Well then get a job and you won't hear

it. And what about Jamie? How will you make a life with her if you have no money?"

"Mom, I know all this! I will find something okay?"

Duncan's mom rolled her eyes and continued her rhetoric. "I don't know why you turned down the scholarship you were offered. You have such potential and you're just wasting it. Anyway, I just put your good clothes in the closet. So dress up so you can make a good first impression."

"I know how to get a job, okay mom?!" Duncan answered in a gruff tone.

"Good, then do so. I will support you in anything except laziness," Shellie said.

"I'm not lazy! What I'm doing is very time consuming and if I succeed, you will see that it has all been worth it," Duncan replied confidently.

"If you succeed, Duncan... I only want you to be happy, and you know that, but you can't live without money."

"I know mom, just give me time, okay?" *It is ironic that the thing I am asking you for is the very thing I am trying to solve the mystery of,* he thought to himself.

"Duncan, time is not going to wait for you. One day you may regret not making use of the opportunities and gifts you have been blessed with," Shellie pressed.

Duncan rolled his eyes as his mother picked up a wad of Duncan's dirty clothes off the floor then turned and left his room. Again, Duncan stretched then slowly got out of bed and pulled on his clothes. He sat down and then blew air out of his mouth in frustration. Downstairs, Duncan's aunt and his mother were sitting at the dinner table working on some homemade hand towels. As they sat and talked about the events of the day, Duncan walked through the house to the dining area.

As Duncan came into the room, he spotted Aunt Sarah sitting at the table. *That explains a lot. I guess that's why mom was so intense this morning and going on about getting a job. Better not hang around here unless I want to hear more of the same,* he thought.

Duncan's Aunt Sarah was always very critical of Duncan. She was a bitter older woman who wanted more out of life than she had achieved and now in her later years, she had little, if anything, to say that was positive. She meant well, but she lacked tact and always said what was on her mind regardless of how it affected others.

Duncan's mother, while she was not entirely pleased with Duncan's behavior, was also a little more defensive of Duncan, especially with Sarah.

Duncan walked by the table dressed in a nice shirt and slacks. "All right, mom, I am headed out job hunting. I'll be back when I can."

Sarah laid down the towel she was working on. "Oh my, you are actually going job hunting? I better mark my calendar," Sarah chided.

Shellie looked toward her. "Sarah, please, he's doing what I asked," she defended.

"Yes dear, but you shouldn't have to ask him to do what he knows he should do in the first place," Sarah said as she picked up the towel and began stitching again.

Duncan, annoyed by the comment, simply said, "Whatever, I'll see you later." He walked out of the front door, letting it slam behind him. He had an annoyed look on his face and headed off to try and find a job.

Sarah sat there with her mouth open, in shock of how lax Shellie seemed to be concerning Duncan.

A moment passed as Sarah looked over at Shellie, who was busy working on a towel as if nothing had happened. Finally, Sarah could not hold back any longer. "Shellie, why do you and Frank put up with his attitude?" she asked with her usual tactless tone.

Shellie looked directly at her and politely said, "He is young Sarah. He does not take life as seriously as we do."

Sarah was less than impressed by Shellie's answer. She fiddled with the edges of her towel.

"Well, he better start taking it seriously. Frank was on his own by twenty-one. He met you and was married by twenty-two. Duncan is twenty-four years old and he needs to act like it," she said, waving her hand in the air dismissively.

"Duncan will find his way, Sarah. He is not his father."

"Well, that is for sure. Frank always did what he was supposed to do," Sarah said, full of pride.

"Ha, not always. Frank had his problems when we were younger, but he grew up and so will Duncan."

"He'd better. This is a different world now, Shellie. It's cruel and cold."

"Yes, it is, and Duncan is dealing with it in his own way. And I know you care, but you're not making it any easier for him. Now can we drop this, please?" Shellie asked politely.

"Okay, but Duncan will have a rough road ahead of him if he doesn't change."

"Perhaps, but no one has it easy. Now pass me the navy blue thread, please."

"Sure." Sarah handed Shellie the thread as she shrugged her shoulders and rolled her eyes in defeat.

Chapter Six

Father Versus Son

Duncan walked down the main street of his hometown, looking at storefronts. The weather was chilly with a low of 50; it was a comfortable break from the normal warm weather of summer and fall. The trees lining the sidewalk swayed in the morning breeze. As he walked, he passed restaurants, parts stores, printing companies, and thrift shops, all of which were teeming with life. Duncan looked around and saw familiar faces, but had no clue where to apply. He didn't even know where to start and there were no 'now hiring' signs in any of the windows within his sight. Undaunted, he strolled into every door he could find, seeking work.

For Duncan, it was not enough to just find a job; of course, for his parents that's all that mattered, but he needed to be in an environment that would allow him to mentally work through the issues of his Time Box while also appeasing his parents. This meant a job with little to no brain power and plenty of down time. This led him to place spontaneous applications in all of the smaller, less busy shops in town.

Duncan walked into the office of a smaller business; a simplistic blend of modern technology filled the room. Duncan could sense that this business was growing, making him even more eager. He approached the reception desk.

"Hi, how may I help you?" the receptionist said with a gleeful, yet tight, grin.

"Hi! I know this is a long shot, but are you guys hiring at all?" Duncan asked with a hopeful tone.

"I'm so sorry, but we are no longer taking applications at this time..." the receptionist trailed off.

"That's ok," Duncan said with a forced smile. "Thank you." He shrugged his shoulders and began to walk away.

After a few stops, he walked into a small bike shop. The doorbell rang, announcing his entrance. There was an older gentleman sitting on a stool behind a counter, his glasses low on his nose as he tinkered with a bike chain over a glass display case.

"Can I help you young man?" the man asked, his eyes looking up at Duncan.

"I was just looking around to find some work. Are you hiring, by any chance?" he asked, clearing his throat.

The man shook his head. "Sorry young man, it's just me in here and I'm not busy enough right now to need any help," he said before he went right back to fixing the chain.

Duncan looked around at the rows of bikes lining the walls and the obvious absence of customers and sighed.

"Okay—thank you, sir," he replied, running his fingers through his hair.

As Duncan left the store, his mind kept drifting to the dark, cool inside of his Time Box and he wished that he was there.

What a waste an entire day this had been, I could have been home this whole time working on my box, he groaned inwardly.

Soon after he had passed nearly all the storefronts in town, he noticed that the sun was setting and he decided he should just head back home.

Not much is happening in this small Florida town to speak of. Why does my Dad think there are jobs everywhere in this dead end town? All day long he had looked for work, but to no avail.

The day passed slowly, but eventually evening came. Duncan returned home from his job search and as he walked up to his house, he dreaded the words his dad would surely say. He rubbed his temples as his head began to pound, but he paused in his front yard for a moment, his gaze fixed on the tall covered box standing there like a hopeful reminder of what could be.

One day I'll show them all, he thought as he dragged his feet up the concrete front steps.

His dad, Frank, and his mom were already seated at the table eating when he walked into the dining room. They were discussing the day's events as Duncan came in and shrugged a sigh, then sat down at the table without a word. He rubbed his legs through his jeans because they were aching from a long day of walking. His stomach rumbled loudly, causing his father's head to turn quickly to stare at him. Duncan didn't meet his glare and Shellie, sensing the tension, fiddled with her napkin.

"So, Frank," she began, "Did you hear that Debbie is filing for divorce? It's such a shame but she—" she trailed off as she noticed no one was listening.

Frank ignored her completely as he looked with disdain at his son. Duncan began digging into pans of food his mother had prepared and filling his plate as his dad looked on. Not a word was uttered until Frank, while tapping his fingers on the dinner table, began to question Duncan.

"Well, I hear you went job hunting. Did you find anything?"

Duncan looked up at his dad momentarily, taking in his disapproving look. "No sir, but I did put in over fifteen applications," Duncan replied as he averted his eyes back to the food.

"Fifteen, huh? Well at least you did something worthwhile today... for a change," Frank commented sarcastically. He scooped up some mashed potatoes onto his fork, the metal scraping the plate.

"Frank, please! He did what you asked," Shellie pleaded as she placed her hand on his shoulder.

"Yeah, today he did! But why should I have to ask him? He is not a kid anymore, Shellie," Frank said gruffly, shrugging out of her grasp.

Duncan was irked by the remark. "No? Then why do you treat me like I am perpetually eight years old?"

"Because you apparently don't know how to act like an adult! Most twenty-four year olds have a job Duncan!" Frank retorted with a snap as he slammed his fork down on the table.

"Dad, I have been working on something very important. It could change our lives!" Duncan pleaded.

Frank offered a sardonic chuckle. "The only thing you have been working on is more efficient ways to slack off. Too bad you can't get paid for that."

"You don't know what I'm working on! And, what's more, you don't even care," Duncan said, looking directly at his dad.

"You're right, I don't care! You're not going to build a future by playing on the computer or working on that stupid box!"

"That stupid box may very well be the thing that brings me the success you so highly covet," Duncan argued, leaning forward hard over the table.

"No Duncan, getting a job is the only way you're going to have success! This house didn't get paid for because I sat around on a computer everyday or spent my time living in some science fiction fantasy!" Frank snapped.

Shellie had seen this same argument play out evening after evening for weeks and tonight she had had enough. She nervously ran her fingers through her shoulder length brown hair as she spoke up for Duncan. "Frank, stop it! He spent all day looking for a job."

"That's great, Shellie! And when he finds one I won't need to say anything!" Frank replied, exasperated. His anger grew with his wife's input; his frustration built upon the foundation of his son's lack of motivation to work and his wife's constant coddling.

For a moment there was silence. Frank grabbed his glass of tea and began taking a sip, but Duncan got a self-righteous look on this face.

"No, you will find fault with me no matter what I do," he reasoned.

Frank's face reddened deeply in anger. "You listen to me, boy! I was working when I was 14 years old, and I have never stopped. You get a job then you can talk," Frank replied as he slammed the glass down spilling a few drops.

"I'm trying, dad. I'm really trying," Duncan

countered, his tone rising in frustration.

"No, you're not! One day of job hunting does not constitute trying as hard as you can!" Frank said harshly.

"Whatever—you'll never be satisfied! You sound just like Aunt Sarah." Duncan said dismissively.

"Yeah? I'll tell you this junior, your Aunt Sarah worked all her life and was able to retire! You on the other hand have not worked in, what, seven months now?"

"That is because I'm working on something which might give me some real success!" Duncan argued once again.

His father sighed in frustration and ran his hand over his face. "Duncan, building a piece of crap is not going to make you a success—hard work will."

"Hard work may make some successful but all it's done for you is make you bitter! You always come home mad and complaining about your job," Duncan argued.

"That's because I work sixty plus hours a week to put food on this table and support *you*, who should be working! And then, to top it off, I have to come home and listen to you make excuses?" Frank yelled as he slammed his palms down on the table.

Shellie jumped at the sound and decided she'd had enough. "Okay, that's enough! Both of you! I am sick of this happening every night." She turned to glare at her husband. "He's right, Frank. You come home with a chip on your shoulder every day. And yes, Duncan should be working, but he is trying!"

"Hold it, why are you taking his side?" Frank asked in a taunting tone.

Shellie threw up her arms in exasperation. "I

am not taking his side, but I have had it with this same thing happening every day. Just drop it!"

"All right, fine. I'll just drop it. Let him get away with whatever he wants," Frank said, spite dripping from his voice.

"Frank, don't start with me!" Shellie warned, giving him a grimacing look.

Frank held his tongue and glared at Shellie who glared right back at him.

"Mom? Where is Linda?" Duncan asked in an attempt to change the subject and diffuse the situation.

Why is Linda always missing when mom and dad are ragging on me? he thought.

Shellie turned her gaze to Duncan, her eyes guarded. "She's out on a date."

This led Frank to become more enraged. "Yeah, she's another one! No one cares about anything but the moment," Frank spouted.

"Frank, she's young! Everyone has their time to be young. Don't you remember the trouble we used to get into?"

"Yeah, I do. And that is exactly what I'm worried about!" he muttered, giving Shellie a snide look. She looked away from his face suddenly, biting her lip in hurt at his hard words.

Duncan, by this time, had enough and had lost his appetite. "Can I be excused? Suddenly I am not hungry anymore and I need to get back to my research."

"Sure, why not?" Frank yelled in anger.

"Why not! All you do is sit in front of the computer or work on that stupid contraption!"

"Frank, why do you have to have such an attitude with him?" Shellie interrupted. "If he does nothing you complain, when he tries, you complain! He's just like we used to be, or have you forgotten?"

"No Shellie, he's not like we were. I worked, you worked! But little Lord Fauntleroy over here thinks work is beneath him!"

"Yes, I know, and now the whole neighborhood knows it, too. We have covered this over and over again! We can't sit down and have a civil meal like a normal family and I'm tired of it," Shellie growled.

"That's because I have put up with his laziness for far too long."

"Nothing I do pleases you, dad," Duncan argued, rolling his eyes.

"Pleases me? That's because you hardly do anything!" Frank half-laughed.

"No, you mean I hardly do anything you want," Duncan clarified.

"What I want is for you to become responsible and make something of yourself."

"I'm trying to do what you want, dad."

"No more excuses, Duncan. I've heard them all. Start acting like a man!"

"Yeah whatever, dad," Duncan snapped.

Frank was not a bad father but he, unknown to Duncan, was going through rough times. Frank placed his hand over his eyes; he was more frustrated with his son than ever. The economy was getting worse and worse and he himself lived in constant fear of being laid off from his job. He was also at the end of his rope with Duncan's attitude.

When his father didn't respond, Duncan stood up quickly and shoved his chair back under the table angrily, the wood screeching against the floor. He carried his plate to the sink and threw it into the reservoir with a clang before stomping into the hallway and heading upstairs toward his room.

Frank stood up in anger at the blatant show of defiance, ready to give Duncan a real tongue-lashing.

"Frank, stop! That's enough—I mean it!" Shellie said angrily, her eyes beginning to water.

Frank sat back down at the table and leaned over to Shellie, his green eyes staring coldly into her light blue ones. "That kid is just like your brother!" he sneered.

"Yeah? And so were you when we met! You had your own ideas, and if I recall, your parents did not approve either."

Frank, realizing he upset Shellie, tried to calm down and be civil. Taking a deep breath, he said, "Those were different times, honey. If Duncan doesn't do something, he's never going to amount to anything. I won't have it!"

"Let him be, Frank. He's trying," Shellie pleaded in a softer tone.

"He's trying my patience. That is what he's trying!"

"You didn't need to get so upset with him. He barely ate anything," she mumbled, looking down at the table in dismay.

"Well maybe it's this roast. What did you do to it? It's like leather," Frank remarked as he attempted to cut the roast with a steak knife.

Shellie now seethed with anger.

She was offended that Frank had decided to take out his anger on Duncan and now on her. She smoothed her skirt with her palms, trying to remain calm. "Oh? Well, you are more than welcome to do the cooking from now on if you can do better."

"No, it's fine honey. It's fine. I'm sorry. Look, I'm

eating it...yum," Frank said as he pretended to enjoy the tough meat, his jaw clenching.

"I thought so," Shellie replied smugly.

Meanwhile, Duncan, frustrated with his dad, walked out to his box and opened it up. He looked inside at all of his hard work; the blinking red buttons and tangle of wires soothed him somehow. *Not long now and we'll show them all,* he thought to himself.

Duncan closed the door and locked his box, his antique key turning with a click. He leaned against the box and drew in a deep breath before he cautiously walked back into the house and made his way to his room, shutting the door behind him.

Chapter 7

Love Hurts

Duncan, still perturbed, sat down and turned his computer on. He was now a man on a mission; however, he needed to do further research, so he went back to the website he had been looking at to see if he could find anything further about time travel theory.

He read from one forum that stated, "Modified pulse emission lasers seemed to have had the most credible results to date when it comes to altering the fabric of space and time." The forum stated that data gathered from thirty-three separate tests seemed to reveal a pattern of opening small windows into time and mapping time via sync sine waves. The writer of the forum had made a note that said, "Look below to see the two most successful patterns of aligning your modified pulse emission lasers. See figure 2 for specs on building modified pulse emitters. For schematics, see Section C figures 1-21."

Duncan sat back and stroked his chin; he paused for a moment, looking at his equipment, and then began to dig in deeper.

The deep yellows and oranges of the sunset began to filter through the window. Duncan barely noticed as the day faded and he continued to read the blog which stated: "However, if you do not have the means to acquire lasers for pulse emission modification, another option in theory is to use four or eight powerful stereo speakers in the 120 to 250 watt range directed at 45 degree angles aimed on one central point, which is referred to as the wave core. This is coupled with a high power amplifier and a sync wave pattern modulator to cause what two separate physicists have labeled as the ripple core wave effect."

Duncan paused and looked to his left and, for a moment, stared at his speakers. He shared a glance back and forth between the speakers and computer screen.

"In theory," the article stated, "the ripple core effect will send pulses—much like those seen in heavy bass vibration—that, by their length, can cause visual ripples in air. This means it is well within reason to suppose that they could disrupt the fabric of the space and time continuum.

Tests have shown that, when coupled with the correct sync modulation and used with the little-known Einstein time theory equation, as seen in Figure 4, these sound and sync waves can cause what some label as amazing results."

Duncan was now more excited then ever and began to write notes; when he finished, he looked out at his Time Box.

Soon, you are going to take me exactly where I need to go, he thought to himself before continuing his research.

The article continued. "Witnesses to three laboratory experiments using this method claim to have seen visions of days past. None of these claims can be substantiated due to the highly secretive nature of these experiments. However, the research continues. See diagram below in Figure 8 for the layout of the Ripple Core Wave Method."

Duncan was fascinated and entranced with what he was reading. His cell phone rang, but he was so engrossed in his train of thought that he jumped slightly in his chair. He looked down at his phone; it was Jamie calling and he quickly answered the phone.

"Hey babe," Jamie said. "What are you up to tonight?"

"Oh, nothing at the moment. I went job hunting and was gone all day. I haven't been home long and I just had dinner. I thought I might try a test tonight on my box," Duncan replied.

"Well, do you need any help? Do you want me to come by?" she asked in a hopeful tone.

Duncan replied, "Absolutely! Come on over. You can help." Jamie agreed, so Duncan said, "Okay see you in a few." He pressed on his phone and rubbed his finger over the picture of Jamie, still illuminated on his screen.

Duncan realized he had work to do and walked over to his closet. He grabbed a box from the top shelf, which was filled with circuits and salvaged parts. Behind the box, Duncan found four high watt speakers, which he had purchased when he had his previous car. *I can use these.*

He left his room and walked through his house with the box of circuits, the four small, but powerful, speakers, and his laptop computer balanced on top. He saw that his dad and mom were watching television as he passed behind the living room and exited through the kitchen door.

Duncan pulled the tarpaulin off the box then opened the door and turned the power on, which lit up the tall, gray box. Without hesitation, he began wiring the speakers in sequence—as he had seen on the diagram—in a configuration under the previously installed home-built laser pulse emitters. He mounted the speakers near the lasers because, in theory, the sound and light pulses should work to his specifications.

Duncan spaced the speakers at the specified angles on a central focal point. Jamie walked up to him and this time let him know she was there so as not to startle him.

"Hey, what are you doing in there?" she asked with a sweet smile.

"Hey, babe. I am just trying to get the speakers put at the correct angles and placement," he answered, his eyes never leaving the circuit board.

"I thought you had a sound system on this thing already."

"I do, but these are for my experiment."

"Oh, yeah, the big secret," she said with an exaggerated hand gesture. He didn't notice her eyes roll at the topic.

Duncan was lying cramped on the floor, his jean-clad legs and white sneakers sticking out of the box. It was a wonder he could fit in there at all; he was so tall. Jamie stuck her head inside to see what he was doing.

"Actually, it should be more of a surprise than a secret." Duncan grinned, "Do me a favor and push the three red switches by my laptop, will ya?" he asked, glancing at her quickly.

Jamie looked and saw several switches, then located the three red ones.

"These three?" she asked, her perfectly manicured fingernails hovering over the buttons.

"Yeah, just don't touch the big gear shift looking

switch though."

"Yes, sir, Captain," she said in a smart aleck tone and saluted him. Jamie turned the switches on and the inside of the box began to sound a deep vibrating tone, which permeated the whole area around the box.

"Wow now that is some noise," she remarked, looking around inside the box as it shook.

"Oh, you haven't seen anything yet. It's gonna take a while, but I'm expecting to see some big results. Well, I hope so, anyway," Duncan said optimistically.

"What's in that big cabinet?" she asked.

"Oh, those are used gel pack batteries. Retz's dad gave them to me, but they still hold a full charge."

"Oh, I see. You're trying to make this where you don't have to plug it in, right?"

"Um, yeah...sort of," Duncan said, not wanting to reveal too much to Jamie.

She sure is asking a lot of questions today... he thought to himself.

"Well it should have fantastic sound, if nothing else," she complimented.

About that time a young man rode up on a bicycle. It was Marshall Martinez. Now, every neighborhood has an annoying younger teen, and Marshall was the terror of Duncan's street. Marshall seemed to delight in annoying and pestering Duncan at every opportunity.

Jamie turned toward Marshall when she heard the bicycle on the crackling leaves. She took in his greasy, dark hair and pimpled face and felt a twinge of pity for him.

"Oh, hi Marshall. How are you?" Jamie asked in

a pleasant greeting.

"Oh no, not him!" Duncan grunted. He stopped what he was doing and rubbed his neck.

"I'm awesome, Jamie C. Hey Duncan, what are you making? Some kind of sound booth or a funny looking Port-o-Potty?" Marshall insulted.

"Not now, Marshall. Can't you see I'm busy?" Duncan spat.

"Oh, you're always busy—busy wasting your time," Marshall replied in a snarky tone.

"Isn't there some traffic you can go play in, Marshall?" Duncan fired back.

"I just wanted to know what you're doing with this thing, whatever it is," he said, twisting his fingers around his handlebars.

"Something you could never comprehend, Marshall. Now take off will ya?" Duncan said condescendingly.

"Sure, but only if Jamie can come with me," Marshall winked at Jamie.

"Yeah, keep dreaming," Duncan replied with snarky tone.

"All right, I'll go for now, but I'll be back. See you later, Jamie. See ya, Dufus!" Marshall rode off into the dark on his bike but never once looked back.

"Oh, thank God!" Duncan said, relieved.

"Why do you let him get to you?" Jamie asked. "He probably just wants to be your friend."

"No, thanks. One Logan is enough. I think they must be related somehow."

"Yeah, but you and Logan are best friends," Jamie mused.

"I know, but I've known Logan for a long time and I'm used to his mouth. Marshall just grates on me and everyone else he comes into contact with," Duncan remarked.

Jamie took this opportunity to casually bring up the subject of marriage again. "So speaking of Logan, will he be your best man when you do decide to get married?" Jamie asked, hoping to provoke Duncan to answer her.

Jamie was a very sweet girl but she had little patience. She had met Duncan through Logan and even before they had gotten together she had been taken with him.

"For the answer to that you will have to wait and see. Anyway, I'm almost done here."

Duncan was tightening a bolt when the screwdriver slipped and he cut his finger. "Ouch, ohh," he yelled.

"Duncan? What happened?" Jamie asked, concerned.

"Ah, I cut my hand. The screwdriver slipped," he answered as he stepped out of the box.

"Is it bad?"

"No, it just hurts a lot," Duncan said, cupping his finger.

Jamie looked to see that Duncan's finger was covered in blood. "You're bleeding. Do you want to me to get a cloth?" Jamie offered as she reached for his hand, but he jerked it away.

"Nah, it will stop in a minute," Duncan said, sticking his finger in his mouth and biting it to dull the pain and to stop the bleeding.

Once Jamie was sure Duncan was okay, she attempted to go back to the subject of marriage. "So, you would not want Logan to be your best man?" she asked meekly.

Duncan heard her but ignored her question and

began ranting about the tool. "I need to get a better screwdriver. This one is useless," he muttered as he threw the screwdriver into the box. It rattled around as it bounced and came to rest on the floor.

Jamie was perturbed by Duncan's lack of attention to her question and the discussion of marriage. "Um, Duncan?" she huffed.

"Yeah babe?"

"Why do you always do that?"

"Do what?" Duncan asked, oblivious.

"Why do you always have to change the subject whenever I mention anything about marriage?"

"I wasn't changing the subject. Did I say something wrong?" Duncan asked innocently, looking up at her in earnest.

Jamie visibly clenched her jaw and sighed. She had waited for Duncan to make a move for their life together, but Duncan had other things on his mind at the moment and Jamie was feeling neglected. "It's not what you just said. It's what you always do when I even hint at us getting married," she moaned, her eyes filling with saddened tears.

"What do you mean? We talked about this yesterday."

"Yeah, for like five minutes! You always find a way to get out of answering me and you act like you care more about this box than you do about me," Jamie cried.

"Babe, it's not like that at all. This is just really important to me," Duncan pleaded.

Jamie was aggravated. She and Duncan were getting more and more agitated as they talked. "I can tell it's important to you. You spend all your time on this thing or researching whatever it is you are trying to do. The only time I ever see you is if I call you and come over here," she espoused.

"That is not true and you know it."

"Really? When was the last time we had any time alone—just you and me, huh? Either this thing is occupying you, or Logan is around. It's like you don't care about me anymore," Jamie proclaimed in a hurt tone.

"Jamie, I care about you more than anything or anyone."

"That's hard to believe, judging by how much time you spend on this thing or with Logan," she chided back.

As the argument escalated, Professor Batton happened to be out walking his dog in the street in front of Duncan's house and unintentionally overheard Duncan's heated exchange with Jamie. His curiosity got the better of him and he stood in a dark spot by the road so as not to be seen as Duncan and Jamie continued to argue.

"Are you actually jealous of this wooden box? And Logan? Seriously, Jamie?" Duncan scathed.

"Why shouldn't I be? They get all of your time and attention. The last time I checked this is not how courtship works," Jamie said, hugging her arms around herself protectively.

"Jamie, you are being unreasonable. We've been together a year and now you want to get married all of the sudden?" Duncan questioned argumentatively.

Jamie stared at Duncan blankly. "Well, there it is. *I* want to get married as opposed to you, who obviously does not!"

"I didn't say that," Duncan said in a calmer voice.

Jamie began to be overcome with emotion and to choke up, large tears forming in her eyes.

"You didn't have to say it. You just said, 'And now *you* want to get married,' as if this is all one-sided," Jamie argued.

"I didn't mean it like that and you know it. I just meant—"

"Never mind, Duncan," she said as she began to cry. "I see now why you've avoided talking about this. I'm sorry. I thought you felt the same way about me as I do about you. I'm going to go," Jamie said in a sorrowful voice as she began to back away. She looked extremely hurt.

She began to walk toward Duncan's driveway but Duncan followed her. He ran up behind her and grabbed her over her shoulders in an embrace.

"Jamie—" he started, but she cut him off.

"Duncan please...just don't," she pushed back.

"Jamie, listen to me, okay? I love you, and I do plan for us to get married—just not right now."

Jamie turned to face Duncan and he could see her face was streaked with tears. She tried to wipe them away but there was no stopping them.

"Duncan, you're wasting your life. You're wasting *our* lives on this experiment of yours!" Jamie tried to reason.

"Jamie, I have worked so hard on this. This might be my only chance to see it through," Duncan yelled in explanation.

"I know you have worked hard on this. I know it's important to you, but now it has become more important to you than I am. Do you know how that makes me feel?" she sobbed.

She tore herself away from Duncan's embrace and backed away from him.

"Jamie..." Duncan pleaded.

"This experiment has replaced me in your heart.

That hurts me in ways you can't even imagine," Jamie explained through her tears.

"Why? Just because I don't want to get married right now? Why is it all you women think about is marriage? We have plenty of time."

"Just forget it, Duncan. Forget me!" Jamie turned and sprinted away as Duncan looked on after her.

"Jamie stop! My experiment involves time travel! It could build a future for us!" Duncan yelled, but to no avail. He watched in dismay as her long brown hair swung behind her.

Professor Batton, still standing in the street listening, was filled with excitement. Not at the poor couple's argument, but rather the words time travel.

"Time travel? What? Time travel is not an experiment—it's a fantasy, Duncan! That's not a future! *We* should have been the future," Jamie yelled back as she continued to quickly walk away.

"Jamie, is this really happening? You are blowing this way out of proportion.   It's like you wanted this to happen," Duncan accused.

"Forget it Duncan…it doesn't matter now, okay?" Jamie said in defeat. She was now walking backwards and throwing her hands in the air in defeat.

"Of course it matters, but you won't listen! You're the one walking away—not me—over a stupid mistake!"

"Yeah, apparently we both made a mistake, Duncan! I hope you and that box and Logan will be happy together!"

Jamie turned and took off running, sobbing out of control. She turned the corner and disappeared from sight as Duncan stormed back to his box, fuming with anger. "Crap baskets!" he yelled. He threw the wrench in his hand down and punched the box, hurting his knuckles. He clutched his hand in pain. "Ohh! That's real, oh yeah, that's real!" he exclaimed to himself as he shook his hand, knowing he had really hurt himself.

When his hand finally simmered down and was only a dull ache, Duncan paced back and forth in front of the box as if he didn't know what to do.

Well, that just happened!

Jamie was gone; she really gave up on him this time. Duncan was now alone at his box and unaware that Professor Batton was still standing in the darkened street and had seen everything. Duncan, still in disbelief, continued to pace back and forth in front of his box with a menacing, hateful, and somewhat baffled look on his face.

I'm just going to put all my energy into my time box from now on. When I finally get it to work Jamie, and everyone else, will see. They'll all see, Duncan thought, his mind racing.

Chapter 8

The Great Experiment

Unknown to Duncan, Professor Wofford Batton had a history in similar experiments with time travel. The professor continued to watch from the street, wondering if he should approach Duncan.

Duncan, now with nothing to lose, at least in his own mind, walked into his box. He turned on his laptop and began to play music through a program, which modulated it into a mechanized noise. The LED lights inside the box reacted to the noise and flashed in pulses. Duncan opened the file with the codes that he had saved from Einstein's equation. He scrolled fast and began to run the program, making a few last-minute adjustments.

Duncan looked down to see that the volume was set on twelve percent, so he turned it up. He threw the yellow switch and pushed the gearshift lever forward slightly—the same lever he had warned Jamie not to touch earlier. The program ran and a curious sound, much like a powerful hum, began to grow in intensity.

Duncan's laptop began flashing with random numbers, which he did not fully understand. He increased the volume even more and began seeing what appeared to be some ghost-like figures that he could not really make out.

He turned the volume to maximum and his box began to shudder.

The speakers pulsed rapidly and the lights flickered as the codes proceeded on the computer. Duncan looked at the screen as more and more numbers popped up randomly on his grid. His heart thudded in his chest as he waited to see what would happen.

Duncan grabbed the mouse, chose a random number, and pushed his lever all the way forward. The batteries began to pulse with maximum power. The beacon light on top of the box began to flash and lights began to emanate from the box. The sound was getting louder, like a jet engine powering up.

Suddenly, the box began to glow green as a phosphorescent light enveloped it like St. Elmo's fire. The light quickly turned to an amber shade and circled in a unique pattern; the box began to phase and started to dematerialize. It grew brighter and brighter as it struggled to dematerialize into the unknown.

Standing at a good vantage point, Professor Wofford Batton witnessed the events, as he stood shocked with his mouth hanging open.

"He is actually doing it!" he said to himself.

Finally, the box disappeared and was gone.

"I cannot believe it. He's done it!" he said in astonishment, pointing his cane in the air and cheering.

He walked over to where the box has just been standing, but it was gone.

Chapter 9

Time for a Surprise

Duncan, inside his box, observed the flashing lights surrounding him and felt the vibrations, but he sensed no movement. He wondered if he was moving at all, or if it was only the loud noise coming from his sound system that was making the craft shudder. His eyes rolled over the entire interior as he tried to locate the source of the light.

Duncan does not yet realize it, but he is in fact traveling in time. Soon, this would become all too apparent. It was the year 2019; it was a cold morning, and Duncan had been missing since the night he and Jamie had broken up—a year and a day earlier.

It was a beautiful, clear, and crisp day. The sky was clear and blue and the sun reflected brightly on the main street in Duncan's hometown. Jamie walked hand in hand with Logan as they enjoyed the brisk morning.

"What time are you getting off work today?" Jamie asked, looking up into Logan's eyes with a smile.

"I am not sure. I will probably be home around five thirty, but no later than six," Logan replied.

"Do you want chicken or steak for dinner?" she inquired.

"Either is fine, or we can go out, if you'd rather. I know this last year has been rough for you," Logan said, running a fingers through her light brown hair.

Jamie looked down. "It's hard to believe he's been gone a whole year."

"A year and a day. I miss him too," Logan lamented.

"I can't believe he would just up and leave like that," she paused, "I talked to his mom this morning."

Logan looked at Jamie and said, "I guess if they had heard anything they would have told us by now."

"I still feel like it was all my fault," Jamie said, her voice full of sorrow.

Logan halted and tenderly embraced Jamie. "It's was no one's fault. Duncan chose to leave without as much as a goodbye. I would have never thought he could, or would, do something like that," he whispered to her softly.

"He was so angry with me..." she began, her eyes welling with tears. "He was trying to tell me about his experiment. It was so important to him." She shook her head slowly, her caramel highlights catching the light.

Logan released his embrace, but kept Jamie's hand in his as they began to walk again. "He had no right to just leave like that. I don't care how angry he was," he huffed.

"I just wonder if—" Jamie paused.

"If what?" Logan asked.

"I wonder if he's okay, or if something happened to him."

"No telling. He took his box with him, though, so maybe he went away to work on it in secret."

"You know that's not like him," Jamie answered stiffly.

"Well, I'm beginning to think it's exactly like him. Anyway, I'm late for work."

"Oh, already? I was enjoying this."

"Afraid so, but we'll do something special tonight, okay?" Logan placed his hand on her cheek and bent down so she would meet his eyes.

"Okay, sounds good."

The two embraced and kissed before Logan jogged across the intersection to his new car. Jamie waved to him as he drove off.

Jamie stood there and watched until he was out of sight. She turned and smiled as she began to slowly walk down the sidewalk in front of the local stores and shops of the main street.

She reached into her pocket and pulled out an MP3 player, as well as a set of headphones. She put the headphones in her ears and pressed on the player a few times until a song began playing— one that was special to her. It was she and Duncan's song. She looked forward again and smiled as pleasant memories of the past flooded her mind.

As she continued to walk, she took in the beautiful morning. The light was shining through the trees, the air was cool but still, and not many people were out. The song had a soothing effect on her, uplifting her mood instantly. She came to the corner of the street that opened into an uptown park. Jamie tapped her headphones as she heard a weird sound, before realizing the sound was not coming from them. She pulled them to one side and clicked pause on her MP3 player.

Across the park, something caught her eye. Suddenly, she saw a bright, amber glow and the still morning quickly changed by a brief atmospheric disturbance. Much to her shock, when the light subsided, she saw something familiar. It was Duncan's box standing in the middle of the field. "Oh my God!" she gasped, as her heartbeat quickened.

Without hesitation she quickly ran through the dewy morning grass over to his box, not caring about the grass blades and dirt covering her feet.

Inside the box, Duncan's curiosity was aroused. The box was only lit by the interior lights, his computer screen, and the unexplained illuminations going on inside the box; however, now there appeared to be bright sunlight pouring into the windows and he couldn't understand what it might mean. Although Duncan wanted to travel in time, achieving and realizing his dream was still somewhat unfathomable.

Unknown to Duncan, he had materialized in his own future. He pulled the battery lever to neutral and his box began powering down. Steam rose from its exterior and it sat in the middle of the park on the cool morning.

Duncan slowly opened the door and stepped out, and, to his surprise, there stood Jamie with a shocked look on her face.

She was confused, but ran up and hugged Duncan tightly as tears began to pour from her eyes. She took Duncan off guard. After all, he had seen her only moments before and she had been very angry with him; yet, there she was in his embrace. He hugged her back, running a hand over her head, and noticed immediately that her hair was different. Was it lighter somehow, or were his eyes simply playing tricks on him?

She took a step back, her hazel eyes gleaming with delight. "Duncan, oh my God—Duncan, it's you!" she exclaimed.

"Well of course it's me," Duncan grinned as he looked around. He recognized where he was but he was still did not fully understand what exactly had happened. "Why is it daylight? And how did I get uptown?" he asked, detecting that something was off.

Jamie was awestruck that Duncan was standing there in front of her, but she was taken aback by his questions.

"Why is it what? Daylight?" she choked through her tears.

"Never mind about that. Listen, Jamie, I'm sorry about last night, okay? You were right; I have been paying more attention to this box than to you, and I said some stupid things. I'm sorry," Duncan said, his eyes filling with regret.

"Huh? Last night? What do you mean?" Jamie asked, her eyebrows rising in confusion. "Duncan, where have you been for the past year? We have all been worried sick."

"Whoa, whoa, the past year? Jamie, what are you talking about?" he asked, his tone confused.

"What do you mean, what am I talking about? Where have you been for the last year Duncan?" she repeated.

"You know exactly where I have been for the past year. Are you all right, Jamie?" Duncan asked, assuming the breakup may have been affecting her.

"It was very irresponsible of you to leave like that, without a word or so much as a goodbye. No one has seen or heard from you. Do your parents even know you're back?" she asked.

"My parents? No one has seen or heard from me? Hang on a minute, will ya? First of all, I haven't been anywhere for the past year. I saw you, like, ten minutes ago," Duncan blurted.

Jamie's eyes narrowed in frustration. "That is lie, Duncan! I haven't seen you in a year, since the night we broke up. How could you just leave like that?" she asked as she wiped tears from her face, smearing her mascara.

Suddenly it struck Duncan that something was very wrong with this picture. He wondered if he had, indeed, traveled through time. He had to know, but Jamie seemed to be ranting. He had to ask her.

"Jamie," he said as she continued to rattle on. "Jamie!" Duncan yelled in an urgent tone.

"What?" she asked, still torn by her emotions.

"What is the date today?"

"Are you serious, Duncan?" she screeched.

"Jamie, please...just tell me. What is the date today?

"It is February eighth, Duncan. What does that have to do with this?"

"What year?" he pressed further, grabbing a hold onto her forearms and staring into her eyes.

"It's 2019, Duncan, duh!" she answered, oblivious to the fact that Duncan had come a year and a day into the future.

"2019? Oh, my God! It worked! It actually worked! I don't believe it, Jamie. It actually worked!" Duncan beamed with glee.

"What do you mean, it worked? What worked? Have you lost your freaking mind? What are you talking about?" Jamie inquired with urgency.

"Jamie, do you remember what I told you about my experiment. Do you recall what I told you the night we broke up?

"Um, no Duncan. I'm sorry, I was a little emotional that night if you remember," she replied hastily.

"You don't remember me telling you that my experiment involved time travel?"

Jamie suddenly had an epiphany. She did remember that Duncan had indeed said that his experiment involved time travel and she recalled that when he went missing, his box went missing, as well. For a moment she conceived it but this was too much for her to believe, and she was more than a little skeptical. *But still what if it is true?* she thought.

"You mean...?" she began.

"Yes, Jamie! I just traveled through time. If the date you gave me is true, I have come one year into the future. That must be the reason why no one has seen or heard from me in a year," Duncan explained.

"Are you joking? Because if you are it is not funny, Duncan," Jamie seethed as she squinted her eyes at him.

"No babe, I'm not joking. I just left you, like, ten minutes ago. Now I know why it's daylight and why we are uptown. It worked!!" he yelled, his voice rising with excitement.

"Are you actually trying to tell me that you came here from the night we broke up?" she asked in disbelief.

"Yes! That is exactly what I'm telling you!"

Jamie put her hands on her head; she was not able to accept this. "No, no! This can't be happening. I must be dreaming!" she screamed.

"You aren't dreaming, Jamie. I did it! I actually traveled through time!" Duncan shouted.

It finally began to sink in, and Jamie had to accept that Duncan was telling the truth. Looking into his clear, green eyes, she knew in her heart that he was telling the truth. It was the worst realization of her life, and because of that, she still resisted.

"Well! That's just great! Congratulations Duncan! We have all been worried to death! Everyone thought you just left or had died or something!" she continued to scream.

"Jamie, calm down!" Duncan pleaded.

"Calm down? Calm down? You ruined my life! You ruined our life! You worried us all to death, Duncan, and all you can say is, Jamie, calm down?"

"Look, I'm sorry, okay? How was I to know what would happen? You stormed off and left me standing there. I was about to try my experiment, but you didn't care."

"So, what? If you hadn't been so secretive, maybe I would have listened, but that didn't give you the right to just disappear without a word!" she continued to rant.

"Jamie, would you please calm down and think for a minute? What has been a year for you have been minutes for me. Please understand what I'm trying to tell you here," Duncan asserted.

"Your point?" she snapped.

"Jamie, from my perspective it's been about ten minutes since you ran off and left me standing in my driveway.

To you, it's been an entire year. Can't you see that I didn't just disappear? It just looks that way from your perspective in time," Duncan attempted to reason with her, but Jamie was so filled with anger that she lost sight of the truth and thought

Duncan was trying to deceive her.

"No, no! I was almost convinced, but this is too much! You are lying, Duncan! Time travel is not possible," she screamed.

"Oh, really? So I have been wearing these same clothes for a year? And look, do you see this?" he held up his finger. "This is where I cut myself, right as we began arguing," he paused, showing her his hand. "Can't you see I am telling you the truth?"

Jamie had no choice but to believe him when she saw his cut finger; the memory came flooding back to her.

"You mean this is real?" she began to tear up again.

"Yes, that's what I've been trying to tell you."

Jamie forgot herself for a moment and embraced Duncan, and then kissed him passionately. She stopped suddenly, remembering all that had happened since his disappearance. She pulled away with a guilt-ridden look on her face, and then began to cry again. She looked down as though she was ashamed.

"What's wrong?" Duncan asked, surprised by her sudden change of demeanor.

"I am sorry Duncan! I am so sorry!"

Duncan had no idea of the truth—that Jamie now had a new man in her life, and that the new man was Logan. Jamie was now married to him and was pregnant with his child.

"It's okay, babe. I know it's hard to accept things like this," Duncan said in a soothing tone.

"It's not okay, Duncan," she said as she averted her eyes.

"What do you mean?" he asked.

"I—I don't know how to tell you this..." Jamie began. She grabbed her stomach as though she was in pain.

"Tell me what?" Duncan persisted.

"Duncan, I'm sorry!"

"Okay...you said that. What is it that you don't know how to tell me? Why are you sorry?"

"Look at my hand, Duncan." Jamie showed Duncan her hand, where there was a golden wedding ring, but Duncan didn't immediately notice the band.

"Yeah and?" he said as if oblivious.

"Look at my ring finger, Duncan."

Duncan looked and saw the ring. His eyes grew wide as a horrible, cold feeling came over him.

Jamie then pulled her coat open to reveal a white, floral dress, and underneath that was a small bump—the telltale sign that no one could deny.

"No, no, no! You cannot be serious!" he exclaimed, his green eyes flashing.

"I'm sorry, Duncan. I am...um, married now."

"You're what?" Duncan yelled, enraged.

"I'm sorry, but you disappeared without a trace. I was hurt and alone," Jamie explained in tears.

"Well, that's just great! Who is he?" Duncan persisted.

"I don't think I can tell you..." she said in shame.

"Jamie, don't play games with me. Just tell me, who are you married too?"

"Logan," she whispered in a broken voice.

"What? Logan? You mean my best friend...? That Logan?" Duncan railed in a rage.

"Yes," she whispered.

"No, no, no. Logan would never do that to me, and you never liked him that way," Duncan barked.

"Duncan, we became close in the days and weeks after your disappearance."

"No, no, I refuse to believe that! Logan wouldn't do that to me, and certainly not in only a year's time."

"Duncan it was not like you are making it out to be," she pleaded.

Duncan paced in front of Jamie. "Well, I guess when we broke up it was meant to be after all. I can't tell you how thrilled I am for you both!" Duncan said in a rage.

"Duncan Sims, if you hadn't left on your little trip in time, this never would have happened."

"Oh, how do you know, Jamie? Huh? Last time we spoke you were just angry enough to pull something like this. I should have seen this coming," Duncan accused.

"You are so wrong, Duncan. Do you have any idea how many nights I stayed up all night with your parents and Logan, waiting on a phone call or any word at all about you?"

"Yeah, it sounds like you were so broken up that you couldn't wait to hop in the sack with Logan," Duncan snapped sharply.

Jamie slapped Duncan hard across his face.

"How dare you say that to me! I waited for you, Duncan! I waited for you to come home or to call! I waited for you! Damn you I kept on waiting, but you never came back," she growled.

Duncan now began to realize the gravity of what he had done in traveling in time.

"I didn't know this would happen! I love you Jamie, but I wanted better things for you, and that's why I pushed so hard for this experiment. And it works, but now I find what our love was really worth—clearly nothing!"

"Duncan, please, listen to me," Jamie pleaded.

"No! I am through listening. I hope you and my ex-best-bud will be very happy. So long, Mrs. Keith!" he yelled as he glared at her.

With that, Duncan abruptly turned around and stormed into his box, locking the door. He immediately activated the program and the sound sync device and began the take-off procedure.

Jamie ran up to the box and began beating on the door.

"Duncan, Duncan! Wait! Duncan, please! I didn't know! I waited for you, Duncan!" she screamed while sobbing uncontrollably.

The box began to power up with an overwhelming noise and within seconds it began to glow. It then phased, finally dematerialized, and was gone. The box caused a strong wind that blew Jamie back, and within a few seconds the disturbance had ceased. Jamie fell to her knees, sobbing. A ghost from the past now ruined her beautiful morning.

Inside his box, Duncan was overwhelmed with feelings of hurt and betrayal. He began to cry. He moved back and forth between rage and hurt as the box proceeded into time. Duncan had no idea where he was going, and now he didn't care.

Chapter 10

Mr. Newman

Duncan switched songs on his computer to a famous classic rock tune. Several points in time appeared on his grid and Duncan chose one at random. Suddenly his box began its landing sequence again.

Duncan was still overrun by emotion, but he wiped his eyes and tried to calm himself down. He had bouts of anger and punched the inside of the box as his rage exploded.

Duncan had no idea that he was about to set forth on events that would change history.

It was a cold, gray, and foggy morning on the dark streets of London in 1963. A television executive named Sydney Newman and his secretary, Grace, were walking down a street, discussing Sydney's busy schedule for the day.

Sydney Newman was a no-nonsense producer who had a made quite a career in broadcasting. He was raised in Canada and had moved to England to take over as an executive at the nation's foremost television company. He was a heavyset man and wore odd combinations of clothing, from his spotted bowtie to his tweed blazer. Though he had little fashion sense, he was a strict, cunning, businessman with an eye for good ideas.

It was to be a busy day for Sydney, but no one could have foreseen what would happen next.

"Did you order the new casting forms from Terrance?" Sydney asked Grace in his business-like tone.

"Yes, Mr. Newman. Now, your schedule for the day is as follows: at eleven a.m., you are meeting with Mitch about the ratings. Lunch is at twelve at Gordon's chateau. At one p.m., you have a meeting with the board of Directors. At ten minutes after two, you meet with Charles from development, and you have a meetig with Sir Niles at three-thirty p.m."

"Sir Niles? What does that old windbag want this time?" Sydney griped as they walked the foggy streets in the extra chilly weather.

"I am quite sure, he was not specific; he only said to make sure that you were free at three thirty p.m." Grace replied.

"Oh, great. That is just what I need, another visit from Sir Moaning Old Goat. Anything else to ruin my day?"

"Well, your luncheon is with the producer Beatrice Clayton. She wishes to discuss this new band from Liverpool."

"Oh, yes, that's what all the kids are talking about these days—long hair and guitars. Whatever happened to the days of Glenn Miller?"

"The same thing that happens to all the great bands. Wait! Sydney, do you hear that?" Grace looked around because she heard a weird, unfamiliar sound.

Sydney and Grace peered in all directions, baffled as to what they were hearing.

"Yes, I hear it. What the blazes is that noise?"

"Whatever it is, it's growing louder," Grace said.

"I know that, you silly woman. I have ears. What on earth can it be?"

As Sydney and Grace wondered what the sound could be, they both began to see a flashing light and the wind seemed to pick up. The atmosphere was disturbed with flashes of amber light. Duncan's box began to manifest itself in an amber and blue glow. Unknown to Duncan, his time machine was appearing right before Sydney and Grace's very eyes.

When it had fully materialized, neither of them could believe what they were witnessing.

"Whaaaat is that?" Grace gasped.

"It's a tall, gray box, by the looks of it. It's reminiscent of one of our police boxes; although, I'm not sure how it appeared there, like that," Sydney replied.

"Well, it certainly is not an ordinary police box. I mean, to be able to appear out of thin air like that. What should we do, Sydney?" she asked frantically.

"Just hang about and let's see what happens."

Sydney was shocked by the seemingly supernatural appearance of this box right in front of him, but he was used to seeing police boxes all over London. A box like this was not uncommon; however, the way it arrived in front of them was more then peculiar to say the least. Sydney paused to think, *Did I actually just see that?*

Sydney had seen a lot in his lifetime and he was a curious man. Therefore, he did not let fear overtake him nor did he run from the unusual occurrence. Rather, he allowed his fascination to hold him in his place and to see what would happen next.

Sydney seemed more intrigued and fascinated, while Grace was shocked. She was slightly relieved, however, when she saw a young man open the box and step out.

"Why, he's just a lad," she remarked.

"Young man, are you all right?" Sydney asked.

Duncan was still angry with Jamie, but he managed to let go of his rage when he saw that he had landed in a place that he had never seen before.

"Yes, sir, I think so, but it's been a pretty rough day," Duncan answered.

"Rough day, eh? Who are you? And how in the world did you make that box appear out of thin air like that?"

Duncan, not knowing who this man was, fumbled for anything to reply. He thought back to one of his favorite TV shows and took the name of one of the characters. "My name is Smith, Doctor Smith."

"I am sorry, Doctor who?"

"Uh, Doctor Smith, sir. I travel in time."

"You what?" Sydney asked again, thinking he had heard wrong. He looked at Duncan as though he was crazy.

"I travel in time," Duncan repeated.

"Well, my boy, you sound like an American to me. Aren't you a little young to be a doctor?"

"Um, I started early," Duncan half-joked.

"Be that as it may, or may not be, but more to the point. Why are you here, Time Traveler Smith?

"My arrival here was kind of an accident."

"An accident?" Sydney asked.

"My machine is a little hard to control."

"I see. Tell me—why on earth, would you choose to make a time machine out of an old, gray box? Were you trying to disguise it as a police box?"

Duncan didn't want to reveal too much, so he stretched the truth. "No. Actually, I had to make it out of something, so a gray box seemed as good as anything else."

Sydney looked at him skeptically. "Do you expect me to believe that?"

Grace was too shocked to speak, and she stood there feeling faint from it all.

"You can believe you what like. You asked me, so I told you."

"Well, in the absence of any other sensible explanation, I suppose I will have to believe you for now."

Duncan was freezing. He was not really dressed for winter in London, no matter the year, and he noticed that it was overcast and foggy.

"It's cold and foggy. Where am I?"

"You are in London, doctor."

"London? Really? What year is this?"

"It's 1963. January, 1963."

"1963? Whoa."

Duncan could not fathom being in London, nor in the year 1963. While time travel was his goal, and he had been one year into the future, it was still new and somewhat overwhelming to him.

"Is that so hard to grasp for a time traveler?"

"No, sir. It's just not exactly what I was expecting."

"Well, what exactly were you expecting, lad?"

"I'm not sure," Duncan replied.

"I take it time travel is common where you are from?" Sydney inquired.

"Not exactly. It's kind of a new discovery."

"So, not quite perfected, then?

"Not quite," Duncan replied.

"Where and when do you come from?"

"All I can tell you is that I am from the future. It wouldn't be wise to say more."

"I find this very hard to fathom; yet, here you are. Tell me, can you go to other worlds, in your machine?"

"I suppose so. I haven't really tried that. I'm not sure there are other inhabitable worlds, and as I said, time travel is kind of a new discovery."

"Would you mind if I had a look inside your machine?" Sydney asked.

"I'm sorry, mister, but I would rather you didn't. It could be hazardous if you did see inside. Trust me."

"Hazardous? In what way?"

"If you were to see things from the future, you could possibly damage the timeline. I can't take that chance."

"I see. I suppose that's plausible."

"I'm sorry I can't show you, but I assure you I mean no harm to anyone."

"I am relieved to hear that, doctor. Tell me, what do you call this manner of time machine?"

"Well, actually, I just call it a time machine for now."

"Hmm, that's very clever. So, in the future, you are brilliant enough to make a time machine, but you can't think up a name for it?"

"Well, I haven't had time."

"I would think time would be the one thing you had in abundance."

"Not exactly. In fact, you must excuse me. I have had a bad day, and I need be going soon, mister—?"

"Oh, I am terribly sorry. Where are my manners? My name is Sydney, Sydney Newman and this is Grace, my secretary."

Duncan was taken by surprise for he knows

exactly whom Sydney Newman was. "Sydney... Newman? *The* Sydney Newman?"

"Yes, my boy. Am I known to you?"

"Yes, Mr. Newman, but I am not at liberty to tell you how or why."

"You are quite secretive, Doctor Smith."

"I have to be; time isn't to be trifled with," Duncan replied.

"Even so, it's an honor to meet you, even in such a strange and unorthodox way," Sydney said politely.

"An honor to meet you as well, Mr. Newman. I'm sorry I startled you. I didn't intend to land in front of you like that."

"Quite all right. At least I have seen something now that no one else has."

"Um, yeah. Anyway, I'd better get going."

"I understand. I do hope we shall meet again. I would love to know what you can tell me about the future."

"Perhaps we will meet again, maybe in a way you do not suspect."

"What do you mean?"

"Sorry, Mr. Newman, but you will have to let the future play out as it is meant to."

"Very well then, Doctor Smith. Safe journeys to you."

"Thank you, sir. Is your lady friend going to be all right?"

"Oh yes, she'll be fine.

She is just a little shocked."

"Yeah, that makes two of us. Please say nothing about this to anyone."

"Ha, who would believe such a thing if we were to?"

"Most likely no one, but better to safe than sorry. I really have to go now. Goodbye, Mr. Newman."

"Farewell, young man—or shall I say, doctor."

Duncan stepped back inside the box and closed the door. He was shivering from the cold. Duncan activated the power, ran the codes, and within a few seconds, as Sydney and Grace looked on from outside, the box disappeared just as it had arrived.

"Now that was extraordinary, wouldn't you say, Grace?" Sydney paused, then glanced at his secretary. "Grace?"

"Just give me a moment to gather myself Sydney. I don't feel well."

"Are you going to be all right?"

"This is too much! A box appearing and then disappearing? Time travel? I think I need to go home, Sydney."

"Certainly, my dear, take the rest of the day. And keep this quiet."

"Indeed, sir."

After Sydney dismissed Grace, he hurriedly walked across the street to a red telephone booth and dialed the phone, making a call to his television company. This encounter had given him a great idea for a new TV show.

"Good morning, Joan, this is Sydney, Authentication

Code, Treble Zero, one, five, three. Give me extension R twenty-one twelve please. Thank you, dear."

As Sydney waited for an answer, he rubbed his chin and pondered what had just happened. He turned and looked, and, standing next to the red booth, was a blue British Metropolitan Police Call Box. Sydney grinned as an even better idea came into his head. Soon Rex, Sydney's assistant, answered.

"Rex? Sydney here. I am on my way to my office, and I want you to meet me there in a half hour. What? I don't care what you are doing, just drop whatever it is and meet me there," he paused, switching the phone to his other ear. "I have a great idea for a new series. You stuffed shirts over the drama department have been looking for something good, and I am about to give it you."

Rex's mumbled reply came through the other end before Sydney replied, "That's right—my office in half an hour, and have David and that new guy, uh, what's his name? ...Yeah, him. Have him there as well. All right, see that you do. I will talk to you then."

Sydney hung up the phone then stepped out of the booth, smiling. He lit a cigarette and looked once again at the police call box, and said "Yes. Yes indeed," then walked on down the street.

Chapter 11

Crash and Burn

Duncan was still in awe of meeting Sydney Newman, but the moment passed and soon reality struck him. He was angry again and had a sour, grimacing, look on his face. He looked around, unsure of what to do next, so he used a reversed application of the trace to trace a song that was unique to him. Before leaving, he had previously set up a method of finding his way back to his own time. The trace was a recording of his mother singing a song that she had sung to Duncan when he was a small boy. He felt a sudden pang in his heart at the thought. He knew she believed in him; she just didn't understand his mission.

Through all the confusion and misunderstanding between him and his parents, he had grown tired of letting them down. Yes, he was onto something life changing, but they were unable to see it yet.

Duncan was attempting to materialize back in his own time. Suddenly, a loud alarm sounded, several warning lights flashed on the screen, the batteries began to overheat, and another more urgent klaxon sounded. The box began to fill with smoke before there were sparks and arcs of electricity. Wofford Batton, who was still standing right where he had been when Duncan had taken off only seconds earlier, began to see a bright amber glow.

As Duncan landed, he noticed even more trouble; his computer screen lit up with warnings of critical failure, and the alarm continued to sound.

Duncan started coughing and his eyes began to water because of the toxic smoke filling his box. Soon, he was overcome by the noxious fumes and could barely see anything. He didn't realize it yet, but his overheating batteries had gone beyond critical. As he began to rematerialize, there was a pop and green-colored fire began to pour out of the two of the battery boxes. Duncan, frantic, grabbed the fire extinguisher and attempted to put out the fire. He was able to do so, but the thick smoke was choking him.

"Oh no, no, no!" he exclaimed as he gasped for air.

Duncan tried to shut everything down but it was too late. The batteries had melted and smoke was billowing out of control. Duncan yanked the door open and grabbed his laptop, which was burning hot, and leapt out of his box, landing flat on his belly with his face to the ground. He was coughing uncontrollably and choking. He rolled over onto his back and lifted his head to look at the Time Box, only to see it beginning to dim. The noise ceased and then there was only silence.

Smoke continued to billow from the now dark box. It was a thick smoke, gathering in heaps around the roof of the box before it stretched out towards the sky. His eyes were watering, his lashes were dusted with black ash, and his face was smeared with soot. His previously white shirt was now stained with grass and dirt. After a moment, he gathered his strength and sat up, continuing to cough. In a daze, he reached frantically for his laptop. Once it was in his grasp, he opened it and felt a rush of relief as the screen lit up, illuminating his face with a familiar, soft glow. Duncan pushed himself up to his feet and brushed himself off. His jeans had green streaks from the grass and he shook his head in shock.

"I can't believe this," Duncan said aloud, his mind spinning with worry. "It's ruined!" He paced back and forth in front of the invention, his fingers interlocking at the back of his neck and the promise of a headache beginning to throb in his temples.

His attention was soon drawn away from the smoking box as he heard the crunching of leaves and the sound of an older man's voice. It was his neighbor, Professor Wofford Batton. "Duncan...Duncan Sims?" the professor called to him.

"Yeah?" Duncan replied, regaining his breath.

"Are you okay? What happened?" the professor asked as he looked over towards the box. Smoke was still pouring upwards as if it were a raging furnace.

"Professor Batton?" Duncan inquired, as he only vaguely recognized the man in the dark. He could smell the cherry tobacco from the professor's pipe, its potent smoke curling in the air. It was a sweeter scent in comparison to the acrid stench that had flooded his nose earlier.

"That's right, Professor Batton. How are you Duncan? You look like you have had a rough night, son," the professor remarked with a pleasant smile, seemingly undaunted by the sight. Duncan appraised him; he appeared to be out of place or time, even, dressed in a dark blue, long-sleeved shirt buttoned to the top and a brown sweater vest.

He didn't know what to make of him.

"That's an understatement," Duncan gruffly retorted as he coughed again.

"Well, what happened son?" the professor asked again. Maybe it was just his round wire-rimmed glasses, but Duncan noticed an odd glimmer in his eyes and wondered if he had seen him appear out of thin air.

"You would never believe me if I told you," Duncan quipped.

"Oh, I don't know, Duncan. I've seen a lot of weird things in my lifetime. Weirder than you look now, anyway, so try me."

Duncan looked at the professor, his eyes still watering and smeared with soot. The man was right; he probably did look a mess. He had known Professor Batton for years, but he had always been a somewhat distant figure and Duncan did not wish to divulge anything about what had transpired. *How would he ever understand? No one would.* Duncan thought.

"I would really rather not talk about it, professor," he half-muttered. "No offense."

"Okay, Duncan, but it looks like you need to talk to someone."

Duncan rubbed his neck, feeling the grit of sand under his fingers. He started to feel itchy all over after his tussle in the grass.

"It suffices to say this has not been my night," he finally admitted.

"Well, I am sorry, Duncan. I kind of eavesdropped on you earlier while I was walking my dog, but did I hear you say something about time travel?" the professor asked.

Duncan, somewhat shocked, looked directly at

the professor while watching him fiddle with cigarette lighter.

"Uh...yeah," Duncan replied, as he coughed once more.

"If you tell me what is going on, then maybe I can help you," Professor Batton offered.

"Help me? Help me how?" Duncan asked, raising an eyebrow.

"Well, you might be surprised, Duncan, but time travel has long been a passion of mine."

Duncan stood up and looked directly at the professor, pondering if he should say anything. He felt that he needed to tell someone, someone who actually understood what he was trying to do, but should it be Wofford Batton?

The professor met his gaze and stood perfectly still, as if giving him an open invitation. "Come on, Duncan. Let me help you."

Duncan stood there for a moment, weighing his options. "If I tell you what happened, it goes no further. Do we have a deal?" he insisted, looking sternly at Professor Batton. At least he would be able to discuss this with somebody that understood what he was talking about.

"Of course, Duncan; you can trust me," the professor reassured. He straightened his glasses and waited for Duncan to speak.

"Well, it all started two days ago. I was working on an experiment..."

From there, Duncan told the professor all that had happened since he began his quest for time travel, but refrained from telling him he had been successful in his endeavor at least for the moment.

"So your time machine failed?" the professor asked.

"No, it worked... but now I wish it hadn't." Duncan said, running a hand through his dark, messy hair.

"It worked? Are you saying you actually traveled in time?"

The professor took a slow drag from his pipe and looked at Duncan intensely, awaiting his answer. Duncan looked up only briefly, his eyes wandering to the smoking box.

"Yeah, I did. But it doesn't matter now. I burned up the whole system. All of that work for nothing...but it's just as well because the future sucks!"

"You went to the future?" The professor's eyebrows rose quickly, clearly excited about Duncan's story of success. "How far into the future did you go?"

"Professor, I really don't want to talk about this."

"Duncan, please. If you *have* traveled in time, I need to know about it."

"Why? What difference does it make?" Duncan began to pace back and forth in front of the box again.

"It makes a big difference to me, son. You see, years ago, before I taught at the university, I worked on a project called Patmos."

"Patmos?" asked Duncan, squinting his eyes and cocking his head to one side, stopping mid-stride.

"Yeah, Patmos, uh huh" the professor nodded, taking another drag from his pipe.

"Never heard of it," Duncan replied stiffly.

The professor let out a brief chuckle. "No, I am sure you haven't. It was highly classified and top secret."

"Wait," Duncan paused, "Isn't Patmos the island

where John saw the future—the one that's written in the book of Revelation?"

"Yes, exactly. We were working on time travel, Duncan."

Duncan's eyes widened in disbelief. "You worked on time travel?"

"Yep," the professor smiled. "I sure did."

"Did you succeed?"

The professor shook his head sadly. "Well, that's the problem—I don't know. You see, they forced me out of the project and sent me off to teach at the university, but we were close to a breakthrough when I left."

"How close?"

"Close. There were twenty of us. My friend, Emmit, and I had come up with a new hypothesis, but they forced both of us out before we could test it. I lost all of my security clearance."

"They just kicked you out?"

"Yes, son. Now, please tell me what happened. What did you see?"

Duncan shrugged and looked down at the ground. "I went to the future and saw my ex-girlfriend. She was married to my best friend. I still can't believe it," he said as he shook his head.

"I see."

"Now do you understand why I really don't want to talk about this?"

"Of course. But Duncan, you should know one thing."

"Yeah? What's that?" Duncan asked in an exasperated tone.

"What you saw was only a possible future. It may have occurred, or been initiated, because of your absence from this time."

"Come again?"

"Well, what you need to understand is that, since you have returned to this time, the future you saw is not the only possible outcome."

"You mean that my presence here, in this time, might change things?"

"Yes! That's exactly what I mean. Just because you saw that future doesn't necessarily mean that it must happen that way."

Duncan squinted his eyes in thought, a small glimmer of hope growing inside of him. "Then I can change things?" Duncan said to himself.

"Duncan, the future is not yet written—only the past is. You cannot change the past, but you can change the future."

His heart quickened. "So that means Jamie might not end up with Logan? There's still a chance..." He resumed his pacing, his mind racing with possibilities.

"I'm sorry, what did you say?" inquired the professor.

"Nothing important. Oh, anyway, this doesn't even matter now. My time machine is ruined, and I don't have the money to rebuild it. It's a hopeless pile of junk," Duncan sighed, his brief feeling of hope beginning to dim.

"Well, maybe not. You see, I think that if we work together, we can make both of our dreams come true. You have traveled in time, and I have always wanted to."

Duncan wasn't convinced. "I am not so sure I want to travel in time again, after having seen what I have. I might mess things up even worse."

"It's true, Duncan. You would have to be very careful, but you've succeeded where so many have failed. It seems a shame to waste such a discovery."

"I don't know, professor. It all sounds good but—"

"But what, Duncan? You have been blessed with a gift from God!" the professor exclaimed, reaching an arm out to point to the Time Box. "You have a very rare opportunity here. Think of all you could see, think of all you could do—that is, if you don't give up."

Duncan looked around in doubt, but his curiosity was aroused. He crossed his arms. "Okay, let's say I agree. What do you have that might help me, professor?"

"I still have a prototype time machine and I have an endless power supply to feed it."

"You built a time machine?" Duncan asked in surprise.

"Yes, yes," the professor waved his pipe dismissively. "But I never was successful at achieving time travel. I tried and retried, but never got anywhere; however, you have. I think we can help each other, that is, if you're up to the challenge."

"Well, it has been my dream for a long time."

"So then, are you in?" the professor asked with a grin.

Duncan turned from looking at his Time Box, and then stuck his hand out towards the professor. "Am I in? You bet I'm in."

Professor Batton grinned and grasped Duncan's hand, shaking it firmly. "Excellent, then come with me. This is going to be fun, Duncan—I can't wait."

The professor spun around and started to make his way down the driveway and towards his stately home. The old man was moving faster than Duncan would have ever thought possible, and he found himself grinning at the sight. He had a feeling they were going to get on just fine. He straightened his rumpled but dirty white shirt and quickened his steps to catch up with his new partner. Neither of them looked back at the still smoking ruins of the Time Box; instead, they were deep in conversation as they disappeared into the night.

Chapter 12

The Pandora 8

One could see the professor's home before even turning the corner. Duncan marveled at the long driveway, the white pillars, and all of the overgrown bushes. It was easy to see how it could seem haunted to the neighborhod kids, especially at night. The professor's experiments probably fueled all of the ghost stories that surrounded the place.

I wonder what Jamie and Logan would think if they knew I was headed to old Professor Batton's house right now, Duncan thought to himself.

The professor unlocked the door to his sizable abode and then reached in and turned on some lights. As they made their way through the professor's home, they came to a staircase that descended downward to the professor's basement. Duncan was a little apprehensive as they entered the professor's lab. They walked in and the professor turned on an old fluorescent light that reverberated with a constant buzz. Dust particles floated in the air and he could see some machinery covered with worn sheets and various intricate pieces laid out on the wooden counter.

"Wow professor, I never knew you had a lab. What are all of these things?" Duncan asked as he walked through the lab, lifting his hand to graze over the equipment.

"Oh, just experiments that I've tinkered with over

the years. Never mind those. This is what I want you to see," he said, leading Duncan to a tall shape covered with a dusty sheet.

Duncan and the professor walked up to the big, covered object. The professor quickly pulled the old sheet off the rectangular shape, revealing what was underneath.

"What...what is this?" Duncan asked in awe.

"It's what you've been looking for, Duncan. It's the golden ticket to all your hopes and dreams—it's your future," the professor announced, his eyes bouncing back and forth between Duncan and the box.

Duncan was amazed at what he saw. The professor stood beside him, wearing a big grin. In front of him was a tall, metallic green box. Two cylindrical shaped extensions were mounted on either side of the time-weathered box. Along the top, etched in white lettering, was the word 'Pandora.' In the dead center of the box were two retractable doors with a silver circle painted on them and the number eight in dark red lettering. It must have been older than Duncan was, but it had stood the test of time.

"Professor, *this* is your time machine?" Duncan asked.

"It is. This, Duncan, is Pandora 8. Originally there were ten Pandora machines each with it's own crew and theory."

Duncan took a step towards the box to get a closer look. He ran his fingers over where "Pandora" was engraved. "What happened to the others?"

"Well, most of them, including the original number 8 box, are probably sitting in a government facility somewhere—under guard, of course, but this one I built while I was at the university. It is exactly like the one I built for Patmos." The professor took off his spectacles to clean them with one of his sleeves.

"You mean the military doesn't know about this one?"

Professor Batton exhaled on the glass, clouding the lenses, and wiped them again before speaking. "No, they do not know. You see, I took the plans that Emmit and I worked on and made copies of them by hand. That way I could recreate this version in secret."

"You said you had an endless supply of energy to power it?"

The professor replaced his glasses on top of his nose and fished an old brass key from his breast pocket. He unlocked his Pandora Box and it opened with a *click* and as he pushed the doors apart the sound of rusted metal grinding made a loud noise. Inside sat an odd-looking device that was made of metal; it looked like a cone with three supports.

"This, Duncan, is my reverse Tesla coil. It gathers energy from anything and everything.

"But isn't that what a Tesla coil is supposed to do?" Duncan inquired.

"Yes, but this one can gather energy from anywhere or from anything. Basically it can gather energy from any source of power."

Duncan blinked in surprise. "What? How?"

"It's a little hard to explain, son. This coil is the Mark IV version. You see, I have improved it over the years; it's more powerful than the one's I created for the machines back in the days of Patmos."

"Well surely it must work off Tesla's principle of ion energy gathering right? Duncan asked.

"Well, as you know, a Tesla Coil takes radio frequencies and ions through an air core resonant transformer and produces high voltages of electricity at low currents," the professor said, motioning to the reverse Tesla Coil and looking at Duncan. "The reverse coil takes the waves of electricity that fill the air from technology, like telephone lines and light sources, and absorbs them in order to power itself. It can even use the sun as a source of power in the event of encountering an area with low electricity. It then recycles the energy back into the atmosphere in order to prevent depletion of electric energy or, in a worse case scenario, solar energy. So it works as an electric conductor and source.

It apparently gathers power from positively charged ions in the atmosphere. It also collects energy from any power source. It can pull power not only from all I have mentioned but also from rocks, or grass, or even trees. In essence, it can never be exhausted."

"How did you come up with such a device?

"I made it from a set of plans given to us at the Patmos laboratory. My coils were the only ones that actually worked and the government paid me ten million dollars for the design."

"Wait—ten million dollars?" Duncan asked in shock.

"Yes, that was a lot of money back then. They use it to power places like NORAD and the bunkers under the White House and other military installations to this day, but I have improved it."

Duncan walked to the side of Pandora and then stood on his tiptoes to inspect the reverse Tesla Coil. "How did you manage to sneak the coil out of

Patmos?"

"I didn't. I made this one after they forced me to retire and work at the university. The only reason I still live on the grid is so they won't suspect anything."

"How much power is it capable of producing?"

The professor smiled. "Enough to power New York, Chicago, and Seattle for the next five thousand years."

"Seriously?"

"Absolutely. It has been collecting energy for the last 42 years, Duncan. It has all the power we would ever need to power a time machine indefinitely."

"Okay. So we have the power, but what do we do now?"

"We take the technology you used to make your machine travel in time and apply it to the Pandora 8."

"That should be easy," Duncan said without hesitation.

The professor stared at him for a moment and crossed his arms. "How did you figure out time travel, Duncan?"

"Well first, I found a code written by Tesla for a different application, but I tried it in an experiment and opened a tiny hole into time. I was amazed, but then later I found one of Einstein's thesis's written as an equation, and I used it with pulse emitting lasers to trace the resonance frequencies of sound sync sine waves," he said simply, shrugging his shoulders.

"What? That is brilliant! So you trace time by musical notes and sound frequencies?"

"Exactly. Wherever a song has been played, the song has left a resonance from its point of origin.

So then everywhere it has ever been played becomes a potential fixed point for a landing."

"That's incredible! Emmit said he thought music would somehow end up being a key to finding time travel, but he used naturally occurring x-rays from the sun to try to trace time." The professor looked off into space with his hand at his chin, clearly lost in his memories.

"I never would have thought of that," Duncan admitted.

The professor leaned on a shelf. He was tired from the excitement. "This has been quite a night, but it's getting late, Duncan, and I am not as young as I used to be. You run along home and get some sleep. We'll meet tomorrow evening and begin formulating a plan."

"Sounds good, professor," Duncan said, the excitement obvious in his voice.

The two walked up the creaking stairs and the professor saw Duncan to the door. As Duncan walked back toward his house, the professor locked up his house as if it were Fort Knox.

Duncan had never seen so many locks and bars on a residence before. Now, besides the professor, he was the only person in town who knew why.

Chapter 13

Letting Go of the Future

The next day dawned, cold and overcast. It was Saturday morning and Duncan awakened earlier than usual. He sat up in his bed, and thoughts of the previous evening raced through his mind.

He quickly pulled on his clothes, sat down at his computer, and turned it on. He bounced his knee up and down while he waited for it to start up and looked at the phone lying on his desk. He placed his hand over it briefly. *Should I try to call Jamie?* he pondered. He shook his head and pulled his hand back. *No, not after what she has done, or rather will do.*

No matter what Duncan did, he couldn't escape the ghosts of the possible future he had witnessed. While Duncan sat there pondering how he would handle this, there was a knock on his bedroom door.

Duncan stood and slowly approached the door. Upon opening it, he discovered Logan lazily leaning on the doorframe with a sly smile on his face. This version of Logan, however, had no idea about the future, or what Duncan had seen.

"Hey bro," Logan greeted in his usual demeanor.

Duncan hadn't expected to see Logan so soon. *Thanks for giving me a heads up, mom,* he thought to himself.

"Uh, hey Logan. What do you want?" Duncan asked, biting his tongue.

"What do I want? Man, somebody got up on the wrong side of the bed this morning," Logan joked, leaning his arm against the doorjamb.

"Yeah," Duncan replied coldly.

"Is something wrong, dude?" Logan inquired.

"No. What are you doing up so early?"

"I just wanted to see if you were okay." Logan put his hand on Duncan's shoulder but Duncan brushed it off.

"Well, do I look okay?" Duncan deadpanned.

"Yeah, you look okay, but I know what happened last night."

Duncan was taken off guard by Logan's comment. He narrowed his eyes. "What do you mean you know what happened last night?"

"Dude, Jamie called me last night and told me you two broke up."

"She called you?" Duncan seethed.

"Well, yeah...she was really upset."

His jaw clenched. "Ah, I see. So she just went running to cry on your shoulder, huh?"

"What, man? What's wrong with you? I came over to make sure you were all right..." Logan said.

"Right. Well as you can see, I'm fine. So you can go report to her that I'm just fine," he replied, backing away from the door.

Logan let his hand fall to his side. "Okay, Duncan. I know this has to be a hard time, but why are you pissed off at me?"

It suddenly occurred to Duncan again that this Logan was unaware of the events that he had witnessed in the future. He could see the confusion in his friend's eyes and felt instant regret.

"Sorry, Logan. It was just a bad night last night." Logan smiled. "Hey, no worries. I have the cure to take your mind off of Jamie."

"You'd like that I'll bet," Duncan said under his breath.

"What?" Logan asked.

Duncan ran a hand through his dark hair in frustration. "Nothing. What have you got in mind?"

"I figured we could go bowling tonight. Don gave me passes to Les Lanes. We can bowl all night if we want."

Duncan shook his head firmly. "Thanks, but no thanks. I am not in the mood and I have other things to do this evening."

Logan tilted his head to one side and asked, "Really? Like what?"

"Like working on my project."

"Aw man, not that again. Jamie is right, you are paying too much attention to that box."

Duncan's eyes darkened at the thought of Jamie confiding in Logan about him. "Well why don't you take *her* bowling, then? I'm sure she would love your company."

"Duncan...what's gotten into you, man?"

"I just don't want to go bowling or talk about Jamie. Is that okay?"

Duncan could see that Logan was puzzled by his anger, but Logan kept on talking. "Yeah, it's fine. Anyway, I think I'll go before one of us says something we'll both regret. See ya later." He abruptly turned and walked away as Duncan sat there stewing in his anger.

Duncan realized he was mad at Logan without cause. He jumped up and ran downstairs to the front door just as Logan was getting into his truck. Duncan stopped outside the door of Logan's truck. He was breathing hard from the sprint down the stairs.

"Hey, Logan—wait."

"Yeah?" Logan didn't meet his eyes, but instead looked straight ahead.

"I'm sorry man, I just need some space right now, okay?"

"Anything you say Dunc. I'll see you next Friday—or sooner, if you get can over this before that."

"Friday?" Duncan asked.

Logan finally turned to look at him. "Yeah, you know, Ryan's party? You haven't forgotten about that, have you?"

Duncan leaned back on his heels and wrapped his arms around a light pole by the driveway. "Oh yeah, right," he paused, "I guess I did forget."

"Anyway, call me if you need to talk," Logan offered.

"Yeah, sure thing. See ya, man."

"See ya, Dunc."

Duncan turned around and walked back inside. Logan sat there for a moment. *Man she really did get to him,* he thought. With that, Logan backed out of the driveway and drove off.

Duncan climbed back upstairs to his room and fell across his bed. He shrugged as he rubbed his face. *How can I have been to the future, but I don't have the slightest clue of what I'm going to do now?* Duncan wondered.

CHAPTER 14

Switching Boxes

That evening, Duncan grabbed his laptop and snuck past his mom and dad, who were engrossed in watching television. He could see them sitting together and he watched the familiar blue light of the TV flickering as he walked past. Duncan wondered if someday he and Jamie might be on the couch watching TV as their son tried to sneak out unnoticed. He frowned slightly as he exited via the back door of his house.

Duncan walked down the street to Professor Batton's home and found the professor sitting on the front porch. The professor lit his pipe and smiled as he saw him approach.

"Ah, Duncan, my boy, I have been expecting you." He gestured his arm towards the lab and slowly stood to greet Duncan.

"Good evening, professor." Duncan smiled and excitedly shook the professor's hand.

"I've cleaned up the Pandora 8. Are you ready to begin?"

"Sure thing. I brought my computer and equations," he replied, shifting his weight in anticipation.

The professor puffed and the sweet tobacco scent drifted over to Duncan's nose. "Excellent, excellent. Let's get started, then."

The professor and Duncan went down the stairs

to the professor's private lab once again, and when the professor unlocked the door Duncan was pleasantly surprised. Now the lab was well lit and the Pandora box stood off to the side, looking as if it were almost brand new, save of a little rust.

"Wow, you did clean this place up."

The professor peered around the room, as if trying to find a clear path. "Indeed. We are going to need room to get the Pandora out."

"Out?" Duncan asked, surprised.

"Why yes, my boy. We will have to take it to your house."

"Why do we need to take it to my house?" Duncan asked, thinking about his dad's attitude.

The professor looked at him over the rim of his horned glasses. "Duncan, you have had a box standing at your house for months. If anyone, especially my old associates, were to find out I was working on such a project, well, let's just say I could get into a lot of trouble."

"You mean the government?" Duncan whispered.

"Well, yes, among others. It won't look out of place, nor draw any attention, at your place."

"Okay, but how do we move this thing? It's big."

"I have a large pallet jack that should do the trick, but we'll have to wait until it gets completely dark."

"Where can we put it at my house?" Duncan queried.

"We'll sit it where your current box is. It won't draw any attention there."

"All right, but that means we'll have to move my box somewhere else."

"No problem. We can bring it back here, unless

you have another place for it."

Duncan began to pace back and forth. "No, my dad would find it if I put it anywhere else in the yard. He would notice if a weed grew in a different spot than usual."

"Fine. We will just exchange them then."

"That might be a problem, though. The Pandora doesn't look like my box."

"It does not have to, Duncan, just keep it covered when we are not working on it. If somebody does notice it, you can say that you made some improvements."

"I guess that would work."

"Come on, let's get the jack so we can be ready."

After dark, Duncan and the professor quickly moved to switch out the boxes. Luckily, in a small town like theirs, very few people would even notice if a tiger tank drove down the road after dark.

Duncan pulled while the old professor pushed, and soon they had the Pandora box in Duncan's yard next to Duncan's burned out box.

Duncan opened his box to the raunchy smell of melted plastic. He looked at the melted batteries and the fried wiring. The professor stood outside but could smell the odor of burnt wiring and the ozone left by the previous night's meltdown. Both of their noses wrinkled at the strong odor.

"Did your laser pulse emitters survive?" the professor asked, hoping for a positive reply.

Duncan frowned, worried. "I'm not sure. I won't know until I send power through them again."

"Well let's pull them out anyway and leave them here with the Pandora," suggested the professor.

Duncan grabbed his tools, unbolted the laser emitters, and laid them neatly in the Pandora box.

"Well, very good. Now all we have to do is get your box back to my lab."

Duncan and the professor covered the Pandora box and loaded Duncan's burned out box onto the pallet jack and slowly began pushing it back to the professor's house. There it stood, Duncan's wrecked box in the basement where the Pandora had been.

Back at Duncan's house, the proud Pandora 8 was covered with a tarpaulin and dormant for a moment. But soon, the two hoped this one would spring to life and make their wildest dreams come true as the first box had done.

Chapter 15

Pandora 8.2

Over the next few evenings, the professor showed up like clockwork as he and Duncan began to augment and build up the Pandora 8. They used a mix of Duncan's laser pulse emitters and the professor's reverse Tesla coil, along with their theories of Einstein. Duncan ran all new wiring and hooked up his laptop via a USB cable, something totally foreign to the Pandora 8's original design, yet still kin to it in technology. The professor provided a brand new set of three-hundred-watt speakers, which the two carefully focused on the core point. All this was done under the cover of darkness. Duncan worked late into the night as he and the Professor Batton worked out the algorithms and rechecked the codes again and again. The two were in sync as partners, working smoothly in unison, and each knowing what the other needed before they asked for it.

The professor held a paper far from his face, squinting to look at some scribbled math. "Duncan? Where did you say you got this equation?"

Duncan leaned over to take a quick look. "Oh, I found a website online—some time travel forum. I found a picture posted there of Albert Einstein with this equation written on a chalkboard." The professor's eyes widened in amazement. "I have never seen anything like this before, I must confess.

This algebra is way above my head."

"It is above mine, too, professor, but it worked with my box."

"Well, I have found something odd in this equation. Perhaps I am misunderstanding it, but it looks like this could conceivably not only go to the future, but also to the past." He looked at Duncan then, waiting for an answer.

"Uh, yeah. Well, I kind of forgot to mention that the other night because I was upset, but I did go to the past, too," Duncan half-laughed and shrugged slightly.

"You did what?" the professor gasped.

"I traveled to the past, professor."

"How far into the past?"

Duncan cleared his throat. "I went back to 1963. I landed in London."

The professor shook his head as though he was now unsure. "Hmm, well this changes things, son."

"How so?" Duncan stopped what he was doing to give the professor his full attention.

"Duncan, when I told you that you cannot change the past, I meant that, in theory, you should not be *able* to go backwards in time."

"Why is that? I thought time was kind of like a river and you could go upstream or downstream."

"From what you are telling me, it is like river. In theory, however, you should not be able to go backwards in time, because if you did, you would pass the point where you had first built your time machine. Thus, you would not be able to travel past its creation—or at least that was the theory."

Duncan's eyebrows furrowed in thought.

"Well, I have been to the past, though."

"I believe you, my boy, but this does present a

problem. We cannot change what has been. If we do, it could cause our own time to change, and it would be a domino effect, that would have far reaching consequences, even into the future."

"Well, I assumed that if anything were changed, that we would know it when we got back to the present. Wouldn't we?" he asked.

"I am afraid I can't be certain that we would notice, Duncan," the professor, exclaimed.

"How could we not notice?" Duncan asked inquisitively.

"Well, consider, for instance, if you went back in time and kept your dad from meeting your mom, then you would no longer exist, and no one would remember or even know you had ever been in the first place."

"I understand that," Duncan nodded.

"Or consider what could happen if time is a certainty."

"What do you mean, professor?

"Well, imagine if you went back and met and earlier version of you. Then let's say you tell yourself about your fight with Jamie, for instance."

"Yeah, go on."

"Well if you did that, then here in the future, things would change and there would be no reason for you to go back and warn yourself."

"Okay, but what is your point, specifically?"

"Well, if you never had a reason to go back and you never went back, then you would not warn yourself and everything would unravel. The future that had been where the fight happened would be again."

"Wait, wait...you said that the future could be altered."

"Yes, Duncan, but I did not know travel in both directions was a real possibility. I mean, it was theorized even by Patmos, but...well, this changes things," the professor warned.

"All right, so what does this mean to us now?" Duncan asked.

"That means we have to be extra vigilant, should this time machine work. We cannot alter what has been or what is, and we must make very sure we do not," the professor warned, placing a hand on Duncan's shoulder.

"Well, I do know this. Nothing changed when I went to the past, because everything here in the present is the same."

"How can you be sure, Duncan?"

"I would have noticed if anything had changed..." he repeated in an exasperated tone.

"Of course you would—if it affected you, or your life, or anything you are familiar with. But what if it was something outside the sphere of what you see?"

"You mean something could have changed and I may not be aware of it?"

"That is a distinct possibility. Did you see or talk to anyone in the past?"

"Well, yes, I met Sydney Newman."

"Sydney Newman? I am afraid I don't know who that is."

"He is the man that created one of the biggest sci-fi TV series of all time."

"You mean that show you were telling me about with the time traveling phone booth?"

"Yeah, that's the one," Duncan nodded, and then paused. His eyes widened and he exclaimed, "Wait, come to think of it, he did see my box land. Oh my

God!" He shot up from crouched kneel.

"What?" the professor asked as he fiddled with the piece of paper still in his hand.

"I told him I was a doctor and that I travel in time and he created that show in the year I went back to."

"Hmm, I would say you had a profound impact on him and time then, Duncan."

"Well, now wait a minute, though. That's one of my favorite shows and it was around before I ever built my box or traveled back in time."

"Either that, or your perception changed when you came back to the present and you only think it was around before."

"No, professor, it was around long before I ever built my box."

"Well maybe it was, but no doubt your meeting with Mr. Newman was instrumental in that show's creation..." the professor trailed off. He pushed his glasses up on his nose and continued, "Hmm, interesting. Perhaps you were destined to go back in time and cause that show to happen."

"You really think so?" Duncan smiled.

"I can't be certain, Duncan, but perhaps it was a loop in time that had to be," the professor theorized.

"Yeah, but now I wonder what else might possibly be a loop or a fixed point that we might change, or have changed, in the past," Duncan pondered.

"I cannot answer that, but I think we better be very careful." The professor began to roll down his sleeves and redo his buttons, his hand shaking slightly. "At any rate, I must go, Duncan. I am not as young and spry as I used to be. I've got to get some sleep."

"All right," Duncan nodded as he powered his

laptop down. "I'll see you tomorrow."

"Yes, I think we are about ready to run some tests. Goodnight, Duncan."

"I will look forward to it. Goodnight, professor." Duncan watched as the old professor walked back down the street, leaning over every other step on his cane.

Duncan stood there for a few minutes pondering if his jaunt into time had really been the catalyst for his favorite show.

Chapter 16

Testing the Theory

Thursday morning arrived, but with it came another cold front. The gray sky opened up as a misty rain poured down, heavy enough to create a dense fog across the streets. There was a slight chill in the house, but Duncan climbed out of bed anyway and put on his clothes. He began to walk down the stairs, rubbing his arms to induce warmth. The wood beneath his feet was chilly and he was bouncing from foot to foot, still half-asleep, when he nearly ran into his mom. She was in a pink bathrobe and house slippers and she clutched her hand to her chest in surprise.

"Duncan? You scared me!"

-"Oh, sorry mom. I didn't see you."

"It's fine; you just startled me. You're never up this early. Are you going out to look for work again this morning?"

Duncan shrugged his shoulders. "Yeah, I suppose so."

"Well, it is cold outside and there is a light drizzle, so wear something warm," she warned.

Duncan rolled his eyes. His mom acted as if he didn't have sense enough to come in out of the rain.

Placing a hand on her shoulder, he gave her a silly but serious look. "I will get my extra waterproof coat and wear my thickest scarf."

She huffed, tucking her shoulder length brown hair behind her ear. "Okay, smarty pants. I just don't want you to catch pneumonia."

"I know, mom. I'll wear something warm, okay?" Duncan said, quickly walking towards the front door to fetch his shoes.

"Fine. By the way, Aunt Sarah is in the kitchen, so you might want to go out the back door," she said with a smirk, gesturing towards the back of the house.

Duncan spun around on one foot and grabbed his shoes by their laces before he turned towards the back door. He nodded his head in her direction so she knew he had heard her. "Will do. See you this evening."

Duncan grabbed his all-weather coat and exited his home through the back door before heading into town to try and find work again.

While he walked throughout town job hunting, his phone began to ring. What had started as a welcome distraction from the endless rejections soon turned to an awkward feeling when he saw who was calling. He hesitated a few seconds when he saw the name Logan light up on the Caller ID, but he had to answer; he had never ignored Logan. He took a deep breath before pushing the green button and saying, "Hey Logan, what's up?"

"What's up? Nothing really. I just wanted to call and make sure you hadn't forgotten Ryan's party tomorrow night."Duncan cringed at the thought;

the thought of running into Jamie made him nervous. "No Logan, I haven't forgotten...but I think I am gonna back out."

He could practically feel Logan's instant reaction through the phone. "Oh no you are not! You have been wallowing in self-pity all week, and I don't want to go stag," Logan argued quickly, sounding as if he had prepared for the argument.

Duncan resumed his steps down the sidewalk, kicking a loose pebble off the curb. "Jamie is going to be there, Logan, and I don't want to see her right now."

"Dunc, you can't hide from life and you can't skip out on me like this. I will be at your house at seven thirty tomorrow and you're going, even if I have to drag you."

Duncan sighed loudly. "All right, all right—twist my arm, geez. I'll go, but we have to leave if there is any hint of trouble, deal?"

"Okay, deal," Logan agreed.

"Anyway, I'm out looking for a job so I'll see you later."

Logan chuckled. "You? Looking for work? Ha."

"Don't you start. You sound like my Aunt Sarah."

"I am just messin' with ya, man. Good luck. See you tomorrow evening."

"Yeah, yeah, see ya later." Duncan frowned as he shoved his cellphone back into his pocket and continued his quest for work. He stopped at the next building and went to open its door, pausing for a moment to look at the sign; it read *Hunter's Feed and Livestock*. Duncan took one look inside the store, got a whiff of the unique store aroma— which smelled like manure—before he shook his head and kept walking.

It took him two hours to ask at every storefront if they were hiring, to which they all said no.

Later that evening, Duncan was back at home working on the Pandora 8. It was cold and windy, but he was undeterred. The professor arrived punctually, as usual.

"Good evening, Duncan," the professor said as he crossed his arms. He was shivering from the cold air.

"Good evening, professor. Is it cold enough for you?" Duncan joked.

The professor looked around at the leaves moving and swaying in the trees. "It's cooler than I expected, but I grew up in Minnesota so I've seen worse. How are you coming?"

Duncan rubbed his hands together in excitement, blowing on them briefly. "I have everything hooked up, even the new inverters for the coil."

"Excellent. We can run some tests tonight then," he stated, crouching down to examine Duncan's work.

Duncan smiled at the professor. "I was hoping you would say that. I know it will work; it should be no different than my old box."

"Yes, I think it will work. I just want to leave nothing to chance—so we test and re-test."

"Agreed. What shall we try first?" Duncan stood up and looked over at the professor. The professor stood and looked Pandora 8 up and down slowly.

"Let's try a test at low power, to gauge how much power is needed to open a dimensional barrier. Start your video camera, please. I want a record of this."

"The camera is on...but, professor, I was able to open the barrier using only 240 volts. Somehow I think your coil can easily handle that."

The professor shook his head. "It's not a matter of if the coil can handle it or not. I want to know if the variables we are dealing with are at threshold of breaking the time-barrier."

Duncan turned to the control panel. "Okay. So what setting should I use?"

"Try 110 volts to begin with, and then let's move upwards from there," the professor suggested.

Duncan's eyebrows furrowed together. "110 volts? That is *really* low power, professor."

"Yes, but it will give us a range to begin with."

Shrugging, Duncan complied. "As you wish. 110 volts comin' up."

The Pandora box began to hum with a low noise. As it powered up, Duncan began running the equation code on his laptop and selected a song to begin the test.

At first nothing happened, but as the power increased, eerie flashes began to illuminate the inside of the box and the garbled sound of voices were heard.

The professor stuck his head in the door and viewed the flashes of light. He cupped his hear with his hand and listened to the garbled voices; they sounded like a crowd clustered together and overlapping one another.

"Ah ha, you see? Even at low power, we are getting some effect," the professor smiled.

"This is what happened in my room when I ran the code," Duncan remarked.

"Try increasing the volume," the professor called out.

"We are at fifteen percent currently. I'm taking it up to thirty." Duncan increased the volume, but little, if any, change was noticed.

"All right. Now try adding power in increments of 10 volts every five seconds."

Duncan began to increase the voltage and called it out as it rose incrementally.

"We are now at 130 volts...140 volts...150 volts."

As Duncan called out the voltage, the flashes became more pronounced and the voices grew louder and less garbled.

"Things are progressing," the professor called out over the noise. There was a certain excitement to his voice.

"They may be progressing, professor, but until I choose a fixed point from this grid, I don't think anything will really happen."

"Nothing is supposed to happen, Duncan—we are just running tests. I assume if you choose one of those points, the machine would probably dematerialize into time."

"Isn't that what we want?" Duncan asked, raising his eyebrows in confusion.

"Yes, but not now. We have to be certain of what we are doing before we commit to launch."

"Okay, but no matter what we test, the machine will go to whatever point we choose. The problem is that we cannot know where or when that point is."

"That's okay," the professor grinned. "Proceed with the voltage increases please."

"We're now at 170 volts...180 volts...190 volts...now 200 volts."

At 200 volts, pressure began to build in Duncan's head, and to his surprise, a portal vortex opened and he saw a blue 1940's Volkswagen Beetle appear before him. He could hear a broadcast talking about "A New Deal for the American People," and suddenly he saw men and women who appeared to be from different time periods. They looked to be from a time before Duncan was born and they were faint, like looking at an old photograph.

"Do you see what I'm seeing? How time is being

broken up into increments?" the professor marveled. "Incredible! Duncan, what I am trying to do is make it so we can choose where we go in time. I think this might be the way!"

Duncan was in deep focus, blinking quickly as he tried to take in what was happening before his eyes. "Understood. We are currently at 210 volts... 220 volts," he continued to call out every few seconds.

Suddenly, an atmospheric disturbance began to form around the Pandora box. The visions that the professor and Duncan were witnessing became vivid, as if they could reach out and touch them.

"Do you see that, professor? That car just flew past me!"

"I did indeed, my boy! Remarkable!" he acknowledged.

"We are now at 240 volts of power."

"Keep going," the professor pressed.

"250 volts...260 volts...270 volts," Duncan said excitedly, his words beginning to come out in a jumble as he watched for the next vision.

Suddenly, the Pandora box began to shake and became almost transparent in certain places.

"What's that?" an unknown voice called out, seemingly from the rift the professor and Duncan were seeing.

The professor realized the machine must have been causing disturbances in other times and places; and, apparently, the people from those times could also see the machine tearing through the walls of reality.

Duncan was still in awe of what he was seeing.

"Did you hear that? Other voices speaking from across time," the professor grinned.

Suddenly the both saw a figure like an officer walking up and looking directly at them. "Who are you and what is this?" the figure asked.

"Duncan! Cut the power!" the professor yelled.

Duncan quickly pulled the lever back and the voltage dropped. As the power grew weaker, the figure and the visions grew blurry, the voices grew more garbled, and the flashing ceased. He didn't dare to blink until they faded away entirely.

He grinned suddenly, his teeth gleaming. "I would call that a pretty successful test, professor," Duncan said, overjoyed.

"It looks like it. I will have to go over the video and review the data, but I think we now have a threshold and a red line of power. Odd, though...I assumed it would take much more power to open a trans-dimensional rift," the professor said, scratching his head.

The comments went right over Duncan's head. "Okay, so what do we try now?" he asked eagerly, having tasted some success.

The professor's eyes wandered to the now still and quieted Pandora 8. "For now, I think we should shut it down. I need time to process all of this."

"But professor, we are so close. I know it will work." Duncan could hear the desperation in his own voice, but he didn't care.

"Duncan, my boy, patience is a virtue. Don't worry; we'll get there. Now, it's cold out here and I am an old man. Give it time. Once this works, we will have all the time in the world," he said with a wave of his hand.

"If you say so, professor," Duncan said begrudgingly, but he couldn't help but feel some doubt in the professor. He powered the Pandora down and stepped out.

The professor nodded his head and adjusted his glasses on the rim of his nose. "All right. Will you lock it up please? I need to go home and rest then I will review this."

"Yes, sir. I will take care of it."

The professor paused to look at his young fellow scientist; his shoulders were drawn in defeat, and a frown hung on his lips. The professor patted Duncan on his shoulder.

"You have done well, Duncan. We're on the cusp of the biggest discovery of all time—quite literally," the professor grinned reassuringly.

As Duncan stepped back from the box, his head rose quickly and he asked, "When do you want to try again?"

The professor paused before speaking. "Tomorrow night, perhaps? If it's not so cold."

"Sure, that will be...no, wait," Duncan paused, shaking his head. "I have to attend a party tomorrow night."

"No matter then. We'll try the night after. If we're lucky, perhaps it will warm up."

"Will you be ready to try a trip into time?" Duncan asked impatiently.

"I will take the tomorrow to review this video and the data. I'll let you know at that time." The professor leaned his cane on the ground and began his slow walk home. He stopped and turned when he heard Duncan's voice again.

"Professor? No offense, but what are we waiting for?" he asked. He hoped he didn't sound quite as irritated as he felt, but he had to get his point across.

"We are making sure that nothing will go wrong

Duncan, that's all. Remember to have patience. One wrong move and we could interfere with time, or worse," the professor warned, pointing his cane at Duncan.

Duncan shrugged, unconvinced. "I suppose so. But I'm eager to try the new machine."

The professor kept his ever-patient look.

"Duncan, Rome was not built in a day. Now, it is freezing out here, so I'm off. Goodnight."

Duncan was a little disappointed, but he knew it was now just a matter of time. "Goodnight, professor," he said as he stood looking at the now dark box.

Chapter 17

An Awkward Night

Friday evening, the night of Ryan's party, was here. Duncan was working on the Pandora box as Logan pulled into his driveway and got out of the truck. It was still chilly, but not as cold as the night before.

"Hey Dunc," Logan greeted as he walked up to the box.

"Oh, what's up man," Duncan replied without looking up.

Logan leaned his arm up against the machine. "What's up? Only the biggest party of the year...so why aren't you ready?"

"I've been busy. I guess I lost track of the time, and I really don't even want to go."

"Don't want to go? Come on man. I don't want to go by myself. I need you there so I have someone to pick on," Logan said in an attempt to lighten the mood.

"Well, I told you, Jamie is gonna be there and I really don't want to see her right now."

He missed her. He missed her being around, even with him being buried in his work it had comforting to know she was always there for him. He even missed the pestering marriage talks because he knew that meant a future with her. But all that went away when he looked at Logan. Duncan still had it fresh in his mind that Logan was her future according to the future he had visited and that angered him. Seeing Jamie for the first time since their breakup was going to be nothing less than awkward, but Logan could never understand the things Duncan had seen, nor could any rational man, so Duncan had to do what he could not so easily handle—deal with it.

"Dude, you can't let her ruin your social life. I mean, okay, not that you have much of a social life, but well, you know what I mean."

Duncan stared up at him blankly. "Yeah, thanks man, I can always count on you to cheer me up."

"Yeah it's a gift. I don't know how I do it sometimes," Logan retorted jokingly.

"Me either," Duncan snorted. He swallowed the feeling in the pit of his stomach and started to wrap his work on Pandora 8.

Logan looked at the Pandora box and noticed something was different. Now Logan was not one to pay attention to detail, but even he could see something had changed.

"Did you do something to your box? I thought it was gray."

"Oh, um yeah. I just gave it a paint job, that's all," Duncan replied, stretching the truth.

"Yeah? Looks like you painted it and added a bunch of parts, and...made it taller too."

Since when does he notice what I'm working on? Duncan wondered.

"Just never mind the box. Anyway, you never paid any attention to it before."

Logan looked into the box and was taken by all the technology. "What is all of this? I don't remember seeing this before," he exclaimed.

"It's just some stuff I added for my experiment,"

Duncan said to take Logan's attention off the interior. He rose from his knees and began to put some of his tools back in the box, noticing how smudged his fingertips were with grease.

"Well your experiment can wait. Now come on and get ready so we can go."

"I'll have to get a shower," Duncan said, holding up his dirty palm.

"Well, whatever, just hurry up. We're gonna be late."

"All right, all right. Keep your shirt on. It won't take me long."

Duncan grabbed his laptop and closed up the Pandora box then threw the tarpaulin over it. Afterwards, he headed to his room to get some clothes before getting a shower.

Logan followed Duncan and waited in his room.

What a mess, Logan thought at the sight of Duncan's room. He carefully moved through piles of clothes and the disorganization. Duncan set his laptop on his bed atop his messy sheets and moved towards the bathroom. He sat on the edge, tapping his fingers against his knees as he waited.

It was not long before his curiosity got the better of him. He took a quick look around the room to make sure Duncan hadn't returned, and then he opened Duncan's laptop and saw a couple of icons on the screen that were labeled "Einstein time code" and "Pandora 8 schematic."

He clicked on the icon labeled "Pandora 8 schematic" and it opened with detailed plans that Logan could make no sense of, but he also saw a folder named "Logs." He opened the folder, which was a log of all that had been done to the time machine, including Duncan's remarks about the power of the Reverse Tesla Coil.

He looked through diagrams and read about Duncan's plans to travel in time. He was so engrossed in what he is reading that he didn't hear Duncan re-enter the room behind him.

"Hey! What the hell do you think you're doing?"

Logan jumped and quickly backed away from the laptop, caught off guard.

He held up his hands innocently. "I was just snooping. Sorry, I didn't mean anything by it."

"You didn't mess with any of my files did you?" Duncan ran over to his laptop and slammed it shut.

"No, I was just looking. So, this thing is a time machine?" Logan asked point blank.

"Uh, yeah. It is an attempt at a time machine, anyway,"

"Dude, you can't be serious. A time machine? Really, Duncan? I mean you can't even keep your room clean."

Duncan's face flushed red and he ran a hand through his damp hair in frustration. "What? You don't believe time travel is possible?" he asked.

Logan blinked quickly as thoughts raced through his mind.

"To be honest, no, I don't. I mean if it were possible, don't you think some scientist would have traveled in time by now?" he asked, tossing his hands in the air.

"And what makes you think someone hasn't? That is not exactly the kind of thing someone would just talk about openly," Duncan remarked, looking him dead in the eye.

Logan stared back at his friend, wondering when he'd lost his mind. He shook his head in disbelief. "Okay, it is official, my best friend is nuts."

"I'm not crazy, Logan. Time travel is possible," Duncan shot back.

"And you think you are going to be the one to make it happen?" Logan asked mockingly, his eyebrows raising on his forehead.

"I *will* be. As a matter of fact, I already have," Duncan boasted. He stood up with his laptop, taking it to his desk. He rummaged through his loose papers with drawings all over them, letting his words hang in the air.

Logan paced over to Duncan, stepping on his clothing now without care.

"Okay, Duncan. I know that when you and Jamie broke up it was bad, but this is off the rails man."

Duncan huffed angrily. "Off the rails? I have been to the past, but even if you don't believe me, what about all the videos and pictures that have recently been discovered that show things that are way ahead of their time?"

"Those are all explainable or photo-shopped nonsense made online by geeks with vivid imaginations," he replied as he moved some junk and sat on he corner of Duncan's desk.

"One day you'll see, and it is going to be sooner than you think. But for now, aren't we late for Ryan's party?"

"Yeah we are. Just try to act sane for my sake."

"I'll do my best," Duncan said in a lightly sarcastic tone and a half-grin to match.

Duncan's mind drifted, and he remembered how the professor had dismissed him earlier, and now Logan doubted him too. On top of that, he still didn't have the job that his parents were pressuring him to get, and nothing else yet to show for himself. Jamie's face also popped into his mind and he felt a sudden wave of weariness wash over him.

I wish I could just go to bed and not think about anything else for the rest of the night, he thought to himself.

The two headed downstairs and encountered Duncan's sister on the way out. She was twenty-two years old and quite beautiful. She and Logan had a kind of love-hate relationship; she was more than a match for his sarcasm and his devious wit.

"Well if it isn't dumb and dumber," she said condescendingly, tossing her long, pin straight brown hair over her shoulder.

"Oh, hi Linda. You still sleeping with my picture under your pillow?" Logan chided.

"Ha, in your dreams, pizza face," she retorted.

Logan leaned against the wall, his arm out in front of her, blocking her path down the hallway. "You know, Linda, a lot of guys want to be me. But you? Ha, you just want me. Admit it, you have had a crush on me since third grade," he smirked.

She batted her eyelashes at him, and placed a hand on his shoulder. "Oh, you got me Logan. I do want you..." she trailed off, their lips nearly touching. "...To high dive head first into a rusty tack," she mocked, her smirk returning.

Logan had no quick retort and just made a face at her. She laughed and pushed his arm down, heading to her room. He nearly lost his balance and quickly looked at Duncan, who was snickering to himself. Duncan turned, shaking his head and continuing towards Logan's truck.

"Yup, she wants me," Logan bragged, matching his friend's pace.

"Sure, anyone can see how she's totally into you, man," Duncan poked.

Once in the truck, they backed out and headed down across town to Ryan's house. Logan played the air-guitar to loud, thumping music as he drove, trying to psych himself up for the party.

As they rode along, the night began to overtake the daylight and there was a golden orange sunset that illuminated the dusky sky.

Duncan suddenly turned the radio down that Logan had at full blast. He turned towards Logan straightly and asked, "Don't do anything to embarrass me with Jamie, okay?"

"Would I do that? Muahaha," Logan jeered playfully as the truck went down the road and made a turn up a street where other cars lined the street.

Logan pulled up in Ryan's front yard, his tires crunching against the loose gravel at the end of the driveway. It was a packed house. There were cars for blocks, and they heard the crowd inside. The two exited the vehicle and heard music playing as they walked up to the door, which opened as others were coming out. Logan caught the door and the two entered the party, where their friend, Chris, was playing live. There were people dancing and others standing around, laughing and talking. The room smelled of cheap beer and even cheaper cologne; there were flashing lights and everyone seemed to be having a great time.

The party was packed with people and Duncan and Logan knew most of them. Others were new faces. As soon as they got into the thick of the people they began to mingle, but Duncan was ill at ease. He knew Jamie would be there somewhere.

He ran into some old friends and chatted with them while Logan headed for every female he could see that was standing alone.

After a short time, Logan saw Jamie moving amongst the crowd. He noticed that she had spotted Duncan and her eyes were fixed on him, so Logan began to move toward her as she was making her way through the crowd. Duncan, being uncomfortable at this get-together, decided to try to distance himself from the events and walked over to the refreshments table. Jamie knew it would be awkward, but she decided to at least say hello and to talk to Duncan.

Unknown to Duncan, Jamie walked up to the table and stopped directly behind him. She stood there contemplating what she could say to him. Logan saw what was going on and quickly came over to ease the tension he knew would come from their meeting.

Jamie's attention turned when she saw Logan.

"Oh. Hi, Logan, how have you been?" she asked with a strain in her voice. She was a little irritated that he there with Duncan; she had hoped to see him alone.

"Couldn't be better, Jamie. How are you?"

"I am doing okay," she replied with a half-baked smile.

Despite the noise, Duncan heard the conversation going on behind him and turned around to face Jamie. The sight of his blue eyes comforted her.

"Hi, Duncan," she said nervously, briefly meeting his eyes.

Duncan, recalling the events of his trip to the future, was at a loss for words.

"Hi," he answered coldly as he looked toward the stage.

"How are you doing?" she asked as she fidgeted

with her fingers nervously.

"I've been getting by, I guess," he said with no real emotion in his words.

"That's good, I just wanted to—"

"Excuse me will you? I need to go talk to Chris while he's between sets," Duncan interrupted.

Jamie was taken by surprise and instantly felt tears sting her eyes when Duncan walked away and headed for the small stage through the dense crowd. He felt his stomach dip from his nerves.

Geez, he thought, *could that have been anymore awkward? What if we argue in front of everybody? I never should have come to this stupid party. I have to stay away from her for a while; it's the only way.*

Jamie watched Duncan's back as he went up to talk to Chris. Duncan and Chris had been friends for years but had grown distant; she knew he was just attempting to avoid her. She wiped her tears away quickly and her hands shook in anger. She felt a hand on her shoulder and turned around, realizing that Logan had probably heard everything.

Logan's eyes looked tender and filled with sympathy for Jamie. "What's up with you two?" he asked, keeping his voice low in her ear.

Her eyes glinted with anger as she looked up at him. "I guess I pushed him too hard, I don't even know. All he seems to care about is his experiment, or hanging out with you." She sniffled and smoothed her skirt, trying to remain calm.

"Uh, news flash, Jamie, he hasn't been hanging out with me. As a matter of fact, he has had nothing to do with me since you two broke up," Logan explained.

"He doesn't seem to care anymore," Jamie

lamented, looking around at all the happy, chatting couples and people socializing. She wished she and Duncan were a part of that.

"That's not true and you know it. I think he's just going through a tough time right now," Logan reassured, patting her shoulder softly.

She inched a little bit away from him and shrugged. "Maybe so, but he won't even talk to me."

Logan stood there debating what to say.

"I'm gonna go try to have some fun," Jamie shrugged, turning around and walking away.

She looked and saw a bunch of her friends dancing in the center of the room. She devised a plan to try to make Duncan jealous. She walked over and one of the guys dancing on the floor—a jock named Riley who immediately asked her to dance. She smiled flirtatiously and played with her hair as she accepted his invitation.

Logan, still standing where Jamie had left him, took notice of what was happening and knew it would not end well, but there was nothing he could do. He shook his head at the disaster that was bound to happen and proceeded outside to try his luck.

Once out the door, he noticed two girls leaning on a car. One of the girls he was familiar with, and in typical Logan fashion, he walked up to them and started chatting.

"Hey Simone, what's up?" he said arrogantly.

She turned her shoulders stiffly towards him. "Um, not much. What do you want, Logan?"

"Who says I want anything?"

"I am not stupid, Logan. I know your reputation."

"Yeah? And I know yours. Big deal. Does that mean we can't talk?" he replied with a slow smile.

Simone made eye contact with her friend. "I guess not," she shrugged, looking back at him.

Meanwhile, back inside, it didn't take Duncan long to notice Jamie dancing on the floor with her jock partner. Immediately, Duncan became enraged and left Chris, who was tuning his guitar, and made his way to the front door.

I guess my trip to the future revealed more truth about Jamie than I wanted to believe, Duncan reasoned in his head.

With that, Duncan threw his drink into a trashcan as he moved to the front door and exited the part. Jamie, mid-grind, was watching out of the corner of her eye and saw Duncan walk out, but she couldn't break away; the middle crowd was too thick for her to reach him in time. She quickly realized that her plan had backfired severely.

Duncan hurried across the yard and came up to Logan, who was still chatting with Simone and her friend. Duncan usually would not have interrupted, but his anger was burning within him. He tapped him hard on the shoulder.

"Logan, we need to go," Duncan interrupted.

Logan turned and looked at Duncan then looked back to Simone in exasperation. This was the last thing Logan needed right now.

"Excuse me for a minute, ladies?" he said with a quick smile.

Logan grabbed Duncan by the shoulder and whisked him over to an oak tree in the yard away from the girls, glancing back to check if they were still watching.

He lowered his voice to a whisper as he spoke. "Duncan, dude, what do you mean we need to go? I am talking to Simone! She has never given me the time of day until now," Logan pressed.

"I am done here Logan, and I want to go," Duncan reiterated, his face blank.

Logan looked at him in desperation. "Well can't you just hang out for a little while? Did something happen in there? Did you get jealous over Jamie or something? I mean, come on bro, we are talking about Simone here, Dunc."

Logan's words meant very little to Duncan at the moment. "Never mind. You stay here, and I can walk." He turned his back on him and began his walk down the driveway.

Logan followed him hesitantly. "Dunc, what's up with you? Just chill man. We'll go in a little bit," Logan assured.

Duncan didn't slow his pace as he navigated his way past all the cars. "Logan, I'm going. It's fine, man. Stay here and talk to Simone. I'll just walk."

"No, that's a long walk. I'll drive you," Logan relented.

Duncan waved a hand in the air, dismissing him. "No need. It's no big deal, I wouldn't want you to miss out on your big chance with her. I'll catch you later."

Duncan headed for the road, his hands now in his pockets.

"Dunc? Wait up man," Logan pleaded, but Duncan ignored him and kept walking.

Logan shook his head and ran his fingers through his hair and then walked back over to the two young ladies.

"Something wrong with your friend?" Simone asked.

Logan huffed and said, "He's been acting weird since he broke up with his girlfriend. I really should take him home."

"Well, okay, but I wish you could stay," Simone enticed.

Logan turned and looked behind him once more and saw Duncan briskly walking down the street.

"Well, maybe the walk will do him some good." He looked back at Simone, smiled, and gently caressed her hair, pushing it behind her ear. Simone blushed and looked down quickly, only to look back into Logan's eyes.

A few blocks away, Duncan was near the main highway through town. There weren't many cars on the road. He kicked a can on the side of the road, which flipped end-over-end, sounding like a cowbell as it tumbled and finally fell into a gutter.

As he continued to walk, Duncan began replaying the vision in his mind of Jamie being married to Logan and being pregnant. The thought of it dug deep into his soul. Then he thought of her dancing with that jerk at the party. He began to heat up with rage and jealousy.

The night was chilly but Duncan continued to walk, passing under amber streetlights, which cast his shadow as he passed under them.

Ruth Delancie was headed home from work on the empty streets when she caught sight of Duncan walking alone. She immediately turned around and went back. Ruth had known Duncan for years, and in truth had a deep desire for him, but she was a few years older than him and knew that he was involved with Jamie. In a small town, though, news got around fast so she knew that the two had broken up. Though Ruth and Duncan were friends, she never let on how she really felt, but she hoped this might be some kind of opportunity.

Ruth pulled up alongside Duncan and rolled down her window.

"Duncan?" she called out.

Duncan turned to see Ruth's familiar face. "Hi, Ruth, how are you?" Duncan asked without any real emotion.

She could tell he was upset about something. "I'm good. What are you doing out walking on the highway?"

"Oh, uh, well...I just needed to think," he answered with a big exhale afterwards.

"Well, hop in. I'll give you a ride."

"That's okay. Ruth. You don't have to. I know you live in the other direction."

"Duncan, I don't mind, really," Ruth said, hoping he would accept.

"Um, alright. I appreciate it."

Duncan got into the car, which was warm. It was a welcome relief from the chilly air outside. Ruth pulled back onto the highway.

"There's not much traffic tonight," Ruth said, trying to break the ice. She had never been completely alone with Duncan before and she felt a twinge nervousness as she saw him put on his seatbelt.

"Yeah, it's weird," Duncan agreed.

Ruth tried to think of something to talk about, but she came up with nothing. Her big moment was quickly turning into a dud. Duncan leaned his head back against the headrest and sighed, but never closed his eyes.

Back at the party, Jamie finally managed to break free from her dance. She quickly moved through the crowd and reached the front door.

As she stepped out, she saw Logan chatting it

up with Simone. Jamie walked up and stood in front of Simone, not caring if she seemed rude.

"Logan, where did Duncan go?"

"He left, Jamie. He walked home," he said in an uninterested tone, looking right back at Simone. Jamie yanked his shoulder in her direction in order to snap him out of it.

"What? And you just let him?" Jamie sneered.

"He is a big boy, Jamie. He'll be fine," Logan said, looking over her shoulder at Simone.

She moved her head back into his line of vision so he couldn't ignore her. "Why did he leave? You two haven't been here long at all."

Logan rolled his eyes. "Oh gee, I don't know, Jamie. Maybe he was upset because his ex-girlfriend was dancing with another guy or something?"

Jamie cringed to herself knowing she had made a bad situation worse. She tucked a lock of hair behind her ear nervously.

"I was just trying to—"

"You were just trying to what? Make him jealous? Congrats, Jamie, it worked."

Her eyes pleaded with him. "Logan, I don't have time for this. I don't have a car. You have to help me."

He stared at her face, so sad and sweet, and realized something deep down in him would not allow him to say no to her. He ran a hand through his hair. "All right, all right, calm down."

Simone got upset with Logan because he now seemed to have taken his attention off of her and it showed in her demeanor.

She stepped closer to him, now in front of Jamie. "Why don't you tell her to get lost, Logan?"

Logan had known Jamie for years. He had introduced her to Duncan and he did not care for Simone's dismissal of Jamie's distress—at least that's what he told himself was the reason.

"You know what Simone, why don't you mind your own business?"

Simone stared at him, incredulous. "Well, you just blew any chance you had with me, Logan Keith."

Logan faltered, but was quick with a reply. "Yeah, that's really tragic. I guess I will just have to find, oh any other female in the world, to replace you, huh?"

Simone's eyes filled with hurt, and not saying another word, she grabbed her friend and walked quickly back to the still raging party. Logan watched her go, feeling like a total jerk. He felt angry with himself for getting involved in Jamie and Duncan's mess. His meddling had cost him a great night with a pretty girl. *Why do I do the things I do for Jamie?* he wondered to himself, but he knew deep down why.

"Logan?" Jamie called to him as she stood impatiently near his truck. Logan shook his head out of his thoughts and grabbed his keys from his pocket. He noticed Jamie looking at him but he didn't meet her eyes.

He sighed heavily and went to unlock his truck with a click, opening the door for her. " Okay Jamie, let's go look for him."

She watched Logan walk around the front grille after he let her in, his face drawn. When he got into the truck and started up the engine, she kept her face towards the window. She knew she had hurt more than one guy tonight.

Ruth was in no hurry to take Duncan home, but as they rode, Duncan kept his eyes straight ahead. Ruth looked over at Duncan several times but he said nothing.

"Duncan, is everything okay?" she asked.

"Yeah, everything is fine," he said still looking forward.

She twisted her hands nervously around the steering wheel. "You don't seem fine. You seem preoccupied."

"I'm just tired," Duncan excused.

"Are you sure? I heard about your breakup."

"Good news travels fast, huh?" Duncan huffed, leaning his head against the window in defeat.

"It's a small town, Duncan. If you need to talk to someone you know you can always talk to me."

"Thanks, Ruth, but I'll be fine."

Duncan pressed a finger down hard on the window panel, but it didn't roll down.

"Hey, can you roll down the window, please? It's really hot in here." he mumbled, pulling at his collar.

Ruth read into his lack of response. "I'm sorry, I didn't mean to bring up anything bad. I just wanted you to know that I'm here if you need me," Ruth said with soft eyes.

Duncan felt guilty at being rash; she did give him a ride after all. "I appreciate that, Ruth, but there is really nothing more to talk about concerning her," he said in a gentler manner.

Ruth turned into Duncan's subdivision and soon arrived at his driveway.

"Here we are," she said in a defeated tone. She looked at him in a way that almost begged him to stay back for even just a moment, but Duncan was too focused on leaving to notice.

Duncan opened the door and stepped out, then leaned back into the car.

"Thanks for the ride, and thanks for the offer to talk, Ruth." His half-smile and distracted eyes changed his sincerity into mistaken indifference.

She smiled back at him, but her facial gesture was as empty as she felt at the moment. "Anytime, Duncan. Why don't you call me sometime?" she urged.

"Will do. Thanks again for the ride. Goodnight."

Duncan closed the car door and Ruth drove off slowly. As she pulled away, she looked in her rearview mirror and saw Duncan walking up his driveway. He hadn't looked back. She felt a little bit let down, as if her opportunity had slipped away. She sighed and drove off into the night.

Chapter 18

Gone with the Wind

Duncan wasted no time. He darted in his house and up the stairs. He grabbed his laptop and a couple sets of clothes—some straight from the floor that he thought were clean enough, and some from his dresser. *Tonight is the night I show everyone,* Duncan thought to himself as he hurried back down the stairs.

Frank and Shellie were sitting in the living room watching a comedy and were so engrossed in the movie that neither of them noticed Duncan as he came through the house.

Duncan sprinted out to the Pandora box and unlocked it. He set his laptop down and turned on the power from the reverse Tesla coil. He activated the programs as the box powered up.

He felt the box begin to vibrate intensely and he touched a palm to the box and felt something stirring inside him—a familiar feeling. He felt that exact same push that he had when he had first time traveled. Everything in him wanted to go some place far away.

He thought of Professor Batton and closed his eyes.

Sorry professor, but this time I really have nothing to lose. Everything as I knew it has changed. I hate to disappoint you but that's all I seem to do with everyone lately...this box is all I have to prove myself. This is what will make it right, once and for all, he thought to himself.

Duncan pulled on the throttle and the box began to make an increasing humming sound as the whirling light on top of the box spun clockwise and the red beacon light above it flashed in a counterclockwise circle like an old fire engine. The two cylindrical shaped tubes on either side of the box lit up in a brilliant blue color. The box emitted a powerful light from the top, which looked like a whirling white tornado and the atmosphere became charged as it caused a disturbance. Lightning began to flash and discharges of power erupted from the Pandora 8.

Frank and Shellie noticed the light show from their living room and wondered if there might be a storm nearby.

"Was that lightning?" Frank inquired.

"I don't know. I don't think bad weather was expected," Shellie replied.

"Well then, what is it?"

"I have no idea."

The two got up and walked to the window, but could not discern where the flashing was coming from. The living room faced away from where the Pandora was standing. Shellie had an odd feeling suddenly, like she had forgotten something important.

Meanwhile, Logan and Jamie were flying towards Duncan's house. They passed Ruth going in the opposite direction. Logan had his foot hard on the accelerator and the truck's engine pulled hard with power as they passed cars darting in and out through traffic and drifting wildly on to side streets.

Jamie looked and saw what appeared to be a

tall, white light whirling in the sky and odd streaks of lightning coming up from Duncan's neighborhood. She knew it was unusual, but for the moment she was clueless as to what it meant. As an increasing sense of urgency overcame her, all she could think about was getting to Duncan.

Logan flew around the corner and pulled into Duncan's driveway as dust flew from his truck's arrival. Both he and Jamie saw the Pandora box glowing and emitting beams of light and the lights on top flashing. Jamie realized this is what they had seen from the highway. She was terrified to think about what this could mean. The trees near the box shuddered in the outflow from the box's power.

Marshall was riding close by on his bike when he saw the light show and heard the sound of the box. As he approached, he skidded to a stop using both of his feet and his jaw dropped open when he saw what was happening.

He dropped his bike to the ground and stepped towards the box. "Whoa, that is awesome," he exclaimed. "What are you up to Dufus?"

The professor sat peacefully in his rocking chair, looked at the flashing light. He squinted his eyes, unsure as to what he was seeing. With his pipe rested in his mouth, he inhaled deeply. He let out a cloud of smoke and continued to watch the flashes of light from outside and slowly rocked in his chair. It never dawned on him that this was Pandora 8 approaching taking off.

Logan and Jamie jumped out of the car quickly and headed for Duncan's box. The lights were now blinding as they heard the roar of extreme power building up and the winds seemed to increase as if a tornado was near.

Inside the box, Duncan pulled the power lever past the point of the red line, which he and the professor had defined only the night before. Duncan looked as the grid popped up with all the numbered choices for possible fixed points in time. He chose one and the trace began.

As Jamie ran up to the box, she recalled what Duncan had said about his experiment involving time travel. She now knew this was not some fantasy, as did Logan. It was all too real.

"Duncan!" she screamed, pounding her fists against the box as her hair whipped around her face. It was already too late. The Pandora 8 was now glowing amber and was being enveloped by a bubble of blue light as it began to phase and dematerialize. Jamie stepped back in fear.

Suddenly, the box disappeared and was gone, leaving Jamie and Logan standing in the darkness, lit only by the front door light of Duncan's house. The atmosphere began to settle down and became still.

Logan was amazed. He knew Duncan said he would be the one to achieve time travel, but he could hardly believe what he had just witnessed.

Jamie began to cry as Logan put his arm around her to comfort her. They stood there in the dark cool of the night wondering what had just happened.

Frank and Shellie came running out of the house, having heard the commotion; yet, they had not seen the Pandora's spectacular departure.

Shellie noticed that Logan was holding Jamie and she was crying profusely.

"Logan, what the hell is going on here?" Frank

growled.

"I—I don't know. He's gone," Logan stammered.

"Who's gone, Logan?" Shellie asked, her voice shaking in fear.

"Duncan. He's gone."

"What do you mean Duncan is gone, Logan? I thought he was at that party with you."

"He was, but he came back here and now he's just gone."

"What are you talking about, boy?" Frank demanded.

"Duncan just took off in his box," Logan tried to inform Frank.

Frank and Shellie looked at the spot where Duncan's box had been standing and they noticed it was now missing.

Frank's fists were clenched. "What is this, some kind of a joke?" he interrogated in an aggravated tone, a large vein popping out of his forehead.

"No, sir. Duncan just took off in his box," Logan proclaimed nervously.

"What do you mean took off? Are you drunk?" Frank railed.

"Can't you see his box is gone?" Logan pointed to where the box had been standing.

"Yes, I have eyes. Where has it gone?"

"I don't know. I only know he said he could make it travel in time."

"What? Are you insane?" Frank retorted.

Shellie put her hands up to her mouth; she knew Duncan had been consumed with his experiment, but she had no idea it involved time travel. She began to cry instantly, thinking the worst—that her son could be lost to them.

Duncan had broken through the dimensional

barrier once again. Though this was his second incursion into time, to him it felt like the first.

Now he had unlimited power and the ability to go almost anywhere.   —

As he monitored his computer, he quickly noticed that something was wrong. Duncan used music to trace fixed points in time and he had chosen a fixed point for a landing, but now the readings were changing and he had no idea why.

He looked down the saw that in his anger he had pushed the power well past the maximum output level. As he looked back to the computer, he saw no fixed points and no references whatsoever.

Now he became anxious. Duncan knew he needed to have something to guide him but there were no readings on the screen. It was blank.

Duncan pushed forward on the power lever and the power level began to drop down to a more normal level, but still no references appeared. The computer seemed to be working, but there were no potential landing points.

He decided the only thing he could do was to cut all power and hope he could land somewhere, no matter how distant in time. It would be better than being stuck in the box perpetually until he starved to death or something worse happened.

Well, I really hope it's nice wherever I'm going, he thought.

Chapter 19

Meet your Lord

Just as it happened in Duncan's first box, the Pandora landed and daylight poured into the small windows.

Duncan had no idea where he was. He braced himself as he opened the doors, only to see that he had landed in a thick grouping of trees that appeared to have some sort of berries on them. Lush farmland expanded all around him. He could hear birds singing high in the trees and felt warmth against his cheeks.

He stepped out of the box and saw nothing but a large grove surrounding him. From what he could see, it was an olive grove. He was taking in the beautiful, deep green of the olives as the soft sound of waves from afar reached his ears. He lifted his nose to the air and smelled salt air and grass. He wondered if he had landed near an ocean.

The terrain was hilly and looked like nothing that Duncan was familiar with. He walked out to the edge of the tree line and saw a great walled city and tall mountains in the distance. He assumed that perhaps he had landed in Italy or some part of lower Europe by the architecture of the only buildings he could see.

*Hmm, it looks medieval. That shouldn't be, though, because I have no music that reaches back that far in time, it must just be an old town...*Duncan thought.

As he walked out onto the only path he could find, he eventually came to what appeared to be a dirt road with thin depressions and hoof marks in the soil. They looked like some sort of horse-drawn wagons might have made them.

He followed the dirt path until he came to a marker in the road, which appeared to be written in Latin and some other languages he did not recognize. Duncan knew a little Latin, but all he could make out were the words Phillipi and Caesaria, which he didn't understand. He continued to walk on the path, hoping he could find someone to tell him where, and perhaps when, he was.

After about twenty minutes, he saw what appeared to be a very large group of people sitting amongst the olive trees. Everyone seemed to be looking at one man that was standing on a hillside speaking. Duncan didn't recognize the language of the speaker.

As he came closer, he saw men, women, and children sitting around small fires and eating fish and bread. They all appeared to be dressed in robes of different colors, with gladiator style sandals. Some looked like Tartan, others looked as if they belonged in old Rome or out a scene from the Bible. The men wore long robes like one might see in the Middle East or India; they were unshaven, and the women had long, flowing, natural hair and wore simple dresses made of a single piece of cloth, save of those who had head scarfs.

Where have I seen something like this before? These people remind me of something. I think I'm in ancient times, but that doesn't make any sense. I need to know what time I'm in, and fast. I hope I am not in an unfriendly country, I like my head where it is, Duncan thought to himself.

As he walked between the people, he got an uneasy feeling because they seemed to stare at him. A number of people motioned to him and spoke, but he couldn't discern their words. He turned his back towards them, quickly pulled his phone out, and saw that he had no Internet signal; his on-board downloaded programs were working, though. Duncan loaded a linguistic translator program, which came with the phone, and tried to find someone who would to speak into it.

Soon, a bearded man approached Duncan and handed him a piece of bread and said, "Lec hem."

Duncan smiled and took the bread, then bowed. As the man continued to speak, Duncan reached into his pocket and grabbed his phone and held it up to the curious man, who stared at the device, a flash of fear crossing his face at the foreign technology. The man continued to speak, and Duncan told his phone to identify the language. The built in software was able to decipher the words.

The application stated, "Language identified as Hebrew and Aramaic mixture."

Duncan looked puzzled. "Hebrew? Aramaic? How can that be unless...?" he asked himself. He assumed that maybe the linguistic program was incorrect, because he had never seen anyone dressed like this who spoke Hebrew, and Aramaic was a seldom spoken language in the modern day.

As Duncan continued to walk through the crowd, the man on the side of the hill was addressing the people gathered. He heard a number of people in the crowd speaking the same phrase: "Yehoshua ben Da veed Meshiach ben Yahoveh Elohim."

These words were meaningless to Duncan, but the program insisted the language was Hebrew and a mixture of Aramaic. Duncan whispered into the phone, "Translate phrase: Yehoshua ben Da veed Meshiach ben Yahoveh Elohim."

The program responded with the translation, "Jesus, son of David, the Messiah, son of God, Jehovah."

Duncan was stunned and shoved his phone into his pocket. He was now more curious than ever. He walked up to where the man who was speaking to the crowd was standing and sat down at his feet. When the man had finished his oratory, Duncan stood up to get a closer look.

Thinking that the man couldn't understand his speech, Duncan said, "So let me guess, you are Jesus Christ?"

Duncan was shaken to his core when the man answered him in English and said, "I am."

"You are?" Duncan gasped.

"Yes, Duncan. I know you and where you come from," Jesus answered.

"How could you unless—" Duncan gasped.

"Unless I am He," the Man said, looking at Duncan without so much as a blink of his eyes.

"Are you Jesus Christ?"

"I have told you," Jesus nodded. "Do you not believe?"

Duncan's eyes widened in disbelief. "Well, maybe. I just never expected to have gone back so far in time."

"You travel in time and yet you marvel at what you see with your own eyes," the Man said.

Duncan lowered his head in respect. "Forgive me. This is all too hard to accept."

"Marvel not that you find it hard to accept, Duncan. From this time, even your own people will find it hard to accept me; is that not the truth?" The Man never broke his calm demeanor.

Duncan could feel his own heartbeat in his ears and his voice trembled as he spoke. "So you are Christ, the Son of God."

The Man smiled and spoke again and said, "A certain man was lost in the desert, separated from his caravan because of a sand storm. For days he walked, his tongue dry from the heat. He thirsted greatly, so he prayed for water to quench his throat from the heat and from dust of the desert.

He soon saw what he thought to be water and he ran as fast he could to reach the flood, only to find it was a mirage. Again he prayed for water to cool his tongue, and soon he saw yet another vision of water. Likewise he ran also to it, but it, too, was an illusion. He prayed the third time, and said 'Oh God in Heaven, let me have a drink so that I do not perish.' He the looked and saw an oasis in the distance, but he believed not and said in his heart, 'This is not real and I will not go to it.' Verily I tell you that man fell there and died, and the desert sand covered his body because of the hardness of his heart. He did not believe that God had heard him, and so he died and was gathered to his people. Yet the water he had seen the third time was indeed an oasis, and if he had only had faith and run to it, he would have lived," the Man finished.

"You speak in a parable," Duncan said in awe.

"I am the Living Water. He that drinks of me shall never thirst again, but shall live forever."

Duncan now knew this was indeed Christ. He was so overcome with emotion that he fell at his

Jesus' feet and wept.

"Now your eyes have seen," Jesus said.

"Forgive me, Jesus. It is not an easy thing to believe that I have seen you," Duncan pleaded.

"You have been given the gift to have seen the future and the past, and yet your heart cannot accept that you can now see me," Jesus said gently, placing his hand on Duncan's head.

Duncan looked up with tears still in his eyes but felt unworthy to speak.

"Many have desired to see me, but in seeing me, they have not believed. You have now seen me and now you believe, but only because you have seen me," Jesus said, marveling.

"But I believed in you even when I had not seen you," Duncan choked on his words, for the emotions he was feeling were overwhelming.

"Then why did you not accept what you had seen with your own eyes?" Jesus replied.

"Because I did not think it was possible that I could be here in this time," Duncan said, wiping his tears.

"You are not of this time, Duncan, but My Father has allowed you to see this time and to behold this wonder," Jesus explained.

Christ's disciples were also there. They came closer and spoke to Him in the Hebrew tongue. His disciples asked Him of this man who wore strange clothes.

Then said Jesus unto His disciples, "He is one that follows me. If any man will come after me, let him deny himself, take up his cross, and follow me. For whosoever will save his life shall lose it, and whosoever will lose his life for my sake shall find it. The Son of man shall come in the glory of his Father with his angels, and then he shall reward every man according to his works. Verily I say unto you, there be some standing here who shall not taste of death, till they see the Son of Man coming in his kingdom."

Duncan did not understand His speech when He spoke to his disciples. "Jesus?" Duncan asked, reverently bowing his head.

"You wish to know what I have said to mine own, Duncan?"

"Well, yes. But I am wondering why was I allowed to come here? Why did I not stay in the times of the music that I used to trace time?"

"You neither know nor understand the ways of my Father, Duncan. Though you have faith, how little you understand that my Father does nothing without purpose."

"Then I am here with you for a reason?"

"You come from the end of times, Duncan. In your lifetime, you shall see the Son of God return."

"I will see that? Then my being here is no accident?"

"In your days, Duncan, shall be great darkness; such as was never seen since the foundation of the world."

"Darkness? Is the sun going to burn out?"

"Duncan, hear my words and relate them not to things which are seen only of the eyes of man. There shall come one before me. See to it you do not fall to him, for he is the wicked one. He shall bring the darkness of which I spoke."

"You mean Satan?" Duncan asked.

"Now you begin to see what has been hidden from the foundation of the world. When he comes, he shall be as warm and peaceful as a dove, but his mouth shall speak great deception and the whole world shall worship him, for he comes in my place."

"How could anyone come in your place, Jesus?" Duncan inquired of his Lord.

"When your travels in the realm of time are complete, search for me in my words. Then will you have an understanding of those things which I have told you."

"Then I will go home?" Duncan asked. At that moment he feared he would not see home again.

"I have said it, and so it is. The things I say are not of me alone but of my Father who sent me."

"Jesus? They will kill you in Jerusalem," Duncan warned.

"I came as was spoken of me by the prophets. I must fulfill all that is written of me. Have you not read that they prophesied that the Son of Man must be lifted up and delivered into the hands of the wicked and killed, but three days later shall rise and walk again amongst men?"

"I know you did this, or rather, will do this. I guess I need to read my Bible a little more."

"You have devoted your life to the mystery of time and the quest for your own glory. Seek you the Kingdom of Heaven first, then what you need shall be added to you," Jesus smiled.

"What should I do now, my Lord?

"Go back and return to the river of time from which you came. You have a destiny there. And pray, Duncan, always pray and love The Father that sent me, and love your neighbor as yourself. Do this and you shall have treasure in heaven."

Duncan walked up and hugged Christ, then fell to his knees. "I will not fail you," Duncan promised.

"I will be with you, Duncan. I will be with all the

sheep of my fold even until the end of the world. Now go and know that if you seek me, you shall find me."

"Jesus, am I a good man?"

"As a man thinks, so is he, Duncan."

Duncan marveled as Christ spoke another parable.

"A man had two servants and to one he said go and do as I have bid you, and the man said, 'I will.' And his servant departed and did his will. To the other, he said go and do as I have bid you also, and the servant said, 'I will do your bidding,' yet he did not. Which servant was a good man then?"

Duncan answered, "The servant who did his bidding."

"Then do my bidding and you shall be a good man," Jesus said with a smile.

"Lord? Thank you for what you will do for me," Duncan bowed, beginning to tear up again.

"Greater love has no man, save he who lay down his life for his friends. Remember when you read of me, Duncan that you are reading of your friend. Until we meet in the great day, Duncan." Jesus walked away, back toward his disciples.

Duncan could not help but keep looking upon Jesus.

"I will wait for you," Duncan vowed.

As he turned and walked away, he kept looking back. He could not control his emotions and wept as he journeyed back to his box. He was in awe that he had actually met Jesus Christ, the Son of God.

As Jesus looked on, Duncan disappeared back down the path and his disciples had many questions about the young man, but Jesus said nothing of Duncan to them. He said, "Write not of this, for it is not given that this should be spoken of."

Within a half an hour of wandering through the olive grove, Duncan had reached his box. He stepped inside and activated the program, only this time, everything worked. His box powered up and dematerialized, but Duncan could still not fully comprehend that this miracle had actually happened.

Chapter 20

Revelation

Now in full transit, Duncan selected a song from 1978 and began a new trace. He was still moved by what he had just witnessed and wiped his hands over his eyes several times to dry his tears. He had never fathomed such a thing would, or could, be possible, but he had to focus on where he was going next. He felt most at home listening to the music of the 1970s and 1980s. This time period was something that he had longed to be a part of. He found that there were tens of millions of choices on his grid that were fixed points in time. He attributes this to the popularity of the song he chose—an early number from his grid—and didn't know what to expect.

The trace completed and prompted Duncan to commence materialization. *Well here goes nothing*, Duncan thought to himself.

As he was preparing for whatever awaited him, he smelled an acrid odor and saw that the main power lead was glowing on the reverse Tesla coil. At once, the lead melted through and the box went dark inside and began a sharp decrease in power. Luckily, Duncan was already in the process of materializing, but the landing was a bumpy one, as if the box had been dropped from a few feet in the air. This jarred Duncan and he was filled with a sudden bout of uncertainty.

The Pandora 8 landed but was not completely dark because the computer battery kept the screen lit. Duncan pressed the door button, but nothing happened; he then remembered that on the schematic of the box there was a manual switch to open the doors.

Thinking quickly, Duncan reached into a pouch on the console and grabbed a small LED light. He clinched the light between his teeth and pulled a panel off of the wall, revealing a small hand crank. Duncan turned the crank with some difficulty and managed to force the doors open, but not fully.

When he looked out, there was only darkness; however, he heard what he believed to be a waterfall nearby and was taken by the curious strong smell of evergreens.

It was slightly chilly, but luckily Duncan learned from his first incursion into time and had brought a coat with him. As he stepped out of the box and looked up, he could see a canopy of millions of stars in the night sky and a beautiful moon. The view was absolutely breathtaking.

He could tell that he was in a wooded area. There were small patches of snow on the ground.

Well I have to find something that I can use to make a new lead for the power line. I hope I am near a town or city, Duncan thought.

The moon lighted the night and all Duncan could see as he walked toward the sound of the water were patches of white here and there and gray outcroppings of rock. When he got closer to the waterfall, he could see the majestic, cascading falls illuminated only by the moonlight. Despite the beauty, he smelled something besides the pleasant fragrance of the forest. It was the smoke of a fire and the enticing aroma of cooking food. His stomach rumbled and he realized he hadn't eaten in a long while.

As Duncan looked around, he could see the amber glow of the small fire only a couple of hundred yards away. He assumed that he was near a campground, or at least near some sort of civilization.

He began to tread through the night as the sound of tall grass rippled against the stillness. He kept his eyes on the campfire. He heard the crackling of the small fire and he saw an orange tent lit by the reflection of flames of the fire. He also noticed a small oil lamp that lit the tent from the inside.

He heard music playing and was relieved because he knew the song—it was the same one he had chosen to trace. Duncan walked up to the tent, hoping someone friendly would be in it.

"Hello," Duncan called, but there was no reply.

Duncan could see a cauldron sitting on the fire and a metal coffee pot beside it, steaming away.

As he sat down to wait for whomever this camp might belong to, he was still preoccupied with his meeting with Jesus and with thoughts of Jamie.

There was a radio sitting near the tent. It was antiquated by Duncan's standards of modern MP3 players. While he sat patiently and pondered his meeting with his Lord, the song ended and a D. J. began talking, which broke Duncan's concentration. Suddenly a voice boomed, "WSTC playing all your top hits all the time. Good evening, Seattle! You are live with the Don, the night crawler, Morrison. It's 38 degrees and it's one minute past eleven o'clock. The news is presented by JTS communications. JTS—when you have something you need to share, they will be there.

The top story for tonight on this May 17th, 1980..." Duncan raised an eyebrow. That date that sounded familiar, but he couldn't remember why. It was about to become all too apparent, however.

"...Is that another 3.2 earthquake rocked the area around Mount Saint Helens this morning, doing only moderate damage and causing a few rockslides on the peak.

Scientists and volcanologists from around the globe have converged on the area in an effort to determine if the old girl is going to blow her top or not. The local authorities are still not letting anyone into the red zone without a pass. Fish, wildlife, and game wardens are patrolling the areas around Spirit Lake and 12 miles out from the summit in all directions.

In an interview with Joan Evangeline this evening, Scientist David Johnston said a massive bulge has developed on the north face of the mountain and is likely caused by magma rising from deep under the peak. Johnston further said that no one can be sure when, or even if, it will erupt, but tensions remain high as loggers from the area are losing valuable wages playing the waiting game.

In other news, two skiers that went missing a week ago have been found alive near the Toutle River. A survey team that was checking seismometers near the river picked them up. The Sheriff's office had no comment on the matter at the time of this broadcast.

Stay tuned for more news and your favorite tunes after this brief message..."

Duncan's eyes grew wide. He had been listening

to the broadcast, but it had not dawned on him until just now that the D. J. had said May 17th and Mount Saint Helens.

No, it can't be...I am just near to Seattle. This could be any camping area. But what if I am anywhere near the mountain?

Duncan knew history well enough to recall that Mount Saint Helens erupted on May 18, 1980, but he tried to reassure himself that everything was fine. He knew that he was in dense forest, but he tried to relax and convince himself that the mountain was miles away.

While Duncan sat pondering his next move, a young man and woman came walking out of the darkness with flashlights.

The young man saw Duncan sitting at his tent. "Hey you, what do you think you are doing?" his voice called out.

Duncan turned to look in the direction of the voice but all he could see was a flashlight in his eyes. He stood up quickly as they approached.

"Oh, I am sorry. I didn't mean to intrude. It's dark and I am lost," Duncan said apologetically.

"Well, just stay right there. Are you armed?"

"What? No, I'm not armed. I saw your fire and I was cold."

The man approached slowly. He stood defensively as he glared at Duncan, his long thick hair and dark eyes intimidated Duncan as he stood with his arms crossed.

"Well, no wonder. Why are you dressed like that?"

Duncan didn't want to lie, but he had to think up something fast. "I had a little accident. I didn't plan to be out in the woods like this."

"What's your name, man?"

"My name is Duncan."

"Duncan, huh? I am Eddie, Eddie Pryor, and this is my wife, Jamie."

"Jamie? Hmm, that's ironic," Duncan snorted.

"Yeah? Why?"

"That's my girlfriend's name. I mean my ex-girlfriend's name is Jamie."

"Well, good to meet you, Duncan. You said you had an accident?"

"Yeah."

"Well are you hurt?"

"No, I'm fine," Duncan assured.

"You must be freezing if you've been walking all this way. The nearest road is over two miles from here."

"Yeah, I didn't expect to end up here, that's for sure."

"How did you get into the red zone?" Eddie asked.

Duncan remembered that the D.J. said that people were being kept out of the blast zone unless they had a pass.

"Oh, I, um, have a pass," Duncan fibbed.

"So you must not live too far then?"

"Actually, I am a good ways from home."

Eddie nodded and walked closer to the fire. "Yeah? You must live up near the lake, eh? I thought they had evacuated everyone."

"Yeah, they have."

"Jamie, get Duncan some hot tea will you?"

"Sure. Are you hungry, Duncan?" Jamie asked. She had short, blond, curly hair and a sweet, round face.

"Um, yeah, kind of," Duncan answered, stuffing

his hands in his pockets.

"I'll get you a bowl of stew, then."

"Thanks, Jamie. That would be great"

Eddie settled down a few feet away from Duncan, letting his heavy backpack hit the ground with a thud. He was a stocky fellow with short, brown hair and a serious jaw.

"So, Duncan, do you think the mountain is gonna blow her top?"

"Yeah, it will," he replied before catching himself. "Uh, I mean, I think so," he stated, clearing his throat.

I've got to be more careful with my words, Duncan thought to himself.

"I hope not. I love this place. Jamie and I just got married and this is our honeymoon."

"Oh wow, congratulations! I'm sorry I interrupted."

"No big deal, man. You couldn't have known you would have an accident."

"How far are we from the mountain?"

"We are 13 miles north."

Duncan began to feel nervous. He knew what this meant, and he knew that 13 miles was nowhere near enough to be able to survive the eruption. He also knew that in about nine hours the mountain would erupt.

"13 miles? How did you get into the blast zone?"

"We snuck in. The barricade was unmanned so we moved it and drove in."

"Drove in? I didn't see your car," Duncan noted.

"My truck is parked up at the North Mill parking lot."

"How far is that?"

Ed narrowed his eyes slightly at Duncan. He

reasoned that Duncan was from the area, so he surely knew where North Mill was. "You don't know where the mill parking lot is?"

"Well not from here, no," Duncan said nervously.

"Oh yeah, I forgot you got lost. It's about a two and a quarter mile hike back to the south."

While Eddie was content with Duncan's explanation, in the reverse, Duncan became perplexed. He knew that they were on the north side of the mountain, and that where they were would soon be buried under hundreds of feet of mud and ash.

What should I do? Can I risk telling them the truth? It's dark and, in the morning, the mountain will explode. Are they supposed to die here, or can I save them? Duncan pondered as he tried to come up with a solution for what to do.

"Here you go, Duncan," Jamie smiled. She handed Duncan a bowl of hot stew and a cup of warm tea.

"Thank you, Jamie. That is very nice of you."

"You're welcome," she said politely with a smile.

Duncan wrestled in his mind as he ate. *What should I do? I can't let them be killed, but what will happen if I save them and they were meant to die? What will it change?*

"Do you need anything else?" Jamie asked. She was so kind it pained him.

"No I am totally chill," Duncan replied.

Jamie and Eddie looked at Duncan as if they had heard wrong.

"You're what?" Eddie chuckled.

Duncan realized he had been hanging around Logan too long. He had forgotten that he was in 1980 and his words were unknown to Jamie and

Eddie.

"Oh, it's a figure of speech. It means, um, I'm cool with what I have."

"I never heard that one before," Eddie replied.

"You will eventually."

If you live that long, Duncan thought to himself. He cleared his throat and asked, "So when are you guys going home?"

"We go back on the 22nd. Until then, we are gonna enjoy nature and do some fly fishing here."

Duncan knew he had to tell them, but how? *Can I tell them the truth? Will they believe me? How do I get myself into these messes?* Duncan pondered.

Soon they had finished eating and Jamie gathered up the trash. Duncan knew it was now or never.

I have to tell them. There's no way I'm going to let them be blown into oblivion, they're good people. And on their honeymoon, no less. I cannot let them die, he thought to himself.

"Duncan, I have a spare sleeping bag. You're welcome to it, but we want to get up and fish early, so we're gonna turn in."

"Eddie, I am concerned," Jamie interrupted. "I have a bad feeling...maybe we should think about leaving,"

"Baby, it's late. We can leave in the morning when we have daylight if you're that worried."

"Eddie, there have been three quakes today and at least a dozen tremors."

"No she's right, Eddie. I think it would be a good idea for you to pack up and get out of here tonight. Ya know, just in case."

Eddie looked at Duncan with a questioning demeanor. "Duncan? Do you know something you are not telling us?"

Duncan tried to urge Eddie to take Jamie and leave without having to tell them the truth, but he could see that wasn't going to happen. "Um, well—"

"Well, what?"

Duncan kept his eyes closed as he spoke. "I am gonna regret this, but I can't stand by and let something terrible happen. The mountain will explode tomorrow at 8:32 a.m. exactly, and this whole area will be destroyed."

"Ha, okay. For a moment you had me going, Duncan."

Duncan opened his eyes to peer at their confused expressions. He took a deep breath before saying, "Eddie, I am not kidding."

Eddie stared at him. "How can you know the mountain will explode tomorrow, and at that exact time?"

"I have no choice now but to tell you. My name is Duncan Sims. I am twenty-four— "

"Yeah, and?" Eddie interrupted.

"I came here from the year 2018. By your calendar, I will not be born for another fifteen years. I did not have an accident, Eddie. I am a time traveler."

Eddie looked at Jamie, his eyes wide. "What? Duncan, hey man. I'm sorry, man but you are talking crazy now."

"I know what it sounds like, Eddie, but I'm not crazy and I'm not lying."

"And why should I believe you? Time travel is science fiction, Duncan," he said, tossing his hands in the air.

Duncan reached into his pocket and pulled out

his cell phone. "Have you ever seen anything like this before?" He handed the phone to Eddie, who flipped it over in his hands. He looked at the pictures and the icons that filled the screen.

"What is this?" Eddie asked, as he looked the phone over.

"It's a cellular phone and iPad. This phone has the date on it. Please look at it."

Eddie looked down and saw the date showing as Feb 12, 2018.

Jamie looked at the phone as well, and then she looked at Eddie in dismay. "Is this some kind of a joke?"

"No, it's no joke. I am dead serious and if you are here tomorrow morning at 8:32 a.m., you will both be killed.

Eddie handed the phone back to Duncan, shaking his head. "I can't buy this Duncan. That device is something I have never seen, but it proves nothing. I mean who knows what that really is?"

"Eddie, I can prove that what I am saying is true."

"How?" Eddie asked.

"My time machine is up by the waterfall."

"And you expect me to just trounce off in the dark, on your word, to see this time machine? I mean for real man, you already lied to us and said you were in an accident."

"I know that, Eddie, but I couldn't very well tell you the truth, could I? If you'll come with me I'll show you my machine," Duncan said, pleading.

"Eddie, what if he is telling us the truth?" Jamie said in a concerned tone.

Duncan stared at them and motioned towards the waterfalls. "It's only a couple of hundred yards and your life depends on whether or not you believe me."

"All right, all right, Duncan, I will go and see this time machine—if it exists. This better not be some kind of trick, though."

"You'll be glad you listened to me, I swear."

"Okay, well then let's go."

The trio stood up, and Jamie handed Duncan her flashlight to let him lead the way. Duncan knew all he had to do was follow the river back up to where the Pandora 8 was standing in the trees.

Chapter 21

My Eyes Have Seen

Duncan trudged up the muddy bank of the little river that led to the waterfall. Eddie and Jamie were close behind him. They were both silent; the only noise from them was the snapping of twigs and branches under their feet. Duncan was using a small LED light to find his way. He heard a howl suddenly, then a bird's wings flapping in the trees. He picked up the pace, knowing that time was growing short.

He reached the area of the falls, which made a comforting, roaring sound. Jamie and Eddie followed closely, whispering to each other and stealing glances at him. Duncan could sense their hesitance about him—not sure if he could be trusted, or if he really knew what he was talking about.

"If I had a quarter for every time someone looked at me like that lately..." Duncan muttered under his breath. He turned his back to them nonchalantly, as if he couldn't still hear what they were saying.

"Do you think he is crazy?" Eddie whispered to his wife.

"I'm not sure, but he seems sincere," Jamie said calmly.

"Just keep your eyes on him for now," he replied, looking at Duncan out of the corner of his eye.

The two young campers closed the distance between themselves as Duncan continued to walk towards the falls. He spotted his box sitting next to a grouping of tall evergreens. "Over here," Duncan implored, motioning for them to follow.

Jamie shined her light on Duncan and soon saw a tall, green box that had the word Pandora written across the top and the number 8 showing on the slightly opened doors.

"Pandora?" Jamie asked, her voice filled with wonder.

"Yeah, I guess it's a reference to Pandora 's box or something," Duncan replied. He patted the box slightly, showing pride for his machine.

"This is what you time travel in?" Eddie asked.

"Yes. I had a box before this one, but it burned up."

"So time travel is not unusual in your time?" Jamie asked.

"Actually, I discovered a code and some websites which led me to the discovery of time travel," Duncan clarified, as they looked he box over.

Jamie crinkled her nose in confusion. "Website? What's a website?"

"Oh, um, it is a place you can go on a network called the Internet. It's only a dozen or so years into your future. You'll like it," he said with a half-grin.

"So you made this Pandora machine?" Eddie interjected.

"Actually, no. I made my own machine, which, as I said, burned up. This one belongs to a friend of mine."

Eddie leaned against a sapling. "Wait, I thought you said this was your discovery."

Duncan sighed and rubbed a hand over his eyes. "Eddie, it's kind of complicated. I did discover the key to time travel, but my friend built this box in the 1970s; however, he was not able to make it work, but I was able to make it work."

"He built this in the seventies?" Eddie asked as he hesitantly approached the machine.

Duncan nodded and cleared his throat. "Yeah. He was part of a government project."

"So then, somewhere, this box is not only here with us, but it is also somewhere else?"

"Come again?" Duncan asked, tilting his head slightly.

"If he built in the 70s and it is here, it must also be somewhere else in this time," Eddie explained.

"Ha, yeah, I suppose it is. I hadn't thought of that." He looked over at Eddie and noticed his hesitance. "Go ahead Eddie, look inside."

Eddie slowly and cautiously peered inside the box with Jamie's flashlight. He saw Duncan's laptop computer and wiring, along with the reverse Tesla coil. Duncan opened his laptop and as it awoke from it's hibernate mode it light up their faces and Eddie was amazed at sight of it.

"Jamie, look at this," he said, motioning with his hand as his eyes were glued to the screen.

Jamie stuck her head in the door, glanced around, and was also taken with what she saw. "What is that, a television of some sort?"

Duncan shook his head and smiled. "No, it's my laptop computer. This is what I run the codes on in order to make this machine work."

Duncan watched as Eddie's brain was working, trying to make sense of all he was seeing, but he was not entirely convinced. His eyes lit up when he thought of a loophole in Duncan's logic. "Wait, how do we know you didn't drag this box out here?"

"What?" Duncan said as he squinted his eyes.

"Eddie, why would anyone drag a box like this out here in the middle of the forest?" Jamie asked.

"It's too heavy to drag. Look around, do you see any skid marks where it was dragged?" Duncan quipped.

"So this is... real?" Eddie asked as he took a step back, looking slightly overwhelmed.

Duncan nodded his head slowly. "I am afraid so, Eddie. I didn't want to have to show you this, but you have to be sure I am telling the truth."

"I am pretty sure now," Eddie replied, his wandering eyes looking at everything inside the Pandora.

Duncan felt relief wash over him and he let out a sigh.

"Well now that you know, you have to get away from Mount Saint Helens. All of this will be buried tomorrow morning under tons of debris."

"Will it really be that bad?" Jamie asked, as if lamenting.

"It will be worse than you can imagine. Spirit Lake will be moved. People will die, and it will be a long time before anything can live here again."

"How much of the area will be destroyed?" Jamie asked fearfully, clutching her cross necklace and twisting the chain.

"Everything for twenty five miles north of the mountain will be annihilated, so when you leave you will have to go east or west, and you have to start now. It's already 1:10 a.m. That means in seven hours and twenty-two minutes this place will cease to exist."

"We can make it to the truck in a couple of hours in this terrain, but we have to pack up."

"Eddie, take only what you need. Do not worry about packing everything. You also have to get clear of the blast zone and you'd better start now."

"We will take only what we need. What about you, Duncan? How fast can you get out of here?" His eyes, which were once filled with skepticism, were now filled with worry.

Duncan sighed and looked at his box. "That is the rest of the problem."

"What do you mean?"

"While I was landing, my power cable burned up the connector. I have to find something to reconnect it."

"Oh man," Eddie trailed off. His eyebrows furrowed together before he exclaimed, "Hey, I have a set of battery cables in my truck and I have some battery connectors, too, I think."

"You won't have time to go and get them. I have no choice—I will have to come with you and try to get back here and fix this before 8:32 AM."

"Then we better start right now."

Duncan, Eddie and Jamie took off in a jog back to the campsite. They ran through puddles, mud, and grass that were knee-high as they followed the river. They heard the occasional howl but it fell on deaf ears; they all were focused on their new mission. Within a few minutes they were back at the camp.

Chapter 22

The Dark of the Night

Eddie broke down the tent while Jamie quickly dumped everything she could into a duffel bag. Duncan grabbed the radio and put new batteries in the flashlight. He was sweating from the jog and quickly brought his t-shirt to his face to clear his eyes. It took thirty minutes or so to pack up and begin the hike out.

Jamie grabbed a small bucket. "I'm going to run back down to the river and get some water to put out the campfire," she announced.

"Don't bother; everything here will be incinerated in a few hours. We have to go *now*," Duncan warned urgently.

Jamie dropped the bucket instantly and it rolled a few feet away in the grass. Eddie lifted a pack onto his back, while Jamie grabbed the duffel bag and Duncan grabbed the suitcase that the couple's clothes were in.

"All right—let's go, let's go," Duncan urged. The three began to walk quickly, trudging up the sides of hills and back down through dense forest and tall grass.

"Eddie, which way?" Duncan asked.

"There is a hiking trail about four hundred yards from here. It leads right to the parking lot at the Mill."

"That's good to know. I will have to follow it back

here."

Lit only by two flashlights and Duncan's LED light, they searched for the path. After about another half hour, they had reached the path that had a small wooden marker painted orange at its mouth.

"This is it," Eddie said in a relieved tone. He bent over slightly to catch his breath.

The three walked for about an hour on the path before Eddie began to look around as though he was lost.

"How much further is it?" Duncan asked, aware of the shrinking safety margin of time.

"We should be close," Eddie answered.

They continued to walk forward for another ten minutes before Duncan broke the silence. "Eddie? Shouldn't we have found it by now?" he asked frantically.

"Yeah, we should have. Something is wrong..." Eddie stated, halting his walk. He pivoted in a circle, his eyes searching earnestly for a sense of familiarity.

"Did we take a wrong turn?" Duncan prodded.

"I don't know. We always hike in here during the daylight; I've never walked this path in the dark."

"Every minute counts, Eddie..." Duncan reiterated.

Jamie was exhausted from carrying the duffel bag; her hair fell in her face and her knees began to shake. "I have to rest a minute," she mumbled as she dropped the duffel bag.

"Well take a breather. I have to figure out where we are," Eddie said, lightly patting his wife on the back while trying not to show his mounting fear. He knelt down next to her and took out a small book with a map of the trail, quickly unfolding a page. "We must have strayed onto the old Johnston trail," he began as he narrowed his eyes to focus on the map. "We have to go back east about half a mile."

"Are you sure?" Duncan asked anxiously.

"There are only two trails, and the marker we saw was the correct trail but somehow we missed the other marker to the Mill trail."

"Okay. Let's backtrack, but we have to hurry," Duncan paused, glancing down at Jamie. "Jamie, can you make it?"

"I have no choice," she mumbled, her voice trembling. She threw the duffle bag over her shoulder, letting out a big grunt.

Duncan grabbed the duffel bag from her and threw it over his shoulder. "I will carry this for a while," he said, knowing Jamie was worn out.

Jamie closed her eyes for a moment. "Thank you, Duncan. We had already had a full day and I'm so tired."

He nodded. "Let's just keep moving"

They all backtracked to the trailhead and this time, they saw that the marker to the Mill trail had fallen.

As soon as they had entered the Mill trail, the earth beneath them began to shake. It was just a small tremor, but it got their attention.

"That can't be good," Duncan remarked, looking off in the distance. The howls they had heard before were completely silent now.

Eddie glanced at Duncan and then into the darkness. "No, it's okay. That has been happening every few hours since we got here."

"And that didn't worry you?" Duncan asked.

Eddie shrugged. "Not really. When you live in

this part of the world, these things are pretty much normal occurrences."

"I don't live here, I guess that is why I'm not used to it," Duncan replied.

"Where are you from, Duncan?" Jamie asked.

"Actually, I'm from Florida. Well I will be when I am born, anyway," Duncan mused.

"Florida? Oh I have always wanted to live in Florida."

"If we make it out of here alive, we will go to Florida. How does that sound?" Eddie asked his wife, offering her a reassuring smile.

Another tremor occurred—this one lasting longer—and forced the three to stop for a moment.

"That was a longer one," Eddie noted.

"Yeah, they are getting more frequent apparently," Duncan affirmed.

"I think we have another half hour on the trail then we should be there," Eddie said.

Duncan took his phone out and saw that it was now 4:48 a.m. *We are cutting it close.*

As they pressed on through the darkness, they started heading downhill.

"We are close now. It is uphill from the parking lot," Jamie blurted.

After ten more minutes on the downhill slope, they stopped when they came to the black top. In the distance, Eddie saw his truck. "We're here," Eddie stated in an elated tone.

"Thank God," Jamie reaffirmed, letting out a huge breath and wiping her hand across her sweaty forehead.

Duncan was also relieved, but he knew he had to track back through unfamiliar territory to get back to his box. Not to mention he still had to repair it within the next three hours.

They were all worn out, but Duncan heaved the duffel bag into the back of the truck. Eddie and Jamie also threw their belongings into the truck. Eddie unlocked the truck and opened a toolbox mounted onto the back. He dug through it, pulled out set of jumper cables, and threw them out on the ground. He continued to dig, but was unable to find the battery terminal connectors.

"I don't see the battery connectors," he said in frustration, his fingers getting tangled in the wires.

"Don't worry about it," Duncan blurted as he leaned down and grabbed the cables. "The jumper cables will have to do. There is no more time."

Eddie nodded and closed up his toolbox. He rounded the truck, got in the driver's seat, and started it up. Jamie hopped in the passenger side.

"Eddie, remember what I told you. Go east or west or further north, but just get out of the area of the blast."

"Will do, Duncan."

"Duncan," Jamie started, "Will you be able to make it back to your machine in time?" Her voice was filled with concern.

"I should easily be able to, Jamie."

"I will be praying for you, Duncan."

"I will make it. Jesus is watching over me—He told me so."

Jamie looked at Duncan and cocked her head. He noticed her hand travel back to the necklace at her neck again.

"You mean you have—"

"No time to explain. You two take care of yourselves and get out of here as fast as you can."

Eddie offered a half-smile. "You do the same,

Duncan."

Duncan turned and got ready to run back up the hill.

"And Duncan?" Jamie called out.

"Yeah?"

"Thanks for everything—I mean, thanks for warning us."

"You bet," Duncan replied with a worried smile.

"Will we ever see you again?"

"That's hard to say, Jamie, but who knows. With a time machine, anything is possible."

Her eyes filled with tears as she spoke. "With God, all things are possible. Duncan, please be careful."

Duncan smiled and took one last look as Eddie punched the accelerator and squealed out of the parking lot onto the road.

Chapter 23

The Long Run

Duncan took off in a sprint up the hill. Eddie had left his flashlight with him and now he had to retrace his steps back to the campground. He was already exhausted from the hike to the parking lot, but he had no time to rest. Every breath was painful and his thighs burned as if he had climbed a hundred flights of stairs. Still, he pushed himself as hard as he could, only stopping for a breather every few minutes.

He reached the trail and pressed on as fast as he could go, but it was still dark. The terrain was unfamiliar and he only had his dead reckoning to guide him. As he ran, Duncan debated within himself as to whether or not he had done the right thing by saving Eddie and Jamie, and what effect it could have on the time continuum.

The words of Professor Batton kept ringing in his head. He lectured him about tampering with the timeline and its implications on the future. He kept thinking about what would have happened if he had made the obvious and stoic choice to leave them—that the timeline did not include them beyond the eruption and forcing them into the timeline beyond that could potentially be disastrous. All of this raced through Duncan's mind repeatedly, but one thing made him shut it all out. His empathy forced him to take a chance on the timeline. He logically could forgive himself for messing up the timeline, knowing that with a time machine, he could fix any earth shattering implications; however, the knowledge that he let such wonderful people perish, knowing their potential fate, was something he could not live with. Aside from worrying about that, though, he needed to save himself.

Duncan kept on the hiking trail, but nothing looked familiar. He was not lost necessarily, but he was also not sure of where he was. He only knew to stay on the trail. He jogged along, out of breath, running into low hanging branches and moving through overgrown areas of deep grass.

If only my phone had Internet I could use the GPS, he thought as he attempted to distract himself from the danger he was in.

On and on he ran, but it was as though the trip back to the camp seemed to take longer than the trip to the truck. He heard twigs snap under his feet as he ran and, though he knew it would all be gone soon, the smell of the evergreens seemed to soothe him.

Duncan stopped. He was out of breath and he was beginning to cramp from exertion. He got down on one knee to rest and to stretch out his legs. While he was catching his breath, he saw an unwelcome site. A faint glow was on the horizon to his east—the first traces of dawn. He stood quickly and began to run again, the trees and grass beginning to show the faint purple glow, it was light of dawn coming. Duncan knew he had to pick up the pace.

I should have been there by now. He began to feel a real sense of urgency, and could hear his own quickened heartbeat in his ears.

Duncan kept moving forward as the light became more pronounced. He no longer needed the flashlight, but there was a damp fog that hung over different parts of the trail. The grass was slippery, and Duncan's pant legs were wet from the morning dew, as well as the sweat that was pouring from him as he ran.

Soon, Duncan came to a fork on the trail that he did not recall. He paused for a moment and looked back and forth; the trails looked identical. Through his panic and frustration, he saw the same trees and the same dirt path down each trail. Now he was torn as to which trail to follow. He remembered that Eddie had said there were only two trails—but which one? He tried to decide in desperation as he wiped his sweaty palms across his pants.

Duncan stumbled on something as he paced and tried to make his decision—the downed orange marker. He was not as close to the camp as he had thought, but even so, now at least he knew where he was.

He ran at full stride, darting between tall evergreens and jumping over little creeks. He knew the creeks must feed the river near the campground, so he took a big risk and followed a little stream. Leaves and sticks crunched under his feet as he ran, gasping for air intermittently.

Duncan pulled out his phone as he was running and looked down. The screen illuminated against the foggy morning, the numbers across the top reading 7:27 a.m. *What? How long have I been running?*

He kept following the vibrant stream, which had

gotten wider and more robust. Soon, he heard a welcome sound—the sound of the waterfall—and within minutes, he had reached the river. The sound of the falls were ambiguous, however, and he had to decide whether to go upstream or downstream. He made the decision to go upstream, hoping it would take him to the falls.

As he continued to run, he wondered where he was getting the energy to keep going. Finally, he saw the prism effect of the tiny droplets in the air from the waterfall, and then he smelled smoke. He had to be close. When he came around the bend, the cascading waterfall overwhelmed him with joy.

He stopped at the edge of the river and knelt down to grab a quick, but refreshing, drink of the pristine, clear water. As he stood back up, he saw two otters playing in the water and his heart sank because he knew what was about to happen.

The two otters seemed to be curious about Duncan, so they came close to him. Normally wild otters would not allow human beings so close to them, but they seemed to have sensed that something was wrong. Duncan removed his jacket, leaned down slowly, and grabbed both of them in his coat. He stood back up, holding them like babies in his arms.

Wow I don't think they're scared of me—they look so calm, Duncan thought as he looked down at them. Two pairs of large brown eyes and black noses with long white whiskers peered back at him.

"Well I guess I'll have to save you guys too, huh?" he said to them with a smile.

Duncan turned to see the tall, green Pandora 8 standing nearby. He didn't want to frighten his new friends but he had to hurry. He moved at a quick pace as gingerly as possible and squeezed in through the door of his box.

Before he put the otters down, he cranked the door to a small crack so that the animals could not get out. He then sat them down gently.

Now down to business, he thought to himself as he tried to ignore the hell that would soon be upon him.

Chapter 24

The Big Blast

Duncan immediately got to work. He peeled back the burned cable, shaved off the rubber coating, and hooked up the battery cables Eddie had given him. He ran a current from the reverse Tesla coil to the Pandora's power inputs. He crossed his fingers and turned the power on and to his relief the lights came on. When he was sure everything was ready, he began the process of take off. He opened his laptop and started to run the codes. He powered up the emitters and selected a song. He began a trace and the computer showed millions of fixed points, but Duncan decided that he was ready to go home. After having seen these places in time, being afraid for his life, and now being worn out, his simple little town did not seem like such a bad place after all.

Duncan changed the song to one he knew would take him nowhere but home. Just before he had begun his quest into time, he had begun a song playing in a loop in his dad's garage on an old CD player. He could still see it in his mind, sitting on the dusty counter surrounded by various tools. It was bright red with metal dings and scratches all over it.

The song was a lullaby that his mother had sung to him when he was a little boy. It would put him straight to sleep no matter what. He briefly tried to remember the last time he had slept soundly and came up blank.

Duncan had taken the song from a cassette tape, burned it to a CD, and set it in a looping playback. He knew that his mother's voice would guide him home.

As he made his final preparations for take off, he began hearing what seemed like tiny pebbles or sleet hitting the outside of the box. At first he thought the otters were simply making noise, but no—this was definitely the sound of tiny impacts from debris.

Duncan grabbed his phone, looked at it, and, to his horror, the time read 8:32:53 a.m. The landslide had begun and the mountain was blowing out its first hints of eruption, but he didn't know it because there wasn't a big blast, as he would have expected. Rather it was eerily quiet; soon, the earth began to move violently beneath the Pandora box.

Duncan jolted from side to side, but the tremor seemed to ease off long enough for him to peer out of the still cracked doors. He was shocked. Darkness expanded all around him in what had previously been a pristine, beautiful, spring morning. Duncan quickly cranked the doors fully closed.

He knew he was seconds from being killed if he did not dematerialize. He pulled back on the power lever and prayed; from this point on, his survival was out of his hands.

Nevertheless, he chose lucky number 8 since his box was the Pandora 8, and the box began to phase. Duncan scrunched his nose up; he smelled a familiar, but unwelcome odor. The power was too much for the jumper cables and, like his previous hook up, one of the cables had melted through and the power had gone off. The Pandora went from phasing to powering down. Duncan grabbed his LED light and clinched it between his teeth so he could look for the problem.

Unknown to Duncan, the mountain had now fully exploded and a pyroclastic flow was heading for his box at more than three hundred miles an hour. It would arrive in less than thirty seconds.

Duncan could see that the cable had melted, but there was nothing he could do. If he only had a piece of metal that could withstand the power.

Suddenly, Jamie's face popped into his mind when she was leaving in Eddie's truck. He couldn't figure why in a time like this, but he yelled in surprise when he realized that he, too, was wearing a cross on a necklace that his mother had given him around his neck. He quickly grabbed the necklace and pulled it over his head. He grabbed a pair of vice grip pliers and bridged the connection between the cable the coil. The necklace began to glow like a heated burner element from the power, but held its form. Luckily for Duncan, his laptop was still running off of its internal battery, so the codes and trace were also still running.

Duncan grabbed the throttle and prepared to push it forward.

Duncan closed his eyes and called out to Christ, "Jesus, please help me. I know I have not been the best man I could be. I know I have caused my parents and my girlfriend and even my friends a lot of grief, but I know you are with me as You said You would be. Please help me now, by the mighty hand of Our Father in Heaven."

When he had said his prayer he pushed on the throttle. The cross suddenly lit up bright white, illuminating the entire interior of the Pandora 8. Once again, the time machine powered up to maximum and began to phase.

As the dark wall of the pyroclastic flow enveloped the Pandora box, Duncan slammed into the side of the box but somehow maintained the connection with the cross in hand. The box suddenly dematerialized and disappeared from the superheated cloud that was enveloping it. Duncan had escaped with his life.

"Thank you, Jesus. Thank you," Duncan cried out.

Chapter 25

Escape to Blitzkrieg

Duncan was in transit once again. He had escaped being incinerated by milliseconds. The Pandora box was hot, as if it were a sweatbox. The heat from the pyroclastic flow had struck the side of the box that had been facing the mountain and it was scorched black. The red light on top had melted completely, but the hardened glass of the lower light ring and the windows had miraculously survived the heat and being pelted by pumice and small stones.

Duncan was burning up and sweating profusely and his shirt stuck to him like a second skin. He was still holding the cross in the pair of vice grips. He could only touch his computer with one hand and his shoulder was injured from being thrown against the wall when the volcanic flow had struck his box, but he could not allow himself the luxury of worrying about that now. He knew he had to land somewhere and allow the Pandora to cool down.

He had thoughts of returning home, but even if his mom and dad were furious with him, it would be a welcome sight compared to the destruction he had just escaped. The heat had also affected his computer and now songs from different eras, which Duncan had loaded into his library, were playing and skipping at random and the grid of landing choices seemed to change every few seconds.

Duncan had not prepared for this and was unsure how to find a safe landing zone, but he needed to land somewhere just be able to get away from the stagnant, heated interior of the Pandora. He had never had any serious doubts about time traveling until now. He thought of Professor Batton and felt an overwhelming bought of regret for not listening to the wise old man.

With no other alternative, Duncan watched the songs change and quickly clicked the trace button on a random number on the next song that popped up on his screen. The computer trace began, but the songs kept changing.

The Pandora 8 began its landing protocol. At this point, Duncan would be happy to land anywhere.

The Pandora suddenly materialized in the middle of a large city.

Duncan, being inside the box, could only see a faint orange glow outside through the frosted window, but he assumed it might have been sunset.

He pressed the open button and the metal doors slid to each side. Once they were fully open, Duncan, now exhausted and sweating, sat the pliers that held the cross down gently on the floor. He could hear a roar outside and he smelled smoke, and he wondered for a brief second if he was still at Mount Saint Helens.

Please, please, tell me this is not what I think, he thought to himself in a panic.

He stepped out of the box, only to see that he was in a big city and that, just across a river, large buildings were burning out of control; yet, no one seemed to be fighting the infernos.

Duncan heard the roar of engines from above.

He looked up and realized there were large planes overhead. He looked to the left and then to the right and saw no one at all on the streets. He could feel the searing heat even from across the river.

Hmm, out of the frying pan into the fire, huh? he thought to himself, still panting.

Duncan began to hear what, at first, seemed to be fireworks exploding, but then the explosions got louder and more pronounced. He could see that the planes flying overhead were dropping bombs and that entire streets were being leveled. Great plumes of smoke were rising into the night sky, causing a dense haze in the air. He could see orange tracers flying into the darkness and giant searchlights circling through the sky, along with what appeared to be little blimps.

He could tell by the sound of the planes that they were older aircrafts, but he was unsure as to where or when he was.

The bombs continued to fall, but they were far enough away that Duncan did not feel as though he needed to take shelter; however, he was worried about the Pandora since it was near the street, and if a bomb were to strike it he would be trapped wherever he was for good.

The Pandora was still hot and covered in volcanic ash and pieces of pumice, so Duncan elected to sit down on a set of stairs on the front of a building that was directly behind his time machine.

Duncan was exhausted and he leaned back on the stairs. Within a few moments, the bombs quit falling and the planes seemed to be moving off into the distance. He leaned his head against the handrail of the stairs and, before long, despite them mayhem, he had fallen asleep.

Duncan awoke to someone leaning over him, their voice pulling him out of his deep sleep. "Oi, you all right mate?" a man asked in a heavy British accent.

Duncan opened his eyes to see a short man with a tall fire helmet standing over him. "What?" he replied as he came to.

"I say, are you alright, lad? You look a bloody mess," the fireman asked again.

"Yes, I'm fine," Duncan replied, wiping his hand over his eyes.

The man smiled and said, "He's a yank. How on earth did you fall asleep during that raid?"

Duncan sat up, noticing that it was now morning. A heavy smoke hung in the air, along with the acrid smell of burning plastic and other materials.

"I was exhausted. I've had quite a night," Duncan explained.

The man laughed, shaking his head. "Aye, I should say so. We all have, young man. You'd better get to a safe zone before tonight," the fireman warned.

"Yes. Thank you, sir. I will," Duncan answered.

The fireman lifted his head, cupped his hands around his mouth, and yelled to the others of his fire brigade. "This one is all right. Keep searching—we have a lot of ground to cover."

The troop of men walked on down the street, and not one of them even noticed the odd looking Pandora box sitting near the edge of the sidewalk. It, too, was scorched, and the light on top was melted.

Duncan stood up, stretched, and began to walk down the river, making sure to take note of the landmarks around him so that he could come back to the Pandora.

Duncan saw people coming up from subway entrances and others carrying injured people away on stretchers. There was trash all over the place and pieces of paper and debris everywhere he looked.

He leaned down and picked up a newspaper that was blowing gracefully in the wind. Duncan read the date—September 2, 1940. He didn't know if the paper was for that day or not, but he knew it was at least a current paper.

The Blitzkrieg! he thought to himself.

Duncan continued to walk. He was hungry and he needed to get something to drink, but all he had in his pocket was some change.

Duncan continued to walk, feeling his legs cramp and his exhaustion increase by the second. It felt like he had lived a hundred days in only one. He clutched his hand to his stomach, feeling it grumble in response.

I gotta find something to eat around here, he thought.

He reached into his pockets and found some lint, a stray piece of wire, a paperclip, the crumpled up receipt from the pizza joint back home, and exactly eighty-three cents in change.

I wonder what this could get me in this time, he thought, before he shoved the contents in his palm back into his pocket.

The streets became a little quieter, and Duncan only saw a person here or there. He wondered where everyone had gone. The farther he moved from the inferno the more he shivered as he walked along in the shadows, rubbing his arms to keep warm.

As he continued to walk, he saw shops, all of

which were closed. Many of them had broken windows or other damage. He could hear glass crunching underneath his sneakers with every step, and he tried not to imagine the violence that had surely taken place there. It seemed like all the good that had been there was long gone.

Duncan turned the brick front corner and came to a park that looked untouched by the heavy bombardment. There, he saw a women sitting on a bench and holding a blanket. She had a bewildered look on her face, but she was absolutely breathtaking. She wore a coat and a floral dress that was slightly filthy.

Duncan thought it was odd that she would be sitting there alone. He decided to see if he could find out exactly where he was.

He walked up to the bench where the woman was sitting. She had not moved, or even so much as flinched, the entire time that he approached her.

"Hello," Duncan greeted.

The woman looked at Duncan suddenly under long lashes that held the warmest brown eyes he had ever seen. His heart skipped a beat in his chest when she slowly smiled at him.

"Oh, hello there," she replied in a soft, sweet voice.

Duncan's head felt fuzzy all of a sudden. He cleared his throat before he spoke, "Are—are you okay, Miss?"

"Yes, thank you. Most kind of you to ask," she answered softly.

Duncan could not stop staring at her. *She is beautiful,* he thought, forgetting to say something back.

"You are American?" she asked, tilting her head

to the side. Her hip length, curly brown hair nearly brushed the ground as she did.

"That's right," Duncan replied, still not taking his eyes off her.

"Oh, how nice to meet you. My name is Victoria," she said. She smoothed her dress with her hands as she spoke, and Duncan noticed how tiny and gentle they looked.

"Hi, Victoria. I am Duncan." He reached his hand out to shake hers, hoping his palm wasn't shaking.

"Duncan? What a wonderful name," she smiled, but it didn't reach her eyes, and placed her hand in his.

Duncan wanted to hold her palm in both of his suddenly; he felt as if her smile was hiding something, some deeper, inner pain. He let her hand down gently, wondering how to ask without offending her.

"Are you all right, Victoria?" Duncan inquired.

"I will be very soon," she replied, nodding her head to herself.

Duncan had no clue as to what she meant, but he continued to talk to her. "Why are you sitting here in the open?" Duncan asked in concern.

"Oh, well it is such a beautiful morning, I just felt like being outside..." she said, looking up at the sky.

Duncan wondered if she was in her right mind. *Had she not been aware of the horror of the night before?*

"Do you live around here?" Duncan asked.

"I did," she replied sorrowfully.

"You did? Well where do you live now?" he pressed.

"I don't live anywhere now. You see, my home

was destroyed the night before last."

Duncan decided to sit next to her—not too close, but enough so that he could be near her and listen. "Oh, I'm sorry, Victoria. Do you have family nearby?" Duncan inquired.

"No, I am all alone now," she said, as a single tear formed and slid down her cheek.

Duncan could see that the young woman carried pain in her heart, but even so, she kept a sweet demeanor about her as if nothing was really wrong.

"I am kind of new here. Can you tell me which city this is?" Duncan asked.

Victoria came out of her daze-like state at this question and said, "Why, you are in London, Duncan. My, you must be lost."

"London? Ha, yes, I am sort of lost. I have only been here once," Duncan stated.

"It's not much to look at these days..." she trailed off in a hushed tone.

"It will look better than before—when the war ends, of course," Duncan assured.

"I would love to see that," she answered.

"Oh don't worry, I am sure you will."

She looked at Duncan and smiled, "Do you believe in the afterlife, Duncan?"

"Yes, I do, Victoria. Don't you?" Duncan replied.

"I always have but the world is very cruel and I sometimes wonder now," she said, as that same glazed look came over her face.

"Why did you ask me that?" he asked curiously.

"Oh, no reason. I just wondered," she smiled again.

"Hey, I have an idea. Why don't we go and find something to eat?" Duncan proposed.

"I'm not hungry, Duncan, and food is in short

supply. I don't wish to take from those who need it," she answered.

"Those who need it? Everyone needs food. Come with me; I could use a friend. I'm alone here, too," he said, rising to his feet.

Duncan extended his hand. Victoria looked at him, slowly reached up, took hold of his fingers, and stood up. "I have no friends anymore," she lamented.

"You have a friend now," Duncan answered compassionately.

As she stood their eyes met. Duncan stared for a moment because, not only was this the first time since meeting Jesus Christ that he had not thought about Jamie in any capacity, but in that moment, he had felt something unfamiliar to him. He had felt at home—just by getting lost in this stranger's eyes, he felt at ease. After a moment, her eyes shifted, forcing Duncan to snap out of his trance.

"You are very kind, Duncan. I would like to spend some time with you," she said with a smile. She hadn't let go of his hand yet, and he hoped she wouldn't.

Duncan's heart began to race. He was instantly taken with Victoria. She seemed to have cast a spell on him. He felt that she was lost in the world, much like him, and there was some kind of connection with he that he longed to explore. He felt a familiarity with her that he couldn't quite explain.

Duncan became concerned for her safety in the midst of all the destruction he had witnessed. "You shouldn't be sitting out in the open like that, anyway. Who knows when the planes will return," Duncan said.

"We are safe. They only come at night. They will

be back, but only after it is dark," Victoria replied.

Duncan was worried about the Pandora, but, for the moment, the only thing that seemed to matter to him was Victoria. She was a kindred soul that was lost and hurting, and Duncan could not stop thinking about her.

They walked back towards the area where the Pandora was sitting. Duncan noticed a crowd of people surrounding a man that was handing out bread and small cuts of fresh meat.

"Hang on, I'll get us some food. You stay right here," Duncan said, grabbing her hand and clutching it for a moment before letting go. He walked up and the crowd was pushing and shoving each other to jockey for their position in line. He felt anger move through him suddenly.

Duncan yelled, "What is wrong with all of you? Have you forgotten your civility just because there is a war going on?" He threw his hands in the air.

The crowd seemed astonished at the words of this American. Some were ashamed and seemed to come back to their senses, while others continued to push against the man who was handing out the food.

"Stop this!" Duncan yelled again, only louder this time. "You are not animals! Quit acting like heathens!"

The crowd seemed to be touched by Duncan's words. They backed away and formed an orderly line.

"That's better," Duncan stated. "The moment you quit acting civil then anarchy will ensue."

The man in charge of the food handed Duncan a small loaf and a piece of cooked beef. Duncan took the food and said, "Thank you, sir." He rested his hand on the man's shoulder and smiled.

"Thank you, young man. We sometimes forget who we are until an outsider reminds us," the man said apologetically.

Duncan nodded his head to the man before he walked back over to Victoria and handed her half of the ration.

Victoria looked at the rations for a moment clearly conflicted. The events that had transpired had ruined her appetite and made her sick; however, she knew that her body needed food. She felt weak and tired, and she needed to eat, despite her lack of appetite.

She and Duncan sat down on the stairs behind his machine and ate the bread and beef. Victoria shoved the food into her mouth, quickly chewing and not looking at Duncan. He felt his heart twinge out of sympathy, realizing that she had probably been significantly hungrier than he was. He waited for her to eat before asking her anything, and felt some relief as the food filled his stomach.

"What is America like, Duncan?" Victoria asked, brushing breadcrumbs off of her dress.

"It's a wonderful place, but we have our problems, too—at least where I come from, anyway," he answered, chewing his last bite.

"Many here wonder if America will be allied with us in the war," she voiced.

"We will. And the war will be won," Duncan assured her.

"I hope so, for their sakes," Victoria said, looking towards the crowd. She put her elbows on her knees and rested her chin in her hands.

"What about for your sake?" Duncan asked.

Duncan waited for an answer but none came.

Victoria simply looked at him and managed a small smile.

"Would you mind if we went back to the park?" she eventually asked.

"No, of course not," Duncan replied.

The two stood up and Duncan instinctively took Victoria's hand without really meaning to. She didn't seem to mind, though, and in truth, neither did Duncan.

They walked slowly back to the park. Duncan told her some clean jokes and managed to get a chuckle out of her. As they walked back into the park, Victoria sat on a child's swing set.

"Would you be so kind?" She asked, wrapping her fingers around the chains and looking up at him shyly.

"Sure," Duncan answered without hesitation.

Duncan swung Victoria and pushed her a little harder each time. Victoria seemed to be having a wonderful time. Her long hair swung with her, the light reflecting off of it. She was a picture—no, a portrait, of beauty and the essence of a deeper heart felt sweetness,

"I used to swing here when I was just a little girl," she said as she smiled.

"There is nothing wrong with reliving good times," Duncan said. He pushed her again and again and, pretty soon, the morning was far spent. After Victoria got off the swing, the two of them sat down under an oak tree.

"What will you do now?" Duncan asked.

"What do you mean?" she asked, glancing towards him.

"I mean where will you go?" he clarified.

"God will have to decide that," she replied.

Duncan found himself staring at her. He looked at her eyes, her lips, and her wavy, brunette hair. She looked up at Duncan and made eye contact with him for a long moment, as if she saw something in him.

"Have you ever been in love, Duncan?" she asked.

Duncan looked down. "Yes, I have," he answered softly.

"I was, too, but when the war broke out, my George had to leave. He was sent to France, but had to be evacuated when the Germans occupied it," Victoria expounded.

"What happened to him?" Duncan inquired.

"He...he fell in love with a French girl that he rescued. It was only a month ago. He sent me a letter telling me we were no longer on," she lamented.

"'No longer on?' Does that mean he broke up with you?" Duncan asked.

Victoria looked down, letting her shoe make circles in the dirt. "Yes. He doesn't want me anymore. He said she was like a 'goddess' in beauty."

"Then he is crazy, Victoria. You are a wonderful woman," Duncan insisted.

She blinked at Duncan. "I might have been once, but not anymore," she said as she averted her eyes.

"Victoria, you are sweet and wonderful and very beautiful, and it is his loss," Duncan defended.

"You are most kind, Duncan. Don't ever change. You will make someone very happy one day," she softly spoke.

"Yeah, that's what I keep telling myself," he replied.

Duncan spent all day with Victoria. He was compelled to stay by her side. They walked the streets and she showed Duncan around. Towards the evening, she pointed to a pile of rubble.

"This was my home. There is nothing left of it now," she said as her eyes welled up with tears.

"I'm sorry, Victoria, but at least you are alive. This can all be rebuilt, and one day it will be," Duncan comforted as the amber of evening engulfed them.

Chapter 26

Togetherness

Dusk had arrived; it was getting dark, and the sound of air raid sirens resounded through the streets as people ran for shelter.

Duncan looked up to the sky to see a flock of birds fleeing, their dark wings flapping quickly against the sliver that was left of the setting sun. He looked at Victoria, who was already looking at him, her eyes filled with dread.

"You had better get to cover, Duncan. The raids will begin again soon," Victoria warned, placing her delicate hand on his arm.

Duncan was worried about his time machine being exposed to the bombs, but he was somehow more concerned for Victoria. He had a strong compulsion to protect her. As Duncan took in her sweet, sad face, he felt a surge of emotion take over him.

"Where can we find cover?" he asked, trying to remain focused.

"If you go to the subway, you can get underground. There is an entrance two blocks north of here," she said, pointing in the general direction of the subway. Her dark hair shifted around her shoulders as she looked towards the entrance.

"Well then let's go there. We can stay there until morning," he beckoned, clasping one of her hands in both of his.

Her feet stayed firmly in place. "No, you go. I will stay in the park," she answered, not meeting his eyes.

He stopped in his tracks. "What? Why would you put yourself in danger like that?" he asked, his eyebrows furrowing together with concern.

"I do not fear death, Duncan. My life is over," she stated with unrelenting certainty.

"Victoria, your life is not over. Don't you want to live and be happy?" Duncan asked, sensing her pain.

"I did want that, Duncan—I wanted it so badly. But now it no longer matters. Please get yourself underground," she implored, wiping quickly at her eyes.

Duncan took a step closer to her, trying to get her to meet his gaze. "Not a chance. If you intend to stay in the park then I will stay in the park with you," he stated matter-of-factly.

Her hair fell in her face as she shook her head slowly. "I do not want you to die, Duncan. You have a chance at happiness but I don't," she said mournfully. She let her hand fall from his as she tried to pull away from him.

"As long as you are alive you have as much chance as anyone else, Victoria. I'm not going to leave you and that is final," Duncan maintained, taking her hand again.

"Then let's go to the graveyard. We will be as safe there as anywhere," she prompted.

"Why the graveyard?" Duncan asked.

"There is cover there. Also, the Germans have mapped London. They will not waste bombs on the dead," she reasoned as she looked at him, pulling her naturally wavy hair from in front of her eyes.

He nodded, understanding her logic. His eyes leveled at hers before he glanced into the encroaching darkness. "How far is it?"

"It's just across this field," she said as she pointed.

Duncan felt the rumbling roar of engines under his feet before he heard them. "Here come the bombers," he cried out. He lifted his head to scan the sky, before he quickly grabbed Victoria's hand. She used her other hand to gather the hemming of her dress as they ran in a dead sprint towards the graveyard.

The planes passed over them and soon the rolling, thundering report of bombs returned. The dark sky was alight once again, the orange fire blazing in the background and dark grey pillars of smoke rising in the air. Dust and ash settled on their hair and clothes like snowfall and bright orange embers floated in the night like fireflies.

Victoria looked back at the ruins of her city and began to weep, knowing what was happening to her countrymen. She lost hold of her dress as she ran and tripped, her hands and knees hitting the ground.

Duncan panicked when he saw her fall. "Victoria, are you okay?"

"I think so. I can still walk, anyway," she said, as Duncan helped her back to her feet.

"Maybe we should head to the country. The city is too dangerous," he suggested.

"Duncan, these are my people," she said as she extended her hands to the city around her. "This is my home. Why is this happening?" She blankly stared into the distance, specks of dirt littering her cheekbones.

"Victoria, evil rears its ugly head from time to

time. Now come on, we're so close. I will not leave you behind like the others. You don't deserve to die just because you were born here. You have to keep going and be strong." He bent down and hoisted her up by the waist, half carrying her as they continued towards the graveyard.

Duncan's heart filled with relief as the tall, wrought iron fence creaked open and they were able to enter. His eyes landed on a sizable crypt that was before them. There were four weeping angels on top of an ornate grave hewn out of stone. They looked beautiful, but sad. Duncan sighed and turned to lean against the wall, the cool stone soothing his back as he slid down onto the ground. He tilted his head back and closed his eyes, trying to catch his breath.

Victoria sat down beside Duncan. She was still weeping and Duncan was moved in compassion to hold her. He embraced her and they sat, watching the spectacle unfold.

In another time and place, the warm, orange glow over their heads might have been a romantic setting, as if it were fireworks on a first date or even a bonfire. What was happening across the field and the river, however, was nothing short of unbridled terror. As Victoria laid her head on Duncan's chest, she flinched and trembled at the noise of the nonstop explosions that echoed their report like thunder.

Duncan held her tightly. He felt as though he never wanted to let go of her. He could not fathom why he felt such an attachment to her, but he didn't care. Even with the horror going on only a short distance away, it felt so good and so natural to hold her. Duncan felt a little guilty because even in the face of all this destruction, he never wanted this moment to end. It was a new sensation; he felt alive and had a deep desire for her, even in the midst of the brutal onslaught.

The bombers came in waves all night long. It was a relentless barrage of death and destruction unleashed. It felt like the entire world was ending all around them.

Duncan was shaking as he held Victoria close and buried his face into her wavy brown hair. It was such a warm, sweet feeling. He had no thoughts of Jamie at all. Right now, his world revolved around himself and Victoria and nothing else seemed to matter. He cradled her as if she were the most precious thing he had ever touched.

The night was long; it felt like an entire year in one. The explosions were both close and far away. Smoke poured into the sky, illuminated by massive walls of flames. Duncan had never experienced war up close, and he was overwhelmed with emotions. He knew people were dying by the hundreds, if not thousands. Their homes and memories were being systematically blown out of existence. He thought of the short fireman he had met that morning. He thought of the people in the bread line. His heart was filled with sorrow as he obsessed on what their fate would be.

His mind finally and suddenly zoomed back to the Pandora 8, and he wondered if it was still in one piece. It was, after all, his only way home, but he remembered the words of Christ and was comforted. However, he was filled with instant panic as he remembered the two otters he had rescued at Mount Saint Helens. He knew they had to be terrified, as they were all alone in a foreign land.

Did I save them from one inferno only to deliver them to another? he pondered. He began to break down at the thought, and a steady flow of tears soon poured from his eyes. Between the fate of the good people of this city and the innocent little animals, it was too much for him.

Victoria could see Duncan was in emotional turmoil and she reached up, wiped his tears, and stroked his hair gently. "This is so unfair," she said, shaking her head slowly.

Duncan choked up. "Even in this time man is supposed to be civilized, but you would never know it by witnessing this."

"Why do you think God allows this?" she asked, her voice breaking.

Duncan looked at Victoria, her face lit only by the reddish glow from the burning city. He touched a hand to her cheek. "God gave man free will, Victoria—to heal or to hurt, to kill or to save. No, this is not God's doing. This evil comes straight from the darkest depths of man's hatred," he answered as he tried to catch his breath from weeping.

Victoria grabbed Duncan in a tight embrace to try and comfort him. She, too, knew there was something more between them, but she was afraid to feel. She was afraid to be close to anyone, especially now with so many people suffering and being wiped from existence.

"You don't belong here. It's as if you came from another world," she whispered, clutching his collar in her hand.

"I am not from this time," he admitted.

Victoria thought she had misheard him. She assumed he meant that he felt like he was not from this time. She also felt out of place. She longed for simpler times when men were chivalrous and were civil gentleman who fought for honor and lived by a different code.

She laid her head back on Duncan's chest and as they wept, they finally gave way to exhaustion and fell asleep, despite the noise and tumult. Intertwined they slumbered as the angels above them seemingly kept watch over them with weeping eyes.

Chapter 27

The Last Day

Duncan woke up startled. His back was in pain from sleeping against the stone crypt wall all night. As he stirred, he looked down to see Victoria's head still on his chest. She hadn't moved an inch away from him, even in her sleep. He gently reached up and stroked her cheek lightly; it still had soot smeared on it and he felt something warm; yet, there was a tickling sensation in his chest—an excitement, a need. Her face was so beautiful in the morning light. Duncan realized his heart was melting for her. Who was he kidding; it had been hers from the moment he first laid eyes on her. Perhaps it was the light he saw within her, or the innocence of her pained heart. Whatever it was, he could not stop thinking about her.

As Duncan laid staring in awe of her beauty and pondering his feelings for her, she awoke with a yawn and sat up slowly with a stretch. She turned away as if she was embarrassed because her hair was frazzled and she was covered in dust. The smell of smoke permeated everything around them.

"Good morning," Duncan greeted her.

"Is it a good morning?" she asked, trying to smooth her dress and wild hair as best as she could.

"Well, we're alive and we're together, so yes. Despite the circumstances, it is a good morning," Duncan declared.

Duncan stood up and his knees cracked loudly. He grabbed Victoria's hand and helped her to her feet, her dress falling around her knees. The two of them looked toward the city, but all they could see was black and gray smoke rising and huge flames. Landmarks that were familiar the night before were now unrecognizable.

"Let's go and see if we can help," Duncan urged.

"We can go, but there is no help for them, nor us," Victoria answered hopelessly.

"You're too young to feel this way, Victoria," Duncan marveled.

"Age doesn't matter in hell," she replied, closing her eyes.

Duncan grabbed her hand and squeezed it in an attempt make her feel better. She looked up at Duncan, moved by his gesture. "We should go," she said softly.

The two walked out of the graveyard and back across the field and across the river. As they approached the street, they could see bodies lying motionless; they saw people running and others sitting, bewildered and lost. They saw sights no human being should have to see.

Duncan looked upon the carnage and said a prayer silently in his head. *Dear God, please help these people and make this evil cease. Let Your tender mercy fall upon Your children, Father. In Jesus name I pray, Amen.*

As they reached a smaller river bridge, Duncan was relieved to see in the distance that the Pandora 8 was still standing proudly where he had left it. He looked around, wondering if anyone had taken notice of it, or were confused by it's presence. No— people simply brushed passed it, indifferent to the oddly shaped green box in the middle of the sidewalk. They were understandably preoccupied by the reality of pain and death all around them; perhaps they thought it to be a type of civil service station or even a police box.

Victoria grabbed Duncan's hand and pried her other hand loose. She realized that they were becoming too close and she could not stand the thought of falling for him, only to have him killed by the bombs.

Victoria watched Duncan staring at the odd-looking green box in the distance. His eyes were guarded, and she wondered what he was thinking. She took in his strong, handsome face and felt such fear at the idea of losing him; she was falling in love, her heart rewarmed by his strength and his tenderness. She worried the world would snatch him away from her like it had everything else in her life. She knew what she had to do.

Duncan seemed to sense her thoughts and immediately grabbed her hand again, as if to let her know he didn't wish to let go, either. In truth, she desired his touch, but she felt guilty for thinking of her own feelings at a time like this. After all, they were stepping over the dead as they walked.

"I'm going to go, Duncan. Thank you for making this time special. I will not forget you," Victoria said as she took a step back.

"What?" Duncan asked, confusion and concern draping over his face. "Where are you going?"

"I have something I have to do. Beware when it gets dark Duncan, the Hun will be back in force," she warned.

"Meet me here before dark," Duncan implored.

Victoria smiled, but said not a word as she

turned and her hand slid out of Duncan's grasp. Duncan's eyes followed her as she walked down the street and turned a corner and then disappeared from his sight.

Duncan felt cold and empty all of a sudden, as if there was a void inside of him. He scratched his chin and was torn. Should he head back to the Pandora 8, or should he follow Victoria? Something hadn't seemed right before she walked away, and he had a bad feeling in the pit of his stomach. His heart wished to follow after her, but he stood there debating what to do, and felt as if there was a shadow across his heart.

Chapter 28

New Lease on Life

Duncan wrestled with his emotions. Back in his own time, there was Jamie, his first love. Here in this time was a breath of fresh air, an angel of a woman that needed someone desperately. Though he had just met this Victoria, he could not get her out of his head, nor did he want too. He knew he needed her and in truth, she needed him as badly as he needed her.

Duncan paused for a moment; he now felt weak. He slouched down onto the sidewalk and kicked a rock back and forth between his feet. For the first time since being in London again in this earlier time, Jamie popped into his head. He was consumed by a warm feeling as he thought about her sweet smile and her unforgettable eyes. With these visions of her came guilt, because although he loved Jamie, he now felt something that he had never felt before, a much deeper tenderness. When he was with Victoria he felt at peace, he felt safe, and he felt at home. It drew him to her in a way that made Jamie seem less magnetic, somehow not as familiar and that hurt him. The woman he once felt so strongly for grew further and further the more he thought about a practical stranger; a sweet stranger he craved, and a stranger that had single handedly changed the priorities of his life. He thought only of her until his attention was stolen away; suddenly a new guilt hit the core of his stomach. "The otters! I forgot about them again! How can I have been so stupid?"

Duncan took off running back to the Pandora box. He ran past people who had begun to stir on the streets and jumped over pieces of debris and dodged smoldering pieces of homes until he reached his time machine.

He wrenched open the door and saw his jacket lying on the floor where he had left them, but the otters were gone. Duncan looked around frantically, but there was no sign of them. He looked towards the river. *Of course!* he thought.

He quickly darted over to the edge of the wall and looked down into the water. There were ripples here and there on the surface, but he could not yet see anything. To his relief, he suddenly saw the two otters frolicking in the shallows a little farther off shore.

Duncan leaned against the wall and began to laugh as the otters tumbled over each other, thoroughly enjoying the water of the Thames. Their dark, wet bodies wriggled together as they played with a stick and flicked their tails happily.

"I'm sorry guys, I just forgot," Duncan called out to them, as if they would understand.

Now, certain that the otters were okay, he began to walk back toward the burned-out, war-ravaged city. A sickly sweet, rotten smell hung in the air, all burnt wood, fire, and death. Duncan felt sick to his stomach and tried to breathe only through his nose as he walked through the rubble in the streets. They had once been beautiful, safe streets with markets and stores and the dwellings of many thousands of British citizens who could not have foreseen that their lives would be forever changed by the outbreak of war.

Duncan felt anger rush through him as he looked upon the burned-out tenements and pieces of people lives and their mementos and memories laying everywhere in the streets, not to mentioned parts of bodies for the previous night's horror.

He felt something squish under his foot and glanced down to see a rumpled doll that had once belonged to someone's little girl. It's black-button eyes and its dirty, torn dress were pitiful, and he felt sadness in knowing what the abandonment could mean. As tears welled in his eyes, he pondered as to whether this child was still alive somewhere, hidden away in some bunker under the once grand city, or if she had been met with an untimely, horrible death in the nights before when she should have been safe in her bed. Either way she was without her precious doll and he knew she felt lost.

Duncan had grown up in America in a time when such things were unimaginable—at least in his small town. This new reality was unreal. He continued to trek through the city, stepping over burnt pieces of lumber and large stones that had once been the fronts of stately buildings. At the end of one block, the road ahead became impassable.

He made his way through an alley and, as he walked past what had been a garbage area, he heard the sound of crying.

He began to feel panicked and followed the sound of the crying, but was unable to see anything or anyone. The mournful sound was muffled and Duncan was compelled to find whoever it was. Finally, as he walked back and forth trying to find the source of the wailing, he stopped at row of dirty, metallic trashcans.

He lifted the lid of the first can, but there was only the normal rubbish one would expect to find. He lifted the top off of a second can and found the same. But when he lifted the top off of a third can, he was shocked to his core.

There was a little girl, no more than five years old, huddled in the trashcan. Her clothes smelled of smoke and they were ripped, as if she had been jerked up and placed in the can. She looked just like the little doll in the street—sad and left behind. Her eyes poured forth a steady stream of tears. Her face was red from crying. Duncan reached into the can, lifted her out, and held her in his embrace.

"Hey, sweetie. What are you doing in the trash?" he asked in a sweet, soothing, low tone.

The little girl was scared and continued to sob, barely taking a breath in between each sob.

"It's okay, I'm going to help you," Duncan said reassuringly.

The little girl wrapped her arms around Duncan's neck and her crying began to subside.

"What's your name?" he asked, running a hand over her hair.

"Sarah," the little girl answered, almost hyperventilating in fear.

"Sarah? Well, that's a pretty name, Sarah," Duncan said as a tear ran down his cheek.

He bounced slightly on his heels, trying to soothe her. "How did you get in the trash can, Sarah?"

"Mummy put me in," she answered, rubbing her small fist over her eyes and sniffling.

"Well, how about you come with me and we will find your mommy. Okay?" Duncan looked into her eyes as she nodded.

"I want my mummy," she replied, looking back at him.

"Okay. Let's go find your mommy," Duncan said as he held the little girl close. He turned and began to walk back through the alley, then came to the rubble in the street.

He walked over the obstacle course of burnt pieces of furniture and things that were completely out of place. He was careful not to drop the small girl or shake her too much in his arms. There were bent nails sticking out from boards that had once been part of something, perhaps someone's bathroom wall or the doorway to someone's apartment.

Duncan made his way back through the mass of debris until he reached the area where the Pandora was standing.

People in the surrounding area blended together in marks of soot, dirt, and torn clothes, but differed with coping mechanisms. Some hobbled through the street with an emotionless look in their eyes.

The ones that really stood out, however, were the ones in denial. They held their heads high as they pursued the day in tattered clothing, socializing amongst one another as if it had been a normal day—as if their only challenge was to find a café that would be open so they could truly start their day. Duncan both pitied and envied them.

He walked into the crowd, hoping someone would recognize the little girl.

"Excuse me, does anyone know this child? Her name is Sarah," he called out, clutching his hand to her back and patting her.

The people gave Duncan and the little girl a

fleeting glance. One man answered. "I am sorry, young man. There are many children like her who have lost their parents in this bloody war."

Duncan felt his heart sink. It began to occur to him that if her mother had placed her there in the can, she surely would have returned for her if she had been able. He wondered if Sarah's mother was even still alive.

A horrible feeling washed over him and his heart broke when he thought of having to be the one to tell her that he she wouldn't see her mother again.

Duncan looked over her little head to the park, and though his mind was heavily laden with concern for Sarah, there sat the only thing that could have made him feel better in a moment like this—Victoria. She was in the park, seated on a bench.

Duncan moved as swiftly as he could and walked into the park. Victoria looked up and smiled at the sight of Duncan coming towards her. "Duncan?" she yelled, immediately rising to her feet and running up to him.

"Victoria!" he exclaimed in his delight to see her again. He wrapped his free arm around her and pulled her to him, kissing her as if she were a refreshing oasis that could quench his thirst. Victoria, taken back by the kiss, paused for moment, unable to process it. Though she hungered for his lips as if they fed some ravenous appetite for emotion, she directed her attention towards the girl instead, blinking quickly.

"Who is this precious little angel?" she asked.

"Her name is Sarah. I found her in a trash can about five blocks away," he replied.

"Aw, hello sweetie. Look at you," Victoria said as she stroked the little girl's hair. "May I?" she asked, opening her arms to take the little girl.

Duncan gently handed Sarah over into the arms of Victoria.

"Oh, you're such a precious little dear," Victoria said, her eyes welling with tears. She rocked the little girl back and forth on her hip.

Duncan smiled because Victoria's spirit seemed to rise as she held the child close. "I have been trying to find her mom," he stated, running a hand through his hair in frustration.

Victoria looked as though she had a new lease on life as she rocked Sarah and kissed her forehead over and over again. It is said that every woman has a natural maternal instinct, but Victoria seemed to bond with Sarah instantly. Victoria felt that Sarah was just like her; she was alone in a heartless world and she needed someone and Victoria felt so good to be that someone.Victoria looked over at Duncan. Her eyes were filled with such joy. It seemed that she had purpose again. She seemed so happy to be holding this child; it was as if she were her very own.

Duncan, on the other hand, knew he needed to find some food for the three of them. They all might have avoided the bombs so far, but death could find them in other ways. London was in disarray and not at all a safe place.

Duncan began to realize that they needed more food, especially for this little one.

"Hey, I am going to go and find us all something to eat. Will you be okay here?" he asked, placing a hand on Victoria's arm.

"We will be fine. Won't we, precious?" Victoria answered, looking down at Sarah on her hip.

"I'll be back as soon as I can, but if I'm not back

by the time it begins to get dark, take her to the graveyard. I will look for you there."

"I'll guard her with my life."

"I know you will. I'll be back as soon as I can," he said, walking backwards quickly. He turned and jogged out of the park, looking for a bread line or cans of food in the street—anything he could find for the three of them.

He stopped at the Pandora box and grabbed his coat. He unhooked his laptop, slid it into the coat, and wrapped it. He also unbolted one of the laser pulse emitters and put it in his jacket as well, just in case the worst happened and his box was hit in the attack that he knew would soon come.

Duncan looked around to make sure no one had seen him and, when he was sure the coast was clear, time to get back to the girls before they were all in danger again. Duncan walked into a plaza that was yet untouched by the onslaught of bombings. There were five Red Cross trucks parked in the center, where people were standing in orderly lines waiting for small boxes of rations.

He walked up, stood behind the rest of the disheveled masses, and waited his turn. It took almost an hour, but Duncan finally made it to one of the trucks and was given a box containing three days worth of rations. *This will be enough to feed all three of us,* he thought to himself.

"Thank you, sir," Duncan said to the man who handed him the box of food.

The man handing out the food was also American. He looked at Duncan and said with a grin, "Hey, you're American."

"Yeah," Duncan replied.

"Where ya from?" the man asked.

"Florida," Duncan answered.

"Oh, beautiful place down there. I have been to Miami twice."

"Yeah, I can hardly wait to get back home."

"You and me both, bub," the man agreed.

"Thanks again for the food," Duncan reiterated.

"No problem. Hope you make back stateside safely."

"Same to you, man," Duncan said, before he turned and walked back towards the road that led to the park.

Victoria was sitting in the park with Sarah, holding her close. She had taken Sarah's mind off of the tragedy that surrounded them by tickling her. The little girl laughed and smiled and Victoria was overjoyed. She now had someone who needed her and she felt as if her life had real purpose. She hoped it would last.

As Victoria continued to play with Sarah, a man and woman walking by on the street noticed the two of them in the park.

"Oh my God! Sarah? Sarah!" the woman called out. The man walking with her yelled, "Is it her, darling? Is that our Sarah?"

Victoria looked up and saw the woman running towards her.

Sarah, upon hearing the voice, wriggled out of Victoria's arms and ran towards the woman, her little legs barely keeping up. "Mummy, mummy!" Sarah yelled as the woman fell to her knees and embraced her in a heartfelt moment of recognition. The man fell to his knees in tears as well, and the family embraced.

Victoria began to cry tears of joy as she witnessed the touching reunion. The woman stood up, cradling Sarah in her arms, as she looked at Victoria with swollen, tear-filled eyes.

"I don't know how to thank you, Miss," Sarah's mother said through her tears.

"You have no need to thank me. I am happy that you have found your baby girl," Victoria smiled.

"We were taken off guard last night and I shoved my sweet pea into a can of rubbish, but we were trapped by the explosions and could not get back to her. We have looked for her all day. I was so scared she was lost forever."

"I am so happy that you found her," Victoria replied.

Sarah's dad walked over and hugged Victoria. "Miss, please come with us to the country. We have a place there, away from all this. It's the least we can do," he offered graciously.

"Thank you, kind sir, but I belong here."

The man nodded; he understood and knew it was useless to insist. "We cannot thank you enough, young lady. God bless you and keep you," he replied.

"Honey, you have saved this family," Sarah's mother choked out through her joyful tears.

"It was my dear friend; he found her," Victoria related.

"Aye, well, where is he? I want to thank him personally," said Sarah's father.

"He went off to find some food for us. His name is Duncan."

"I hope we have the pleasure of meeting him. I'll bet he is at the plaza," Sarah's mother stated.

"Come with us, dear. You look a mess and you are more than welcome," Sarah's dad pressed again.

"I have to wait here, but may God be with you

all." She touched a hand to her chest.

"And with you, Miss. Here, what is your name?"

"Victoria."

"Aye, well Victoria, we are headed for the dales. If you change your mind, we well be in Truxton. Come and see us, won't ya?"

"I will, if I'm able," Victoria replied.

The reunited family turned and walked across the park and back onto the road. Each parent held one of Sarah's hands in one of theirs, both of them not looking away from their little girl. Victoria was truly happy that Sarah had been reunited with her family, but as soon as she was gone, a dark void overtook her. She realized she was alone again and her newly found lease on life had suddenly expired. Fate had been generous and cruel all that the same time.

Chapter 29

Night Falls

It was now evening; the skies turned red in the setting sun because of the smoke rising perpetually into the air and Duncan was making his way back to the park. Driven to provide food for Victoria and Sarah, he walked as briskly as his tired legs would allow. He was calm, and even a little excited to see Victoria again, when in the background he heard the faintest sound of an airplane. Suspicious as it was, he trudged on. Suddenly, a blast thrashed into the atmosphere. Duncan stopped in his tracks and turned to see a fiery inferno illuminating several yards away. The planes became louder and the explosions became more frequent. Duncan began to sprint to the park.

He was in the midst of falling bombs that were leveling buildings in all directions. Great fireballs, glowing with an orange amber light, flashed all around him. Vast clouds of smoke once again poured into the sky in huge gray and black plumes.

The people on the streets scattered for shelter and ran down into the subways, trampling each other as they ran for cover.

Duncan jumped and ran as hard as he could for the park, knowing in his mind that Victoria and Sarah would still be there since it wasn't yet dark.

Huge sides of buildings and bricks shot by miniature missiles fell right in front of him, destroying everything around him. Duncan could feel the searing heat of the fires that the explosives had ignited. The smoke began to dim out the evening sun as if an eclipse had overshadowed the city.

He ran down a side road to the river, feeling this would be the safest place to move across the city with the chaos that was ensuing.

He reached the street that was the closest path to the park and began to run up the hill towards the buildings adjacent to the once peaceful play area.

When he came to the far end of the park, he saw Victoria standing out in the open—but something was different. Sarah was not with her. A thousand horrible scenarios began to play through Duncan's mind as he dodged debris trying to reach her.

The blasts were getting louder and closer and Duncan was terrified—not only for himself, but for Victoria and for his only way home, the Pandora 8. Everything seemed to be moving in slow motion and he felt as if a massive force working against his progress was holding him back.

As he got closer to where Victoria was, he began to yell for her. "Victoria!" She was unable to hear him for the loud reports of the bombs as they fell by the hundreds. Duncan attempted to jump over the park fence, but one the decorative fence spires caught his leg. By the time he got over the fence and was almost freed, he was witness to the thing he feared the most.

A large bomb hit where Victoria was standing. The explosion was so bright that it blinded Duncan for a moment and the percussion of the blast disoriented him and blew him hard to the ground. He was dazed and his ears rang loudly.

When he regained his senses, he realized that Victoria was gone. The massive explosion had vaporized her. "Oh God! NO! Oh my God! NO!" he yelled, as his heart was ripped apart in an instant. Another blast behind him blew him to the ground again and his world faded to black as he lost consciousness.

Several hours later, Duncan awoke in a maelstrom of burning buildings and debris laying everywhere around him. He sat up and the reality struck him in the dense, smoky air. Victoria was dead—her gleaming light extinguished. He grasped his head in his hands and began to cry uncontrollably. He crawled onto his hands and knees and punched the ground as hard as he could.

He screamed, "Jesus, help me." So overcome with emotion and pure grief, he began to vomit.

"Oh God, please wake me. Please God, wake me," he screamed, but to no avail. "This is not real! This is not real!" he cried as he desperately tried to convince himself it was a nightmare, but the horrible truth could not be denied. His pain gave way to a long sob until he was depleted.

Duncan sat in a daze the rest of the night, breaking into bouts of heavy sobbing and then going back into a catatonic state of denial.

When the sun began to dawn, Duncan stood up and walked to where Victoria had been standing. Only now, instead of lush green grass and a beautiful bench and swing, there was a great depression in the earth still burning with fire.

Duncan was covered in dust and there was dried blood on his shirt from a small injury he had received in the heavy bombardment.

He knew there was no hope. He slowly walked out of the demolished park. To his surprise, there stood the Pandora 8, still untouched by the bombings; however, the building behind it was now a burning mass of rubble. Duncan sat down on all that was left of the building—a set of stairs that now went nowhere. He began to cry once again and lay his head in his hands.

"God help me. Oh my God, please help me. I cannot take this pain," he pleaded. He felt a cool wind rush past him and a newspaper wrapped around his leg. Duncan reached down and pulled the paper off of his leg and was about to throw it away from him, but something caught his eye—a picture of Albert Einstein.

The headline under the picture read, "Professor Albert Einstein to speak at Oxford." Duncan continued to read the article, which stated that the professor would speak against the war and against the atrocities being committed by the Nazis on September 9th at Oxford at 2:00 p.m.

Duncan realized that this was the current date. *If anyone can help me undo this, he can,* Duncan surmised. He stood up and ran back towards the city as fast as he could. He looked everywhere for a car or a truck or anything he could use to get to Oxford.

Duncan found a man loading some supplies from a warehouse into a flatbed truck. He walked up to him and cleared his throat. "Sir? Sir?"

The pleasant looking man turned to Duncan with a smile. "Yes, young man. What can I do for thee?"

"Can you tell me where Oxford is from here?"

"Aye, it's about 90 kilometers north and west of

here."

"I'm sorry, what is that in miles?"

"Um let's see, it's about, um, 55 miles."

Duncan sighed and hung his head in exasperation.

"Dost thee need to get to Oxford?" the man asked in an old English Yorkshire accent.

"Yes, sir, I need to get there as soon as possible."

"Well, thee are luck then. I am headed near to Oxford as soon as I finish loading me truck."

Duncan gasped, "You will take me there?"

"Aye, thee looks like thee has had a terrible night. I will help thee lad," the man replied.

"Great, I'll help you finish loading," Duncan said.

"Very well, grab those bags of peat and we'll be off."

Duncan grabbed the bags and threw them onto the bed of the truck without hesitation.

"I'll tell thee, I have seen somewhat in my days, but thou is a strong young man. Come along."

Duncan shrugged and grabbed the door handle, hoisting himself up into the truck. The man was still staring at him openly. He started the truck up and it rumbled to life.

"Are thee a yank?"

"Yes, sir."

"What's thee doing in London, with all this mess about then?" He waved his hand in the general direction of all the destruction.

"Oh, I'm just observing," Duncan replied.

"Observing, eh? Aye, much more observing and thee will end up underground, and not for the better laddie."

Duncan was focused on getting to Oxford, but as they rode along at the truck's top speed of about

35 miles per hour, Duncan's mind turned back to Victoria. Though he was sitting next to a total stranger, Duncan began to weep. The man looked over at Duncan.

"Eh? Now there, lad. Somethin' bad happen back in old London town?" he questioned in his heavy accent.

Duncan tried not to let out a sob. "My true love was killed last night."

"Oh, very sorry, lad. Still, let it all out. There is no shame in the laments of a loving woman."

Duncan continued to weep, but tried to regain his composure.

The man tried to change the subject. "So, where are thee off to at Oxford?"

"The University."

"Uh, are thee an exchange student, then?"

"No, sir. I just have to meet someone there."

"I see, I see."

"Is the University near where you are going?"

"Nay, but I will drop thee off at University just the same."

"Thank you, sir. I very much appreciate this. "

"Aye. The good Lord giveth and the good Lord taketh away, but worry thee not, lad. God always gives thee some better in the end."

"Yes, sir," he replied.

Duncan shut his eyes in an attempt to fall asleep, wanting the next three hours to pass by quickly. The tears came even then, wetting his shoulder through his t-shirt. He awoke with a jerk as the truck came to a stop.

"We're here lad. Go off and do what thee must. I wish thee good luck," the man said with sincerity.

Duncan nodded and rubbed his eyes. "Thank

you sir, and the same to you."

He clamored out of the truck and shut the door, heading towards the University with hope in his heart as the old man drove off.

Chapter 30

The Man with the Plan

Duncan stood at the gates of Oxford University. He quickly broke into a sprint and ran down the narrow road and looked for the auditorium where he knew Einstein would be in a few hours.

He stopped and squinted into the sunlight, placing a hand over his eyes and craning his neck back to take in the looming, sand-colored pillars. The cathedral-looking dome was at the center of the landscape and sunlight streamed into the golden windows. Duncan glanced at the position of the shadow against the great stone steps that led up to a large wooden door.

Hopefully I'm not too late, he thought to himself with worry.

The gate creaked slightly as he pulled it open; the black metal was hot to the touch from the sun. He retracted his hand quickly and inspected his palm, only glancing up when he felt eyes on him. There were students scattered about on the green lawn, and they stared at him over their large textbooks. He looked down at his torn, soot, and bloodstained blue jeans and shirt.

"This has got to be something to see..." he muttered, as he attempted in vain to brush off and tuck in his shirt. A young man wandered up to him.

"Ello, I'm William, but you can call Will. What

happened to you, then?"

"Uh, I'm Duncan. I was in London last night during the attack, and I've just arrived at Oxford."

"Oy, you were really there? What is it like down there now? I've heard the most dreadful things."

"It's total devastation," Duncan moaned.

"The Bosch Bastards!" the young man said, anger clouding his voice.

Duncan's mind ran a mile a minute. "Can you tell me when Professor Einstein will be here?"

"He is already here. He's in the campus dining room preparing his speech. He's due to speak within the hour."

"Would you please show me where that is?" Duncan asked, perking up.

"Sure, follow me," the young man agreed.

William turned and led Duncan straight across the lawn and up some stone steps. He didn't hesitate or use the large brass knocker to enter the great wooden doors, he just turned the golden handle and ushered them indoors. Inside was one of the most beautiful hallways Duncan had ever seen. The stained glass windows spanned floor to ceiling and streamed light softly into the building, washing everything in a warm glow. He had never felt more out of place, and as he tried to straighten his shirt, he wished it had occurred to him to ask someone for a change of clothes. There had just been no time. William abruptly turned left and stopped at an ornate door, knocking twice before entering. The conversation stopped as twelve gentlemen laid their eyes on them. Duncan's eyes found those belonging to the one man he traveled all this way to speak to—Professor Albert Einstein.

Duncan walked up to the table. He was covered

in dust and looked as though he had been beaten or had too much to drink the night before. William backed away slowly, nodding his head to the gentlemen and leaving the room. Duncan was speechless for a moment while he looked at the professor. He looked just like the poster he had in his room back home, just a tad younger. His white hair was fluffed around his head like a halo and dark at the roots. His black mustache, flecked with silver, hid his upper lip completely. He touched his fingers to his chin as he looked at Duncan, leaning forward on his elbows. Duncan cleared his throat, hoping his voice didn't betray him. "Professor Einstein?" he prompted.

The professor lowered his hands on the table, keeping his fingers together. His downturned eyes had less wrinkles than Duncan was used to seeing in photos. His dark pupils had a twinkle in them, like he knew something that everyone else didn't. He didn't look shocked at Duncan's wild appearance—just curious.

"Yes?" the man answered, his accent thick. "What can I do for you, young man?"

Duncan moved a step closer to the table, making some of the gentlemen glance at each other quickly. "Professor, I've traveled a long distance to find you. You have no idea. I need your help."

One of the other men seated at the table, Sir Gerald Stanton, stood up suddenly, his chair squeaking loudly against the wooden floor. "Here, you cannot just barge in here and speak with our honored guest while you look like that. If you have questions, save them for the after the oratory. Also, I would suggest that you get yourself cleaned up before then."

Duncan glared at the man and laid his jacket gingerly on the table. He ignored the man and looked only at the professor. "I have just come from London. I was in the attack last night, where my girl friend was killed. I'm sorry for my haggard appearance, but it is imperative that I speak with Professor Einstein."

Sir Gerald moved toward Duncan as if he intended to remove him.

"Sir Gerald, leave him be. I will speak with him," Professor Einstein said in a calm voice, waving his hand dismissively.

Duncan looked around at the group of men that all stared at him in dismay.

"Professor Einstein, I must talk with you privately," he said, his voice low.

"I forbid it! We have no idea who you are, nor what you want," Sir Gerald exclaimed, slamming his palm down on the table.

"Sir Gerald, please," Einstein implored, catching a piece of chalk that was rolling towards his lap.

"He could be anyone, professor. For all we know he could be a Nazi spy," Sir Gerald insisted, his eyes filled with suspicion.

Einstein shook his head and his mustache turned up slightly at the corners. He smiled and turned to Duncan. "What does this concern, young man?"

Duncan leaned over and whispered into Einstein's ear. What he said caused the professor's eyebrows to raise, then the professor looked at him straight on.

"Of course, I will speak with you at once." The professor then turned his gaze to the men seated at his table "Gentlemen, please excuse us for a few moments," he said hastily.

The old professor stood up and steadied himself by holding onto Duncan's arm. Duncan grabbed his jacket and the two walked over to a corner while the men seated at the table grumbled as to what this could be about. Professor Einstein and Duncan stood alone at last.

The professor looked out for a moment through one of the grand, stained-glass windows towards the impeccable green landscape outside. He seemed to make up his mind about something and turned to Duncan. "All right, young man. You said you are from the future and you can prove it? How do you intend to do so?"

"I will show you technology from the future, but you must not reveal what I will show you to anyone."

"It is agreed. But first, who are you?"

"My name is Duncan Sims. By your calendar I will be born in the year 1994. I will be the first, that I know of, to achieve time travel."

"1994? Well, judging by your appearance, I would say you are in your twenties. So then you claim to be from the 21st century?"

"That is correct, sir."

Professor Einstein simply nodded, as if Duncan was telling him something that would not interest anyone but himself. "Very well then. What proof can you offer?" he asked, tucking shirt his sleeves under his navy sweater.

"Look at this, professor," Duncan said. He pulled back his jacket and showed Professor Einstein his laptop computer.

"What is this? Some sort of device?" asked Professor Einstein, his voice filled with wonder.

"This is a computer. It was made in the year

2016." Duncan opened the laptop up and the screen immediately lit, casting a light blue glow in Professor Einstein's face.

Even Einstein, with all that he had seen in his life, could not have imagined anything like Duncan's laptop computer. It was a marvel to him. He jumped slightly, and brought a shaking palm to his chest. "Fascinating. Is it all self-contained? My goodness, it would take several large rooms to make such a computational device in this time!"

Duncan smiled, sharing professor's enthusiasm, and leaned closer to him. "It will be many years from now until this kind of technology is available, but these are very common in my time," he said in an excited whisper.

"Magnificent! Your time must have many wonders," the professor said, still gawking at the laptop.

"You could say that, but a man of the nineteenth century would be astonished at your technology, professor," he said with appreciation.

"The point is well taken," Einstein surmised, his eyes roving over the laptop.

As the professor looked on, Duncan used his fingerboard to navigate to, and then open, the picture of Einstein next to a chalkboard.

As the professor looked on, Duncan used his track pad to pull down his notes tab, where he could reveal his desktop background. It was the classic picture of Einstein next to a chalkboard, smiling at the camera.

"Oh my, could that be... me?"

"Yes," Duncan grinned. "It is."

Einstein's eyes widened in shock, and he hovered a finger over the chalkboard behind him in the photo. "That is my time thesis equation—I recognize it. But how ever did you come by this photograph? I do not recall posing for this," the professor inquired.

Duncan shrugged. "Maybe this picture has not been taken yet. I don't know, I found this photo on an electronic medium called the Internet. From the device that saved this picture of you, I was able to write it down and add it to an algorithm that opened a doorway into the space time continuum."

Einstein touched his palm to his forehead and swayed slightly. "You were able to do all this through the Internet? Is that what you called it? And so, via this Internet, you simply walked through this time doorway?"

"Well, not exactly. I have a vessel that is able to pass through time," Duncan explained.

"A vessel? Is it some kind of ship?"

"Actually sir, it is more of a time box."

Einstein blinked a few times, trying to imagine what a 'Time Box' could possibly look like. "If you can do marvelous things such as travel in time, then what help can I possibly give you?" he asked, looking at Duncan with eyes that were filled with confusion.

"Professor, I have traveled in time to five destinations, but I have run into a real problem."

"What type of problem, my boy?" asked the professor.

"Professor, I need to be able to move through time in smaller increments. As it is right now, when I travel in time, I land in random locations. I don't know how to control where or when I land."

"You said you are the first to achieve time travel?"

"Yes, sir—or I am the first that I know of, anyway."

"Well, young man, I suspect if you have been successful at achieving time travel, that one day you will also perfect it and be able to land where you desire."

"Yes, sir. You may be right, but I have an urgent problem now that I need to fix," Duncan pressed.

"Ah, so you have disturbed the flow of time?" Einstein asked, crossing his arms.

"No, sir—or at least I have been careful not to do so."

"Then speak plainly to me, young man. What do you need from me that made you come all this way to seek my help?" Einstein inquired.

A student walked by and Duncan paused and looked down to be less conspicuous. When the student moved away, Duncan began to explain.

"Professor, I met a woman in this time. She is a lonely, heartbroken woman and I fell in love with her. Last night she was killed in the air raid. A bomb hit and she just vanished, like she had never existed at all."

"I am very sorry, young man," Einstein said, laying his hand on Duncan's shoulder.

"Professor, I need to be able to move my machine through time and go back to yesterday, before she was killed."

"Ah, so you wish to go back and save her. Is that it?"

"Professor, I know what this must sound like to you, but she means everything to me. I don't want to live without her," Duncan urged.

Professor Einstein patted his arm. "I understand your feelings, young Duncan. But what if by changing history to save her, you also alter it?"

"I have weighed the consequences of that,

professor, but she was alone in the world. She had no family, no friends, and no love. Everyone would assume that she was killed, as she was. But if I can save her, I can take her with me, and I can give her the love she deserved."

"But Duncan, my boy, what if it was indeed *meant* for her to die? What if her death was destined?"

"Professor, have you ever been in love?" Duncan asked, looking straightly at Professor Einstein.

"Of course I have, my boy," the professor grinned as he patted Duncan's arm.

"Then can't you understand what this means to me? Can't you understand that she could come with me in my time and find happiness?"

"I understand that you believe that, Duncan, but I also know that time should not be meddled with," the professor pointed out.

"What if my being here caused her death? What if I'm the only reason she is not alive right now?" Duncan pleaded.

"I am afraid neither you, nor anyone, could possibly know that for certain," the professor answered.

"Professor, you are the only man who can help me. You are the one that made time travel possible for me. You must know more about how to control its flow."

"Listen to me, young man. Suppose I were to help you? How can I know what use you will make of time travel? Suppose you were to abuse it?"

"You have only what you can glean of me, professor, but I am an honest man with no ill intentions."

"Yet you are asking me to help you change an

event that has already happened. Even the best intentions can have dire consequences, you must know that."

"I know what I am asking of you, professor. I needed her and she needed me, and I was not there for her. I have to make this right. I owe it to her."

Professor Einstein stood and looked at Duncan directly. Duncan had such a sincere and hurt look on his face. Professor Einstein weighed the possibilities and tapped his shoe against the wooden floor.

"Please, professor. You are the only one who knows how your equation really works. Please help me," Duncan pleaded.

"Where is your time vessel, Duncan?" the professor asked.

"It is in London, professor, and it is in grave danger of being destroyed," Duncan warned.

"Ah, very well, Duncan. I will help you. When I have made my speech here, I will have my chauffeur take us to London. I would love to see your machine and help you in so much as much as I am able."

Duncan broke down in tears and felt a sense of peace he had not known since he last held Victoria in his arms. "Thank you, professor."

"Meet me in the front of the auditorium after I have concluded."

"Yes sir, I will," Duncan agreed, a wave of relief washing over him.

—

An hour later, the professor approached where Duncan was waiting on the grand stone steps. He had his briefcase in hand, his stick of chalk tucked into his front pocket, and his jacket hung over his forearm. Duncan stood up quickly and followed the professor away from the University and past the front gates. The tires of a shiny black car crunched the loose stones on the dirt road and came to a sudden stop in front of them.

If only my dad could see this.

It was a Morris Isis & six Saloon, one of the best cars ever made. Duncan only knew the model because his father loved cars from the early 1900s. To Einstein the car was new to Duncan it was an antique relic but he quickly got in the backseat with the professor and set his laptop inside his jacket on his lap for safekeeping. The driver switched gears and the car rumbled on as they settled in for the two-hour drive to London.

When they had arrived in the ruined city, the sun was already low in the sky.

They were stopped at a checkpoint, but allowed to pass into the city when the officers saw who the passenger was.

"I think it would be prudent to remain on the outskirts of London until morning. There will be less danger of being killed then," the professor suggested kindly.

"I guess that would be best," Duncan reluctantly agreed.

"In the meantime, you can tell me more of how your machine works."

"I will be happy to," Duncan replied.

Duncan and the professor bid farewell to their driver and walked a short distance to an all-night pub. There was smoke and the sound of darts being thrown. Glasses filled with mead thumped onto tabletops as men stroked their beards and chatted about the war.

There were few people and the atmosphere

seemed relaxed, but there was uneasiness about the place. The old professor and Duncan sat down at a dimly lit, wooden table and Duncan took a while to explain how his machine traced time through music and through laser pulse emitters modulated to sync sine waves.

The professor was astonished and only interrupted to ask some questions to make sure that he understood. He had never heard of such a thing, but it piqued his interest the more that he listened.

"That is brilliant, Duncan," the professor said as he clasped his hands together in delight.

"Yes, and it works, but I can't control the flow of time. I end up wherever the music takes me."

"What you need are intermediate points in time between the fixed points which you trace."

"How would I locate such intermediate time points?"

"Well it seems to me that since time is like a river and can be traveled up or down, as a river can. So then there must also be ripples, or what you would call folds in space time."

"What makes them, and how can I trace them?"

"Duncan, the marvels of our universe are too vast for our limited minds. Creation, in its divinity, is the promise to have no fear when facing the wonders of the world. It is in our aspirations for the truth that we find peace and understanding in the wake of all this cosmic mystery. The ripples have been and will always be—just as time itself. As for tracing them, that is another practice entirely."

Duncan looked at the professor with a surprised expression.

"Have I said something amiss?" Einstein asked

at Duncan's puzzled look.

"No professor, I just thought someone like you, who knows so much about the universe, would have seen God intertwined within it."

"I am a man of science, Duncan. I believe that higher power you would call God is not as you think but is within us. I do not believe in a benevolent being who judges souls as good or bad. To me, the real miracle, if you want to call it that, is the enduring spirit of man who strives for knowledge and not some supernatural being."

Duncan looked down as if what he had heard from the mouth of perhaps the greatest scientist in the world had let him down.

"I see," Duncan replied.

"I take by your expression that you number yourself with the faithful who believe in this deistic God?"

"Well, to be honest, yes, I do. I am somewhat shocked that you do not, given your knowledge of the universe and the complexity of it."

"But why should that shock you, young Duncan?"

"Because professor, with such complexity there has to be a Creator; it could not have happened by itself. And you have now witnessed something that, even by scientific standards, would have to be considered a miraculous feat. I am a man from the future who came back to this time—a time long before my birth even—and you believe in me because you can see me and know that I am. Yet, even bearing witness to the proof of things you have never seen before, such as a time traveler, you still cannot conceive of the wonder of God."

"Duncan, if there was a God, surely such horrors

as we know to be true would not be present in any world He created. Why would a God who created such a marvelous Universe allow such things?"

"Why do believe that, professor? God made man with free will; they do not have to kill or to steal or do harm to anyone, yet they do. Is that the fault of the God who made them?"

"It is an interesting question you pose, young man."

"Professor, would it surprise you if I told you that I had met Christ?" Duncan asked sheepishly.

"You met Jesus Christ?" the professor asked, as if he was taken off guard.

"Yes. I accidentally went back beyond the point where I should have been able to reach and I saw him face to face and I heard his wisdom."

"Well, young man, I have no doubt that you met someone. Perhaps you did meet a man named Jesus, or perhaps you even believe that He was the Son of God; however, what if He was just a wise man, liken to Aristotle, or Ptolemy, Plato, Socrates, or even Confucius?"

"No professor, he was so much more. I could debate with you all night, but I can see you are unmovable. Maybe if you could have seen Him, you might've changed your mind."

"Well, Duncan, perhaps the answer to such a profound question such as, 'does God is exist?' is too big to be solved at a pub table."

"Agreed. Please know that I think that you are a brilliant man, professor, but perhaps you have filled you mind with so much science that there is no room left for God or faith."

"I wish I knew the answer to that, young man; I wish I knew."

Suddenly Duncan looked up at the roof as if he could see into the night sky.

"Wait, do you hear that?" Duncan asked.

"Why no, my boy, I hear nothing," the professor replied.

"Exactly. No air raid sirens. No bombs dropping. Nothing but quiet."

A bar patron who overheard the comment said, "Perhaps Jerry has taken the night off."

"Perhaps so, or perhaps they have chosen another target for this night," the professor remarked in response.

"But that means that we might be able to sneak into the city and work under cover of darkness," Duncan suggested.

"How far is it?" asked Professor Einstein.

"It is within blocks of the London Bridge."

"That is only three miles from here," the professor said, his eyes showing his excitement. "I will get my driver to take us into the city."

"We will only be able to go so far, but I think we can get within a few streets of my machine."

"Splendid! Let us go then." The Professor summoned his driver by waving his arm wildly in the parking lot. Duncan suppressed a laugh at the large, infectious energy of the short professor. They got into the car as soon as the driver drove up and they were on their way. The city, besides the parts that were still burning, was dark and foreboding; the absence of electricity made a difference that Duncan hadn't anticipated.

There was a constant orange glow from fires that had been burning for days, but the area around Duncan's machine seemed safe enough.

Chapter 31

The Time Brake

The driver used his skills to navigate the debris filled dark roads so that he could get Duncan and Professor Einstein only a block and a half from the Pandora 8. As soon as they opened the door of the car, the acrid smell of burnt wood and death hit their noses. They tried to breathe through their mouths and began the short walk.

It took some time because Professor Einstein, much like Professor Batton, was no longer a young man. Duncan let the Professor lean on him as he tried not to trip over the large bricks, mortar, pieces of burnt wood, and debris that were scattered everywhere. There effort paid off when they finally arrived at the Pandora box.

"So this is your machine?" Einstein asked as he approached the box slowly, looking the tall box over with a sense of wonder.

"Yes, this is her," Duncan replied.

"An extraordinary design...but tell me, why is the light melted on top? Was the fire that close last night?" Einstein asked, running his fingers up and down the side of Pandora 8 and still looking in astonishment.

Duncan exhaled lightly. "Actually, that happened at a volcano in the year 1980."

"Need I ask?" The professor raised a wiry eyebrow.

"Please don't. It suffices to say it was a close call," Duncan hinted.

He walked into the box and Professor Einstein stuck his head in after him. He looked around while Duncan shined his LED light. Dust specks shone in the air where the light stream touched.

"What is this unit?" Einstein asked, extending a bony finger towards the coil. "It looks like familiar, like something Tesla might have designed."

"Well actually it is–round about, at least. That is the reverse Tesla coil."

"Reverse Tesla coil?" the professor asked, his brows rising in confusion.

"Yeah, I'm not really completely sure how it even works. I only know it has enough power to last for generations," Duncan explained.

"Indeed. So this is the source of your machine's power, is it?"

"It is," Duncan said as he hooked his computer back up and placed the laser pulse emitter back where he had removed it. He grabbed the vice grips with the cross still in them and bridged the power connection.

The Pandora flashed as if it had a surge, then began to power up and made its signature sound as the reverse Tesla coil came up to nominal output. Suddenly, the computer and the power screen lit up with a blue glow that filled the surrounding space.

Professor Einstein was astonished at all the technology contained inside Duncan's little machine. To him, is was so compact.

Duncan turned and began to run Einstein's equation. The white text ran up the length of the screen; the code ran faster than his eyes could track. He pulled back on the lever but did not initiate a time trace. The blue glow that was in the room grew brighter and the light began to shift. Duncan blinked quickly as he began to see shapes and figures that were not from the current time. He heard the rumble of traffic and honking, as well as the voices of men and women talking and laughing.

Professor Einstein stood in awe of what he was witnessing. He rubbed his hands together anxiously and leaned his weight on the back on the wall of the Pandora. He, too, saw visions of the past and the future, like a collage of broken images. He saw jets, and muscle cars from later years; he saw images of wars and everyday events that were less terrifying and he was amazed and lost in the moment.

Duncan pointed to the laptop's screen and had to break Professor Einstein's gaze at the visions to watch the screen. But he did watch intently as his own equation ran as a code on the computer. He saw the grid pop up and the selection of numbers as Duncan explained all that was happening over all the commotion. When the codes repeated—now slower—the professor noted a possible solution in his mind.

"Back the power down please, Duncan," the professor requested. Duncan did as the professor asked. He looked at him straightly. "Do you see each of these sets of values, I mean these blocks of numbers and letters?"

"Yes," Duncan answered quickly.

"As you increase the sum and power, the more blocks you seem to have," Professor Einstein pointed out.

"Yes, I had noticed that," Duncan acknowledged.

"Well, don't you see? With each new number that pops up, you are picking up the ripples in the fabric of time."

"But how do I tell which is which?"

"It should be a matter of adding the rest of my equation to what you have."

"What? There's more?" Duncan gasped.

"Yes, Duncan. A good scientist never reveals all the knowledge he has to the world, at least not at first, because others will claim it as their own," the professor explained, waving a finger in the air.

"How much more is there?" Duncan asked, shocked.

"Duncan, time is like the equation of PI. In theory it never ends, but it keeps flowing. For how long, however, we cannot say."

Duncan shook his head slowly. "Okay, so what do I need to do?"

"Can you put this machine into a neutral state?"

"Yes, of course," Duncan answered.

"Then do so."

Duncan didn't hesitate and pushed up on the lever. The machine began to power down to the minimum operating power usage.

"Now add these digits exactly as I call them out to you. That should stabilize the time matrix to where you can back up or go forward by increments of minutes, hours, or days."

"That would be fantastic professor—just what I need."

Duncan opened the 'run' window and then the code to add the additional digits.

"Are you ready?" the professor asked.

"Yes, professor," Duncan replied with his fingers ready on the keyboard.

"Add in exactly as I say: E over Mc minus 1 = 3.153, Y over T subtract A, add X to M plus 3 then minus out Zed," Professor Einstein called out.

After only a few seconds of adding characters, the Professor said, "That is it."

"That's all? What will this block of code do?" asked Duncan.

"Well, now when you activate these codes, if my calculations are correct, you will have a time brake."

"A time brake?" Duncan exclaimed.

"Yes. This is what you wanted, is it not?

"Well yeah, but what will I use to brake or to release the brake?"

"Your power lever without the trace activation, of course," the professor shrugged.

"You mean the brake will only work once I have landed in a given place or time?"

"Precisely. The more power you apply, the less brake you use. The less power you use, the more brake you apply," the professor explained.

"You mean it's that simple?" Duncan grinned.

"Well, simple is a relative term. It will, of course, be incumbent upon trial and error to get it exactly right, if I understand your time machine correctly."

"Okay, okay, but how do I back up from this point in time in order to arrive where I need to be?"

"Simple. You are currently in what you have referred to as a 'landing zone.' Simply activate the power again, but reverse the power's polarity and you should be able to back up in increments."

"Great! Shall we try it?"

Einstein paused. "I am afraid I will have to leave the box before you do."

"But why? Shouldn't you, the one who figured out this code, at least get to travel once in time?"

he asked, completely baffled.

"Duncan, sometimes a man's work is never realized in his lifetime. I have been fortunate that mine has. And you have shown me that it will go on into the future. I shall be content with that. Besides, if we go back in time, I will exist two places at once. I dare say I am not prepared for that," he admitted with a light chuckle.

"Then I will exist in two places also?"

"Correct. So now you have a new set of variables to worry about. Just do not abuse time, Duncan, my boy," Einstein said, wagging his finger at Duncan. Professor Batton briefly came into his mind and he made the decision not to argue this time.

"Thank you, professor–for everything."

"Thank *you*, my boy. I never thought I would live to see my own future, but through you I have and it is a bright one. Now, go and save your love. Good luck, Duncan Sims," the professor's eyes shone and his smile was one Duncan would never forget.

"God bless you, professor," he said. He grabbed the professor's hand and shook it firmly as the professor stepped out of the box.

"And you, my boy. If there indeed is a God, Duncan, He has surely smiled upon you," the professor said, giving Duncan a grin and a wink as he turned.

The professor stood back from the box, but watched as Duncan proceeded.

Within a few seconds the box had powered up once again and the bottom ring light atop the Pandora began to spin, illuminating the professor with a blinding, whirling strobe light. Duncan looked at the professor to see his silver hair glowing with light, his trusty stick of chalk still in his front pocket. Einstein slowly faded from Duncan's vision as the light that usually stayed on until take off dimmed and then disappeared completely.

"Fascinating!" Professor Einstein murmured as he turned to walk back to his waiting car, a smile on his face and his small briefcase swinging behind him.

Duncan left the door ajar and he could see time backing up before his very eyes.

Dusk began to expand again and the sun rose from the west as the Pandora went backwards in time. He saw fires that had gone out burn back up to fresh intensity. He witnessed smoke pour down from the sky and back into the flames and he watched as buildings that had fallen stood back up. He saw explosions in reverse and soon, the sun set in the east. As he continued to watch, the sun rose in the west again. Even the smell of the air changed from slightly less acrid into a smoky, sweet, wood-burning smell, filling his nostrils with just the promise of imminent disaster.

He knew he was close to where he had to slow the machine, so he began to power the Pandora down until the moment he relived his worst nightmare in reverse. The bomb that had killed Victoria swallowed itself. His heart pounded wildly in his chest as he tried to prepare himself to see his love again. He saw her then, and he immediately stopped the machine by pushing the lever to low power plus .001. Time began to move forward again, but at a substantially reduced speed.

Duncan jumped from the box as it pulsed and time, still slowing, froze around him. He ran over to Victoria, who was almost motionless. She looked very sad, as though she had lost something. She seemed as if she was there, but also a million miles away at the same time. Duncan had not gone back far enough to see Sarah depart with her parents.

As he started out, he thought it was curious that he was able to move in an almost still world.

He looked all around him and had a realization that Professor Einstein hadn't prepared him for. Despite being in the nearly frozen landing zone, he was still molecularly linked to the running time machine; that made him able to move at a normal rate, despite the slow moving time around him. "Whoa, this is incredible," he said aloud as he touched a piece of flying debris that was floating over the ground.

He looked over from where he was bent down and saw his earlier self caught on the fence, looking towards Victoria. He lost himself for a second as he remembered the pain of the moment that Victoria had been vaporized, but he quickly recovered. He wanted to run to Victoria then, just like his past self was, but he reasoned in his mind that he had to take Victoria precisely at the moment the bomb had enveloped her. It was either that or else he would not go back in time to meet Einstein and upgrade the Pandora. "I've got control of time itself, but only one chance to do this right," he said, trying to talk through it.

Duncan stood there, looking up to the dusky sky. He saw the bomb that had killed Victoria hanging in the air above them between the plane and the ground where Victoria, and now he, was standing. The dark grey cylinders had fallen from the belly of the aircraft in groups of threes. Great plumes of smoke rose into the air as the bombs touched the ground in super slow motion. Although

Duncan wasn't physically suspended in time, his entire body froze in fear as he waited for one to come down on them without moving. *Is this what she felt, knowing it was coming?* he thought as pure panic hit him. He waited until it came down, and as it struck, there began a graceful slow expulsion of fiery inferno. He went to grab Victoria, and, as soon as his fingertips made contact with her skin, she increased to his speed with full force. They landed together on the ground in a heap.

Victoria lifted herself up in surprise. "Duncan? Where did you come from?" she exclaimed. "How—how did you do that?" she asked in complete wonder. Before she could say anything else, he grabbed her in his arms and kissed her as tears ran down his face.

Duncan was overcome. She was alive again and his heart raced with excitement and relief.

To her, he had appeared out of thin air and she could barely make sense of it. As they kissed, the bomb began to envelope them in an eerie, orange-amber, slow-moving fireball. He could feel the heat from the explosion-in-progress move at a super decreased speed.

"No time to tell you now. Where is Sarah? We have to move now!" Duncan warned.

"Her parents came and found her," Victoria answered.

"Thank God," Duncan said in relief. "Come on."

Victoria now realized that she and Duncan were moving through a slow motion world as she looked all around her. She was shocked by the reality, but she trusted he knew what he was doing.

As the bomb continued to expand its fireball, they were able to simply walk ahead of the oncoming burst of fire.

"How is this possible?" she asked as she watched everything happen in slow motion. She looked back behind them, staring in awe at the exploding bomb and its slow expanding blast.

"I will tell you everything when you are safe."

Victoria looked and saw the earlier Duncan caught on the fence. Her head swam with disbelief. "What is happening here?" she begged.

Duncan moved directly into her line of vision and said, "When you are safe, I'll explain everything. I promise. Now please, just trust me." He put his hands on her shoulders to steady her and made sure her eyes were focused on his before he moved.

She was confused beyond reason. "But how can you be in two places at once?" she asked, beginning to act slightly standoffish.

Duncan let out an exasperated sigh. "Victoria, please just come with me and don't ask any more questions for now."

Duncan had planned all this out. By taking Victoria without his earlier self perceiving that, he would ensure that his previous self would believe Victoria had been killed by the bomb. Thus, he would go and find Professor Einstein and bring about the events that were now taking place.

Once they reached the Pandora box, Duncan went to work immediately. He cranked the lever upwards and increased the forward speed. Victoria looked on in awe; she saw time passing at a very fast speed. Her eyes tried to track the movements and she quickly became dizzy.

Duncan went past the time where Professor Einstein had departed, and then he stopped the Pandora box and shut the power down. He then turned to Victoria and embraced her tightly, his emotions pouring forth again as he burst into tears.

Victoria was so deeply moved by Duncan's pain that she wrapped her arms around him and tightly embraced him back. "Duncan, what just happened?" she asked shyly.

He took a step back from her. "Victoria, it's time you knew the truth about me." Duncan took her by her hands and looked her directly in the eyes. "I am a time traveler," he revealed.

"You are what?" she asked in total dismay, letting go of his tender grasp.

"I'm a time traveler. I have been through hell the past few days trying to save you. I saw you die right in front of me," he admitted, his eyes filling with sorrow.

"I died?" she asked, her eyes widening for a moment before she released a sigh of relief.

He closed his eyes. "Yes, and it felt like the end of the world."

"You should have let me die, Duncan," she said in her tender self-denial.

"What? Why would you even say something like that?" he scolded.

"There is no happiness here, Duncan. There are only horror, heartbreak, and the coldness of death," she answered, her eyes welling with tears.

"Victoria, it doesn't have to be only horror, heartbreak, or death. There are wonderful things that you have only forgotten," Duncan testified emotionally. He took her hand again, hoping she didn't pull away this time. "What is life without the warmth of love or friends that care about you or a purpose for being? Devoid of those precious things, it is only existence," he said with a hopeless look.

Victoria avoided his gaze and shook her head. "Come with me," he pleaded, "and I will show you warmth and I will fill the emptiness of your heart and I will show you things you never would have believed possible."

"What can you show me, Duncan?" she asked, sniffing her tears.

"What can I show you? Victoria, I am in love with you. I have been since we first met. When you were killed, my world ended. There was nothing more to live for. I have been through hell to come back in time and save you."

"Why would you do that for me? How can you love a hopeless soul like me?" Victoria asked, though his warmth moved her heart.

"How could I not love you, Victoria? You are the most precious woman I have ever known."

"Duncan..." she began, but Duncan grabbed Victoria's cheeks tenderly in his hands and kissed her with all the passion he felt in his heart. She collapsed into his arms as though nothing else in the universe mattered. They fell out of the Pandora onto the pavement, gently drowning in the fire of sweet emotion, but did not break their kiss.

When their lips parted from their kiss, Duncan looked into her eyes. "Victoria, I can show you that love is real and the friendship and the purpose you seek can be found. I do not wish to be parted from you," Duncan said as his emotions poured forth like an overflowing river.

Victoria looked deep into Duncan's eyes and gently stroked his face. "Who are you, Duncan Sims?" she whispered.

"I am the answer you seek, Victoria, and you are the true love I have sought. I wasn't sure of that until right now," Duncan answered, never breaking eye contact.

"A few days ago we were strangers–two lost souls in this world–and in the blink of an eye you have made me love you," Duncan said. He wrapped his hand around the back of her head and pulled her face into his neck.

Victoria pulled herself even tighter into his embrace. "Please, tell me you are real. If this is a dream I do not want to wake up," she pleaded.

"I'm real, Victoria. You are a gift from God. Life will be beautiful again for both of us," Duncan assured her.

"Do you promise?" she whispered, looking up at him with tear-matted eyelashes.

"I swear it, Victoria. This is our destiny," Duncan said, and he kissed her on her temple. He stood up and took her by both hands and pulled her up to him and kissed her again.

"I'm afraid, Duncan."

"Why?" he whispered, tucking her hair behind her ear.

She looked at the ground. "Because you are someone I could fall in love with."

"Is that a bad thing? If you know I'm in love with you?"

"It shouldn't be, but I am afraid to let anyone get close to me."

"Victoria, why? You deserve love as much as anyone."

She shrugged sadly. "Love always ends up hurting me. Can you understand?"

"Yes, I believe so, but why fight such a wonderful, warm feeling that's so rare to find?"

She looked him in the eye then, like she had

made up her mind. "The warmth I feel is wonderful, Duncan, and I want it so badly, but I know eventually it must turn cold and the heat will fade away," she explained through tears.

"Are you afraid to release yourself and let love take you?"

She lowered her head, wiping a tear that was falling down her cheek. "Yes, Duncan, it kills me inside. I crave to be held and touched and to feel that wonderful belonging, only to run from it for fear of losing it."

"You don't know that you will lose it."

"No I don't know that, but I'm still afraid of it."

"Victoria, everyone needs love."

"But they don't get it, do they? All of my friends that died never lived to know love. All of the people buried in the rubble of this place had hopes and dreams and they wanted to be loved. They wanted this warmth, but all they got was death...and for what?" she scoffed.

"The world is unfair, Victoria."

"Precisely, Duncan. So why do I deserve love above any of them?"

"Because you are here and you are alive and you have someone who is in love with you. You can't let survivor guilt keep you a prisoner."

"What makes love happen and why must it be denied to some? Or come to an end?"

"Only God knows what makes love happen or why it ends, Victoria," he paused, tilting her chin up until their eyes met. "But in all of time and space, you are the answer to the need of my heart and soul."

Victoria kissed Duncan's neck. "Only God could create a love this deep. I have been so starved for this feeling, but it puts such fear into my soul," she answered.

"I know you're afraid, but I also know that this is real and I don't need to know anymore than that. Don't run away from it, Victoria. It is such a wonderful and precious thing to know."

"Please just hold onto me for a little while," she pleaded.

Duncan embraced her and he was now more confident than he had ever been. He did not even feel any guilt or remorse over Jamie. He knew that whatever happened, things would take care of themselves. He had found the jewel of true love.

Victoria felt it so deeply, but it was ripping her apart inside. Could she love this stranger—a stranger she had just met?

Even if he had saved her life, she wondered what it was about him that grabbed her heart and held it firm. She never wanted to be apart from him; she could not imagine her life without him and she did not want to. Duncan, likewise, wished there was some miraculous way to keep this tender, sweet moment forever. He held her close.

She was the only bright and good thing in his

life. He knew the night would bring horror, and he contemplated all the ramifications to time if he followed his heart and took her away from all of this.

Would it change history? Would it even matter so long as they had each other? He no longer cared. His love for her was too strong and, consequences or not, he wanted her with him always.

Chapter 32

A Time for Everything

The stars glinted against the night sky and a light, cool breeze blew through the air. Both Victoria and Duncan knew that soon, the German bombers would bring havoc, chaos, and death into the grand city. Duncan knew it was time to tell her the rest of the truth. He took her to the Pandora box to reveal the truth about his machine. Odd as it might sound, not a single soul had so much as noticed the tall green box standing in the middle of war-ravaged London.

Much to Duncan's surprise, the two otters had left the river and returned to the Pandora.

Victoria suddenly let out a delightful squeak, pointing a few feet ahead of them. "Duncan, are those...*otters*?" she asked, a large grin spreading across her cheekbones.

Duncan grinned. "Well yes, they are, but they are not from here. It's time I told you about the Pandora 8," he said as they both entered into the box.

"I wondered what this thing was," she said, looking away from the otters and taking everything in. Duncan laid a hand on the side of the box, patting it with pride. "This is the Pandora 8. It's my time machine."

"So this is how you travel in time? Is that how you went back to save me? You moved through time?" she asked, her eyes widening as she began to understand.

"Yes, that's how I was able to save you," Duncan explained, nodding solemnly. He watched her look around the box in awe before he asked, "Victoria, do you trust me?"

"How could I not trust you?" she replied.

"The truth is, I came here from the year 2018," he admitted.

Victoria took one look around the box and knew that what she was seeing was not of her time. She saw all the technology and equipment, including Duncan's computer. She had seen it when she was rescued from death but it still had not quite sunk in. Her eyes drifted back to his and she smiled hesitantly. "I believe you, Duncan," she said.

Duncan leaned toward her and they embraced tightly. "Will you come with me then, far away from here?" he asked.

"Yes," she answered. "I would go anywhere with you."

Duncan turned his head to whisper in her ear, "I'm in love with you, Victoria."

They held each other tightly again. Victoria leaned back to look at Duncan, never letting go of his hand. With their hands intertwined, Duncan gazed over at Victoria and squeezed her hand.

"I feel like I belong with you—like we belong together. I have nothing here anymore. Are you my miracle?" she asked, tears swimming in her eyes.

"If you allow me to be, then yes, I am."

"So what is next for us?"

"Let's go home," he answered.

Victoria smiled and said, "Home. I will be home if I am with you."

With that, the box began to phase, and as the German Luftwaffe began attacking London, a number of the planes saw the huge, white, tornado-like vortex rise into the sky. A large number of the bomber planes were affected by the lightning emitted from the Pandora 8. It acted as an electromagnetic pulse and the pilots could see electrical arcs moving all over their plane engines. Many of Nazi bombers shut down and simply fell from the sky, crashing into the burned out ruins they had bombed only nights before.

Duncan and Victoria did not witness this, however, but they did hear the voices of many cheering them on as the Pandora box dematerialized from their time.

Duncan looked over at Victoria. She looked as beautiful as he had ever seen her. Her long, dark hair was gently blowing behind her and she had a happy blush to her cheeks.

"Are you excited?" he asked.

"Yes, yes, I am. I cannot wait to see the future and escape this hell," she replied.

"You will never hurt, nor be alone again, Victoria," Duncan promised.

Victoria smiled and said, "I believe you, Duncan. You have saved my life. You made me want to live again. I will go anywhere you go."

Chapter 33

Shades of Things to Come

The Pandora 8 honed in on the signal and Duncan prepared to materialize, hopefully back in his own time. The box began its landing sequence and soon materialized. Victoria held onto his arm tightly, trying not to get disoriented.

Duncan opened the doors, expecting it to be the dark, but it was daylight. He blinked quickly in the harsh sunlight. He once again laid the pliers down and readied himself for what he feared would be an awkward situation. He would no doubt have to confront Jamie and his parents.

Much to Duncan's surprise, Logan greeted him.

"Well that was quick," Logan said as if surprised.

"Huh?" Duncan asked. Victoria stepped out of the Pandora and stood behind Duncan.

"What happened to you guys? Are you okay, Victoria?" Logan asked.

Duncan was confused—Victoria was as well, but she had no idea who Logan even was. Duncan looked at Logan straightly. "How do you know Victoria?" he asked.

Logan cocked his head to the side, thinking that he was missing something. "How do I know Victoria? What's wrong with you, bro? Why are you so filthy?" Logan mused. He wrinkled his nose and shook his head. "You smell like smoke again."

Duncan suddenly realized that something was

not right.

Suddenly, Jamie walked up and stood next to Logan.

"Are you two okay? Where is the professor?" Jamie asked. She was clearly concerned and seemed as if she was familiar with Victoria, also.

"The professor?" Duncan asked.

"Yeah, you guys just left a minute ago," Logan explained.

Duncan had to gather his thoughts. He could almost feel a headache coming on from this new reality.

"Who are these people, Duncan?" Victoria asked in a small whisper.

"They are my friends," Duncan replied.

Jamie and Logan looked as if they were completely confused. "Duncan, what's going on here?" Jamie inquired.

"I'm not sure, Jamie," Duncan replied.

"How long were you gone this time?" Logan asked.

"Wait, wait—Logan, you said you know who Victoria is," Duncan said.

"Of course, bro," Logan replied.

"Why are you asking such strange questions?" Jamie asked.

"Well, honestly, because neither of you should know who Victoria is yet."

"What?" Jamie gasped.

"We've known her since you came back," Logan added.

"Since I came back?" Duncan asked, still confused.

"Yeah, you brought her with you from 1940. Don't you remember telling us about meeting Jesus and going to Mount Saint Helens and then meeting Vicky in London?" Jamie elaborated.

Suddenly it dawned on Duncan. He had chosen a random number from his computer grid and, obviously, he was now in the future.

"When exactly was it that I told you all of that, Jamie?" Duncan asked.

"Seven months ago when you came home," Jamie answered.

"Duncan, what is going on here?" Victoria asked.

"Apparently I overshot the time I meant to return to," Duncan replied, running a hand through his wild hair.

"What are you saying?" Victoria asked, not understanding anything about the effects of time travel.

"I have landed in the future," Duncan answered.

Jamie looked at Logan and then back at Duncan.

"What are you trying to say, Dunc?" Logan asked.

"What I'm trying to say is that I haven't made it back home yet. I haven't told you about any of those events, and Victoria hasn't met either of you yet. Seven months ago I did make it back, or rather I will, if that makes any sense to you," Duncan explained.

"So wait a second...you are not the same Duncan that just left here?" Jamie asked. She let out a half-laugh; the entire process was confusing to her.

"Well, I'm the same Duncan, but from an earlier time," he stated.

"You mean you are from before you returned seven months ago?" Logan asked.

"Exactly, Logey."

"That explains why you look the way you do

then," Jamie laughed.

Duncan met Jamie's eyes and furrowed his eyebrows. "Jamie, you are not angry with me?" he asked.

Jamie tucked her hair behind her ear, a thoughtful look covering her face. "I was, Duncan. I was furious. You hurt me very badly. I cried for weeks, but ultimately, you were right," she replied, shrugging slightly.

"I was?" Duncan asked.

"Yeah, you said that you and I were not meant to be, and that someone would make me happier than you ever could," Jamie replied.

Duncan smiled and looked back and forth between his two friends. "So you and Logan?"

"Yeah, we're together now," Jamie said as she put her arm around Logan.

"Are we okay then?" Duncan asked nervously.

"Yes, Duncan. It was a little rough at first but it turned out to be the best thing," Jamie smiled.

"I'm glad, Jamie. I'm glad we're still friends. We are still friends, aren't we?" Duncan asked.

"Of course we are," Logan answered, holding up his hand for a high-five. Duncan grinned and slapped Logan's palm.

"I don't understand, Duncan. What does all of this mean?" Victoria asked.

"It means we have landed seven months into the future from my time, but everything is going to turn out fine," Duncan said, relieved.

"So what do we do now?" Victoria asked.

"Well, we just have to figure out which number will take us back seven months," Duncan replied.

"It's number eight, Dunc," Logan piped up.

"How do you know?" Duncan asked.

"Because you told me the choice you made to get home was selection eight from the grid," Logan answered.

"Did I tell you about this meeting?" Duncan asked.

"No. You said you had one thing you couldn't tell me but that I would find out eventually," Logan answered.

"This is beginning to make sense now," Duncan exhaled. "Well, Jamie, Logan, I'm happy for you and I love you both. But now I have to get home so that I can get us to where we are right now, if you catch my drift," he smiled.

"Yeah. Finally I know what you were talking about," Logan said.

Duncan walked over and hugged Jamie and Logan. "Thank you guys. No matter what time I'm in, I know you are my true friends," he said softly.

"We always will be. Now go home. Your parents and our earlier selves are worried sick," Jamie said.

"Yeah, and you smell like smoke," Logan chuckled.

Duncan turned, and he and Victoria re-entered the Pandora box. Duncan took one last look.

"See you guys in the past," Duncan smiled.

"Yeah, yeah, see you then. And Duncan?" Logan paused.

"Yeah, Logey?"

"You owe me one for what happens three months from when you get home," Logan said as he cracked a grin.

"What happens then?" Duncan asked.

"I can't tell you. You know the rules about revealing too much about the future," Logan answered.

"Oh yeah, you're right," Duncan answered.

Duncan waved to Jamie and Logan before then the doors of the Pandora slid shut and the box powered up and dematerialized.

"What did happen three months after he got back?" Jamie asked.

"Nothing. I just wanted to mess with his head," Logan laughed.

Jamie embraced Logan and kissed him. "That's why I love you—you never change," she grinned. She and Logan turned around and she wrapped her arm around his. Resting her head on his shoulder, they slowly walked away from Duncan, Victoria, and the Time Box.

In the Pandora 8 Duncan shrugged. "Well, that was weird."

"Maybe one day you can explain all of this to me," Victoria said with a smile.

"I hope so. For now, let's hope Logan was right about the number eight."

Duncan chose the number eight from his grid and the landing sequence began again.

Chapter 34

The Reckoning

Back in the present day, Logan and Jamie were standing in the front yard with Duncan's parents. To them, it had only been moments since Duncan disappeared in his box after he had left the party and beat them to his house.

Professor Batton had seen the lights flashing and the tall vortex from his window when Duncan had activated the Pandora 8 to leave.

He grabbed his trusty cane and walked down the small block to Duncan's house as fast as he could. As he reached the end of the driveway, he could see Frank, Shellie, Logan, and Jamie standing in the front yard. As he walked up the driveway to get a better look, he noticed the Pandora box was no longer there.

The professor walked up to where the four were standing. As he did, a car turned into the driveway behind him.

"Wofford Batton?" Shellie asked.

"Hello Shellie. Hello Frank. How are you?" he said with a slight smile.

"I'm not too good, Batton. My son has disappeared," Frank said with a grimacing look.

"He has disappeared?" the professor inquired.

"Yes, he got into that box of his and vanished."

"I see. So he tried the experiment," Professor Batton said in a relaxed tone. He lit his pipe and balanced it between his lips, his eyes scanning the night sky.

"What do you know about his experiment?" Shellie asked.

"I've been helping him. Your son is quite smart," he said nonchalantly.

"You've been helping him? Helping him do what, Batton?" Frank asked angrily, his temper escalating rapidly.

"I have been working with him on his time travel experiment. He is a brilliant young man."

"You mean you are responsible for this?" Frank growled.

As an argument ensued, the car that pulled into the driveway sat with its lights on. They were shining on the group, yet nobody seemed to notice.

"Professor, where did he go?" asked Jamie, instantly forgetting her previous judgments against him.

"Oh, I wouldn't know that, my dear. Anywhere in time he wanted, I suppose," he replied, shrugging.

"Wait a minute—are you saying this hare-brained idea of time travel is real?" Logan blurted out.

"Oh, yes. Quite real, young man," the professor said, never losing his composure.

"This is utter nonsense. Time travel..." Frank trailed off, shaking his head incredulously. "No way, that's not possible. Where is my son, Batton?" he pushed, his face deepening with color.

"As I said to this young lady, I have no idea where or when he went."

"Have you all lost your minds? There's no such thing as time travel," Frank reiterated angrily.

"Frank, Duncan mentioned he was working on something big, but we didn't believe him. What if

Professor Batton is telling the truth?" Shellie asked quietly.

The doors of the car opened and two figures stepped out, but still no one noticed.

Frank scoffed. "Shellie, please. Duncan did not build a time machine. Time travel is fantasy, not reality."

"Duncan *did* say said he was going to be the first to travel in time," Logan interjected.

"The night we broke up, he mentioned his experiment involved time travel, but I didn't believe him..." Jamie announced.

Frank grabbed Professor Batton by his jacket in a threatening manner. "I will ask you once more, Batton, where is my son?"

"Unhand me at once, Mr. Sims," Professor Batton demanded as a puff of smoke exhaling from his pipe.

"Take your hands off of him," a voice yelled from the dark.

Frank's attention, as well as everyone else's, was directed towards the voice.

"What? Who the hell are you?" Frank asked, still seething.

The two figures walked into the light; Jamie smiled and quickly walked towards them. "Grandpa! Grandma! What are you doing here?"

"Hello, baby girl," the voice answered.

Jamie ran over and hugged her grandparents, but she was still at a loss as to why they were even there.

While this was happening, an atmospheric disturbance of wind and turbulence blew up suddenly, and, as the whole group stood and watched, the Pandora 8 began to materialize.

The whirling lights on top of the box illuminated all of the onlookers, and they watched in awe as the box became fully visible and materialized right in front of them. The box was scorched black on one side and was covered in volcanic ash and tiny bits of pumice.

The Pandora began to power down and the doors slid open like an elevator, revealing Duncan, who was holding a jacket in his arms.

As Duncan stepped out, Shellie and Jamie ran to him. They wrapped their arms around him tightly, their eyes filled with tears. Logan also walked over in his cool fashion, but quickly forgot his ego and joined the hug.

Jamie embraced Duncan lovingly. Her heart sank, however, when she could feel that love had not been reciprocated; it was not the hug of a man in love.

"Is something wrong, Duncan?" she asked, her eyes searching his face.

"Uh...we have things we need to talk about, Jamie," Duncan replied, looking at her absently. As if on cue, Victoria stepped out of the Pandora box and everyone was shocked. Her beauty was timeless, but her clothing was definitely not.

"Uh, this is Victoria, everyone," Duncan introduced.

Jamie looked at Duncan as if she had been pierced through the heart. She took a step back and crossed her arms tightly, tears welling in her eyes.

Frank let go of Professor Batton and walked over to the group. "Well, where have you been?" Frank asked, hiding his emotions. "And who is this?"

"I will tell you later. Right now I am just glad to

be home."

"I'm glad you're home too, son. You had us all worried," Frank admitted.

"Well, my boy, you did it again. I'm glad to see everything is okay. Also, what a charming young lady," Professor Batton said pleasantly.

"Yes, sir. It worked better than expected."

"I will be anxious to hear about it, but for now I will leave you to your family. Come and see me when you can."

"I will come see you soon and tell you all about it."

Professor Batton tipped his Gatsby and sauntered back down the driveway.

Shellie walked over and laid her head on Frank's shoulder. "I think maybe we should be a little more supportive of him from now on," she whispered.

"Yeah, but I still say that this is a lot of nonsense," Frank smirked.

"Get a grip, honey," his wife retorted.

Logan stepped back into his usual haughty demeanor. "Glad you are okay, bro. Where did you find the hot chick?"

Jamie stood there stiffly, her eyes drenched in tears. "Duncan who is she?" she asked. She ran her hand under her eyes to wipe away the tears, but they continued to flow down her cheeks.

"Jamie, she is um—" but Duncan stopped short of telling her. He exhaled and looked at Logan. "Here, hold these."

He handed Logan his jacket with the two otters inside. Logan looked down at the animals. They squeaked softly at him and their whiskers tickled his forearms. "What are these?" Logan asked

"Two friends I rescued," Duncan replied.

The otters began to climb up Logan's shirt, looking up at him as if he was their toy. "Um, Duncan...Duncan?" Logan called out nervously.

But Duncan had other things on his mind; chiefly, how he could tell the present day Jamie the truth about Victoria, though he knew it would eventually be okay. He knew that the news of Victoria would be very painful to her.

Chapter 35

Bittersweet Reunion

Duncan saw two unfamiliar people standing in his yard.

"Hello, Duncan. Welcome back," an oddly familiar-sounding voice said.

Duncan squinted to see an older man and woman standing before him. Victoria also looked, but had no clue as to who these people were. "Um, thanks," Duncan said, puzzled.

Jamie turned and looked at her grandparents. Though she was getting a bad feeling, she kept her composure. "Duncan, you remember my grandfather and grandmother. You met them only last month," Jamie said in a slightly aggravated tone.

Duncan only vaguely remembered the meeting and he had forgotten Jamie's grandparent's names. "Oh yeah, I remember now. I met them when we went to the beach."

"Yeah, it was too cold to swim but it was still beautiful," Jamie said, wiping her eyes and casting a glare towards Victoria.

Victoria knew nothing of Jamie but tried to be polite. "Hello there," she greeted, her voice innocent and pleasant.

Jamie said, "Hello, Victoria—whoever you are."

Jamie's granddad continued to talk to Duncan. "Actually, you met us long before that, Duncan."

"I did?" Duncan asked, not recalling any such

meeting.

"Yes, Duncan. It's because of you that we are here today."

Duncan was puzzled. He had no idea who these people were, other than Jamie's grandparents. He studied the man's face and tilted his head to the side, something seeming oddly familiar. It then hit him like a ton of bricks.

"*Eddie?*" Duncan asked.

"That's right, Duncan. Eddie and Jamie from the campground."

Jamie the elder walked up. "Hello again, Duncan," she said, her eyes twinkling as she fingered a cross necklace at her neck.

"Eddie? Jamie? Seriously?" Duncan laughed as he embraced them both, hugging them tightly. "So, you're *my* Jamie's grandparents?"

"That is correct, Duncan. You saved us from the mountain, and, when we met you a month ago, we knew you were the same Duncan who had saved us from certain death."

"But, you're Jamie's grandparents!" Duncan said. He was still shocked.

Jamie also listened to this in complete shock. She had never known about this.

"Yes. My daughter, Joan, named Jamie after me," related Jamie the elder.

"So that means I didn't screw up time by saving you guys," Duncan said, exhaling deeply.

"Apparently not," Eddie grinned. "We've been waiting a long time. We have patiently looked forward to this day."

Victoria heard this and knew that Duncan must have intervened, at some point in time travel, and affected these people's lives.

"How did you find me?" Duncan quizzed.

"Fate has an odd way of working things out. We tried for years to find you, but it wasn't until Jamie introduced us to you that we realized who you were. We found you quite by accident."

"So you knew I would time travel even before I did."

"We did, and we have been watching your progress. When we saw your first box, we knew the time was near. We drove by here every day. A few days ago, we saw the Pandora 8, but we had to wait until you actually went back before we could tell you," Eddie stated.

"This is incredible. If I had not revealed to you what was going to happen—"

"Then our granddaughter would have never been born and we never would have met you."

Duncan thought he had seen it all, but this was beyond his wildest dreams. He had to take it all in. "So you did come to Florida after all?"

"Yes," Jamie smiled. "We moved down here in 1981."

"I'm just glad you believed me."

"We have been back to the mountain several times over the years. It was horrifying to see what had become of our little honeymoon spot. It was all completely gone, just as you said it would be.

"Well, you know. I actually did save a little piece of it."

"What?" Ed asked.

Duncan turned to look at Logan who had calmed the two otters down in Duncan's jacket. Victoria had wondered how the otters played into this. "Logan—come over here, will ya?"

Logan walked over carefully and Duncan took

the jacket from Logan and handed it to Eddie.

"These little guys were at the campsite and I couldn't let them be killed."

Jamie the elder burst into tears. "Eddie look, it's Tazzy and Snazzy."

"Oh my gosh, it is them," he replied. The otters uttered a sound of delight upon seeing Jamie and Eddie. Jamie grabbed one and held it tight.

"You know these two?" Duncan asked, handing over the second otter to Eddie.

"Yes, we do! They were there every time we went to St. Helens. We were heartbroken at the destruction, and we thought for sure they had been killed. We tamed them and they were there every year to greet us."

Duncan shook his head in disbelief. "Well I guess, like you said, fate has a strange way of working things out."

"I have always believed that with God all things are possible, and here are two little miracles to prove it. I hope they can adapt to life in Florida."

"We'll take them back to St. Helens. We're going back there for our anniversary. It seems only right that we should take them home. I can't believe you saved them," Jamie the elder said joyfully, her eyes tearing up.

Frank and Shellie walked toward the house, but Frank paused and walked up to Victoria. "Welcome to our home," he said, much to surprise of Shellie and Duncan and everyone else present.

Victoria said, "Thank you, Mr. Sims," with a small curtsy.

Shellie shook her hand. "You're British?"

"Yes, ma'am," Victoria replied.

"Well, as my husband said, welcome!"

Victoria began to tear up as she smiled warmly. "Thank you."

Frank turned and looked at Duncan. "We've got a lot to talk about, young man," he said.

"Yes, sir," Duncan acknowledged.

"And Duncan?" Frank added.

"Yeah, dad?"

"Good job. Even your aunt Sarah would be pleased. I love you, son."

"I love you too, dad."

"But I still want you to get a job," Frank jabbed lightly.

"He doesn't need a job, Mr. Sims. He has one," Eddie declared.

Duncan turned and looked at Eddie in surprise. "I have what?" he asked.

"That's right, Duncan. I own the third largest computer software production company in America, and I know you are good with computers. How does $120,000 a year sound to you?"

Duncan's eyes widened with disbelief. He stammered, "It sounds awesome. I—I don't know what to say."

"No need to say anything. If it weren't for you, we wouldn't even be here."

So, see you Monday morning, Duncan. Come on, Jamie; let's leave these two alone. I am sure they have a lot to talk about," Eddie said with a smile.

"I'll be there, Eddie—and thank you," Duncan said with a smile.

"See you later, grandpa and grandma," Jamie said, now looking downtrodden.

"See you, sweetie," they replied as Eddie and his wife got into their car with the two otters in

Duncan's jacket. They then backed out of the driveway and drove off.

Jamie looked Victoria over. She had a bad feeling growing in her gut. She looked back at Duncan and asked pointedly, "Duncan, who is Victoria?"

Duncan looked down and walked over to Jamie. "Jamie, there's just no easy way to say this, so I am just going to say it. I fell in love with Victoria. She is from a different time."

"You *what*?" Jamie exclaimed.

"Jamie, I have seen the future. I know certain things that you don't. I still care about you and I always will, but the truth is, we were just not meant to be."

Jamie took a step back and burst into tears.

Victoria went over to Jamie to comfort her but Jamie lashed out. "Get away from me," she snapped, waving her arm at her dismissively.

Victoria backed up and Duncan put his arm around her comfortingly.

Jamie fell to her knees and began to sob.

Victoria placed a hand over her chest and frowned. She glanced at Duncan and whispered, "Jamie seemed so happy when we met her before."

"She will be; she just doesn't realize it yet. This is the harsh part of time travel," Duncan answered.

Logan felt bad for Jamie and walked over to her. He leaned down and put his arms around her.

Duncan also leaned down and put his hand on Jamie's shoulder. "Jamie, I know this is hurting you right now and I'm so sorry, but trust me— things were meant to happen this way, and one day you will understand," Duncan revealed.

"You said our love would never fade, Duncan,"

Jamie sobbed.

"I know what I said, but you have a brighter future with someone who will love you better than I ever could," Duncan explained, his eyes pleading with hers to understand.

"That's not true, Duncan. It was supposed to be us," Jamie sobbed harder.

"I know how this looks, Jamie, and it's tearing me up inside. This is the way it has to be, though, and if you never speak to me again I'll understand," Duncan said softly.

Logan took Jamie by the hand and they started for his truck. "It's gonna be okay, Jamie," Logan said soothingly.

Logan walked around the truck and looked at Duncan. "Hey, Logan, are we good, man?" Duncan called to him.

"Always, bro. Things will work out," he grinned in his usual Logan way. "But for now, Dunc, I'm going to take her home."

Duncan walked over to Jamie. "Hey, everything will work out for the best, Jamie," he said as he rubbed her arm.

"You have destroyed me, Duncan," she said, in a mournful tone.

"Please believe me, Jamie. I have been to the future. I promise you that you will be very happy," he reassured.

"I hope you're right, because right now I just want to die."

"I'm sorry for that, Jamie. I hate to sound cliché, but time does heal all wounds. You will find love with someone better for you than I ever would have been."

"I'll see you later, Dunc," Logan assured.

"Take care of her, man," Duncan replied.

Logan backed out of the driveway and drove off. As Logan was driving Jamie home, he stopped in the middle of the road.

"Hey, I will be here for you. No matter what, all right?" Logan assured.

Jamie leaned over and cried on Logan's shoulder; they embraced and Logan soothingly stroked her hair.

Victoria and Duncan walked into the house and sat down with Duncan's parents. Duncan told them of all that had happened—of his miraculous meeting with Jesus Christ and Professor Einstein, how he had been to the blitzkrieg and witnessed its horrors, and how he had narrowly escaped death at Mount Saint Helens.

Duncan showed Victoria where the bathroom was and she took a shower. Duncan did likewise in the downstairs bathroom. Shellie gave Victoria a nightdress and robe and she settled down in Duncan's bed. Duncan slept on the living room couch.

The next morning dawned, cold and overcast. Duncan walked up the stairs and opened his bedroom door, expecting to find Victoria still sleeping, but to his surprise, Victoria was dressed in a stylish top and blue jeans. She looked absolutely beautiful. Her hair was freshly styled and she had on a sweet perfume.

Duncan's mother walked out from the closet. "Well, what do you think?" Shellie asked.

"I can't believe my eyes," Duncan replied, still shocked.

"We got up early and I outfitted her with some of my clothes and I gave her hair a nice wave."

"Your mother has made me feel quite at home," Victoria said with a smile.

"Duncan, why don't you take Victoria into town and show her around? I'm sure she will be thrilled to see the modern world."

"Great idea, but we'll have to walk."

"No, it's chilly out this morning. You can take my car," Shellie offered.

Duncan was shocked—his mom had never offered to let him use her car.

"Really? You are letting me use your car?"

"Duncan, you have more than proven yourself. We should have listened. You dad is very proud of you—we both are."

"I don't know what to say," Duncan replied.

"Don't say anything. Just go and have a good time, you two."

Duncan's mother exited the room and pulled the door closed.

"Your mother is very sweet, Duncan," Victoria said as she pulled at the hem of her shirt. She glanced down at her outfit and shifted her weight before looking back up at Duncan.

"I know," Duncan said as he walked over and embraced Victoria then kissed her in a long, slow, passionate kiss. "By the way, you look *beautiful.*"

She smiled up at him and he said, "I am going to show you things you never would have dreamed possible."

"I love you, Duncan," she whispered.

"I love you, too. You captured my heart from the first time I saw you," Duncan whispered back. "Now let's go. You have seventy-eight years of catching up to do."

Duncan took Victoria into town and showed her

the modern world. She was amazed at how far technology had come. She was astonished at modern cars and all the luxuries of the modern day. She even found classic music of the eighties to her liking.

But something still bothered Victoria and she had to get it off her chest. "Duncan, were you in love with Jamie?"

"Well, that's kind of complicated. Why would you ask that now?"

"I only wondered where your love for her went."

"Truthfully, yes, I loved her and I thought she was the only one for me."

"Then what changed?"

Duncan sighed and narrowed his eyes as he looked down the street. "Victoria, Jamie is wonderful and sweet, but she never touched my heart like you have. You showed me a passion and fire in true love that I only had glimpses of with Jamie."

She borrowed my heart for a time, but it never really belonged to her the way I thought it had. Until I met you, I had not fathomed really how deep love can reach."

Victoria glanced at Duncan. "Is your heart full now?"

"With you, it will never be full. There will always be a little room for us to fill with passion."

Victoria leaned over and looked Duncan in the eyes as she tilted her head and they kissed in the sweetness of the love that would last them throughout all time to come. Duncan leaned back and looked at Victoria; he took her hand and squeezed it three times.

"Why'd you do that?" Victoria asked with a smile.

"Do what?" Duncan asked, squeezing her hand

three times again.

"Squeeze my hand three times. Does it mean something?"

"It's something my mom did every time she would take my hand as a kid. Her mom did it with her, and so on and so forth. She would say it's her way of saying, 'I love you,'" Duncan paused and looked into Victoria's eyes.

Victoria, being at a loss for words, took Duncan's hand and squeezed three times as they continued to walk.

Later that night, Duncan was lying in bed. Victoria was asleep with her head on his chest, but Duncan couldn't sleep for he was thinking about all that had transpired. Victoria stirred and noticed that he seemed too keyed up to sleep.

"Something bothering you?" she asked, lifting her head up on one elbow.

"I was just reliving the past few days."

"You have every right to. No one has accomplished what you have."

"Yeah I guess," Duncan said as he laid his head back and thought.

It's funny; yesterday I was miserable. Today, I'm happy, but I realize that happiness comes at a price. I accomplished what none have done before me; I have broken the barriers of time. I have met my Lord and Savior face-to-face. I have stared into the jaws of death and have overcome it by the grace of God. I have seen man's inhumanity to man but I have grown from it. I have found a deeper love than I ever thought possible. I dreamed of living my fantasy,

and now, having done so, I see that time travel is not the glorious adventure I thought it would be; in fact, it's scary as hell. It is a river that man was

*probably never meant to cross, and with good reason.
I have grown up in a single day. I have learned the
greatest lesson that I ever will, and that is nothing*

*compared to the simple things that make up a
life—my deep faith in God, my true friends who
care about me, and the love of family through the
good and the bad. There is beauty right here in a
child's laughter, in a glowing sunset, in the first storm
of summer, in the beauty of the autumn leaves that
God made on His canvas of creation, in the first
snowfall of winter that falls gracefully in its
splendor, and in the rare jewel of a true love worth
living for.*

Victoria laid her head back down. "Will you ever
travel in time again?"

"Hmm, according to future Logan I will, but for
now I know I belong right here in my quiet little
suburban town. It might not be the most exciting
place on the earth, but it is home and there is no
place I would rather be. I would not trade it for any
price."

"Well, you may not, but you have done something
iconic."

"Yes. I have built an iconic Time Box, but even
so, the real treasure I have discovered is this simple
life and the eternal one to come. It will be glorious.
The things written by Solomon are true—for
everything there is a time and my time is now."

Victoria pressed her palm against his cheek. "No,
it's *our* time now," she whispered.

Duncan smiled and laid his head back as Victoria
ran her fingers through his hair. "And we have
plenty of it."